# CRIMES

## OF

# COMMISSION

Diana Rittenhouse mystery 3/5

# **Kate Merrill**

## Crimes of Commission

Cover art: Kate Merrill
Photo: zimmytws/thinkstock

**Merlin-Janus Studio, Inc.**
Mooresville, NC

Publishing History
First Edition 2016
**Second Edition 2022**

Print ISBN: 978-0692509029

Published in the United States of America

For Ginger

ONE

## *Road rage…*

Who said road rage was unique to big cities?

Diana slowed to a crawl behind the cement mixer hogging the middle of the road while the thermostat needle in her brain crept into the red zone. Her temper overheated as the road crew holding the *Stop* and *Slow* signs chatted and smoked cigarettes. Did those guys care if the line of traffic backed up on her tail stretched to Kingdom Come? She longed to lean on the horn or make an obscene gesture, but every fiber in her being prevented such indulgences.

Instead, she turned up the air conditioning, took a deep breath, and contemplated the real reasons for her discomfort. Viv, her elderly mother, would call her peevish, a condition similar to an itch you can't scratch in some intimate part of your anatomy.

The cement mixer backed off the road and the crew waved her through.

Diana's first problem was Matthew. She longed to be with him, relax in the warm comfort of his arms, and take that delayed vacation to Wilmington. They had put it off so long the idea had become an obscene joke. No joke to Matthew, however. He blamed her for stalling and was becoming more than a little peevish himself.

She picked up speed, guided Queen Vic, her Ford Crown Victoria, onto Schoolhouse Road, and then drove to the end of the peninsula. Suddenly a white MacDonald's bag hit her windshield, scattering greasy French fries all over the glass.

She cursed, swerved, and turned on the wipers as the red pickup truck dead ahead belched out another load of trash. Beer cans clattered onto the pavement. At least these were patriotic litterbugs, with not one, but three American flag decals plastered on their bumper. A naked Playboy bunny bobbed from their rearview mirror, a decorative touch that filled Diana with loathing.

Only yesterday she had traveled this same route and had seen a gang of inmates working. They wore orange safety vests over traditional black and white striped jailhouse garb and laboriously picked up every scrap of trash along this posh boulevard to The Point. Today the prisoners' orange bags were neatly stacked along the road waiting to be collected.

Diana made a mental note of the red truck's tag number as it peeled off into a side road. She imagined how good it would feel to report those idiots to her old pal, Sheriff Wayne Bearfoot. She had passed his office a half-mile back and now enjoyed a vision of the misguided patriots being served a whopping littering fine. But then what? Would they come after her seeking vengeance?

*Get over it, girl!* It wasn't the traffic congestion or the local litterbugs short-circuiting her nerves, it was her job. Had to be. Ever since her young partner Liz and she had finally earned their brokers' licenses, life had been an endless headache.

The bankers had extracted a pound of flesh at an exorbitant interest rate before allowing two women to purchase an office condo in Deer Park. The place was brand new and within easy walking distance of Diana's condo at Lakeside, but the lenders' attitude still rankled. Neither her years of experience in Philadelphia nor her reasonably good character cut any ice with the banker boys. They infuriated Liz, who, unburdened by Diana's inhibitions, said: *Fuck 'em all! We will succeed big time and show those assholes!*

*Showing those assholes* was the motivation for today's mission, and Diana was determined to list the luxurious waterfront home of ex-banker Harold Havers. If Liz and she sold this property, their commission would pay the mortgage for six months, to hell with the skeptics.

She eased off the boulevard and turned into Country Club Drive. Dead ahead Lake Norman was a dazzling shade of blue beyond the ninth green, reminding her once again of the stark contrasts inherent in her new Carolina home. This development, The Point, was one of several elite communities cropping up like mushrooms around the lake's impressive five hundred mile shoreline. The heady odor of wealth and privilege wafted across the manicured golf course and glinted off polished brass fittings on the yachts gently bobbing in the marina.

At the same time, a crew of Mexican gardeners labored in the hot sun to insure that all the lawns be cut on the same day, so that each blade of grass be the same height, a regulation in this never-never land where the perfect symmetry of perfect lives must never- never be disrupted.

*Get over it!* It wasn't like Diana was a stranger to wealth. She had been its poor cousin all her life. She had rubbed cashmere elbows with the rich coeds at Bryn Mawr College, although she was a lowly scholarship student. She had even owned a horse, and when she used to gallop across her father's farmland, she pretended she was landed gentry long before the truly rich city folk flocked to Chester County. Finally, she had married wealthy Robert Rittenhouse. He had been her entrée into Philadelphia society, the father of her two children, the man who betrayed her.

If the divorce taught Diana anything, if her forty-three years on this earth had yielded any lesson, it was that money can't buy you love. Trite, but true. Normally she abhorred such clichés, but just now she was too damn irritated to avoid them.

She sighed and tried to concentrate. She didn't want to miss the turnoff to Crow's Nest Court, but suddenly a work van came careening around the corner, so she was forced to swerve to avoid a head-on collision. Ladders clattered against the van's white paneled sides and a curly-haired guy in a paint-spattered ball cap stared out at her. For a split second, their eyes met.

Something was familiar about the man, but before she could sort it out, the reckless driver sped out of sight. Clearly he was a would-be NASCAR star, like so many other kids here in Mooresville, dubbed Race City USA.

Damn fool! As she struggled to compose herself, she remembered what Matthew once told her about how it used to be. Not long ago, before these miles of blacktop, still stinking of new tar in the heat, the land had only dirt roads bisecting cotton fields. And Lake Norman, which now attracted Yankees and pleasure seekers like a magnet, was once the sleepy Catawba River. It meandered through the Piedmont, silent but for the drone of crickets or the occasional squawk of a crow.

Before Duke Power built the dam and created the lake, there were cows, cornfields, and watermelon feasts instead of traffic jams and personal watercraft wagging jet stream tails and spewing gasoline into the lake. That was before greedy developers began building waterfront communities cheek by jowl, polluting the lake as fast as crooked politicians could issue permits for highly suspect processing plants.

Progress, politics, and greed equaled road rage. The equation reeled in Diana's brain like a mantra of doom. At the same time, as she turned into the long driveway leading to Harold Havers' mansion on the Main Channel, she fervently prayed that even though she was both a Yankee and a Realtor, she would not contribute to that corruption.

To top it all off, this Indian Summer—or whatever term the natives used to justify ninety degree heat in mid-October—did nothing to sooth her jangled nerves. Humidity clung to her body as she stepped from the car. What on earth had possessed her to wear a long-sleeved blouse, blazer, and slacks? It seemed a reasonable choice, considering the season, but she was still unaccustomed to the vagaries of the Carolina climate. Would she ever learn?

As she followed a winding pathway leading to the pseudo Tudor monstrosity, which Harold Havers called home, a spectacular sunset dropped through the sky above the far shore. The brick mansion had none of the environmental qualities— natural wood, earth tones, architectural harmony—one would expect in a lake home. Instead, the formal garden belonged behind an English manor, and the whole package, according to Diana's mental calculator, appraised at upwards of 2.5 million, which would net them a tidy commission.

Her conscience barked. *You're a money-grubber like all the rest, so crawl off your high horse and get that listing contract signed!*

Next, she wondered if Liz should be the one going after this listing. After all, she knew Havers, while Diana had only met him briefly two years ago, at a local restaurant. She remembered him as a distinguished-looking gentleman with hair as thick and white as a cotton field. That day Havers had been tipsy from a multiple-martini lunch. Drunk as he was, he'd still maintained a haughty, superior attitude.

Havers was CEO of all the Wells Fargo branches in the Lake Norman area. Everyone called him Happy Harry behind his back, but showed him deference face-to-face. Apparently, his ruthlessly shrewd banking practices had earned him every penny of his fortune, not to mention a young trophy wife.

It was the wife who rubbed Liz the wrong way, and the wife who had caused her to avoid this client altogether. Janelle, the new Mrs. Havers, had grown up with Liz in a tough Charlotte neighborhood, and the two were longtime adversaries. Liz had called the woman everything from *bitch* and *slut* to *shameless gold digger,* but Diana suspected Liz's problem with Janelle went much deeper than simple material jealousy. Be that as it may, today Liz's problem had become Diana's problem.

She pressed the doorbell and heard Westminster chimes pealing faintly through the house. She shifted from foot to foot as beads of perspiration slid down the valley between her breasts.

*C'mon, already!* Havers' secretary had confirmed her appointment for five thirty, and Diana was right on time. She tried the brass knocker, cast in the shape of a fouled anchor, and noticed how the door inched inward with the pressure. A slight push released the latch, and the door swung open to a cool, silent foyer.

"Anybody home?" she called out. "It's Diana Rittenhouse. I've come about listing your house...?"

No response. She called again, but the place remained quiet. Years on the job, of inadvertently bursting in on clients who were not supposed to be home, had conditioned her to knock hard and holler louder. But something told her that this time, instead of surprising clandestine lovers in bed, she was more likely to discover her newest client sleeping off a drunk.

Perfect. Just what she needed.

"Mr. Havers?" She rapped on several closed doors as she progressed down the Persian-carpeted hallway. For all she knew, she was banging on closet doors, making a fool of herself.

"It's Diana Rittenhouse!" Her voice echoed through the state-of-the-art kitchen and drifted into the great room, where it vibrated off stone walls decorated to resemble a medieval castle. She passed through a wrought iron gate, guarded on both sides by faux gargoyles, and entered an inner sanctum, which clearly belonged to the king of the castle. A masculine black leather chair with brass studs replicating an antique Spanish throne was pulled up to a heavily carved dark oak desk. Only the computer was out of place in the artfully contrived setting.

"Can anybody hear me?" Her voice had lost its bravado and her skin was a mass of goose bumps. Too cold in here. And the faint odor of smoke, along with a sweet floral essence, hung in the still air.

She was sure the next door, which was slightly ajar, led to Harold Havers' private office, the place where he did his real work. Many men, including her ex-husband, reserved a room which was strictly off limits—a place for highly personal phone calls, a venue to plot against the competition, or simply to escape. Diana had trespassed in such havens before, so why did she hesitate?

By now she knew she was alone in a deserted house, but if everyone had left, why hadn't someone taken the time to lock the front door? Summoning her courage, she pushed into a room much larger than she had expected. And darker. Mahogany paneled walls and a deep burgundy carpet added to the gloomy effect. The only illumination came from a green glass desk lamp, and from the sunset staining the mullioned picture window on the west wall. The only sound was a faint electronic buzzing.

As her eyes adjusted, she sensed an eerie presence in the room and her pulse began to race. Something was wrong. She felt it in the pit of her stomach, even before her eyes registered the broken glass window behind the desk.

The crimson sunset filtered through the fractured shards, matching the abstract splatter of bright red dribble on the jagged edges of glass. Diana was transfixed as her eyes wandered to the green lamp. She followed its glow to a cotton field, where fluffy white hair grew from what was once a human face. This pulpy red horror was attached to the dark mountains of the dead man's shadowed shoulders.

Bile rose to the back of her throat when she saw a gun in his right hand. His wrist and arm were twisted at an improbable angle from the force of the blast that took off the back of his head. Before she fainted, she lifted her eyes once more to the window and understood...

The red abstract splatter was Harold Havers' blood.

## TWO

### *A body at rest…*

"Poor bastard." The young deputy stepped gingerly behind Havers' body, tiptoeing to avoid a puddle of blood pooled on the plastic chair pad. "Happy Harry blew his mind."

"Shut up, Billy, and don't touch anything," Sheriff Wayne Bearfoot growled at the kid, then turned his dark gaze on her. "Jesus, Diana, were you born with the gift, or do you go out of your way to be at the wrong place at the wrong time?"

She pressed the cold washcloth Wayne had provided against her aching forehead. How had she managed to throw up and black out at the same time? Her mess was embarrassing, to be sure, but hardly comparable to the catastrophe at hand.

"Feeling better now?" Bearfoot was six feet of towering intimidation leaning over her as she slumped in a side chair.

Diana nodded, but wasn't convinced. She'd feel much better once she was far away from the body. Unfortunately, her old friend, Wayne Bearfoot, was right. Since she moved to North Carolina, violent death seemed to stalk her as relentlessly as her own shadow.

"At least you had the presence of mind to dial 911. I was just leaving the office when we got the call."

"I used my cell phone…" She recalled opening her eyes and lifting herself off the burgundy carpet. Then she had crawled up level to the desktop and heard the staccato buzzing of the phone receiver near the dead man's left hand. *If you wish to make a call, please hang up and try again,* the mechanical operator had pleaded to the corpse.

"I couldn't very well use *his* phone, could I?" she babbled.

"Guess not." He eyed the desk where the blood-spattered receiver still lay out of its cradle.

"Just hang up the damn phone!" Diana knew she was being unreasonable, but the incessant yammering of the recording made it impossible to focus.

He squatted down, compressing like a powerful spring, bringing his face level to hers. "You up to answering a few questions, Diana?"

His next words guided her gently backwards through her afternoon activities, coaxing out the why, when, and how she'd come to be on the scene shortly after Harold Havers met his Maker. According to Bearfoot, the fresh scent of gunpowder and still-warm body proved he had just died.

"You sure you didn't hear the gunshot? Must have happened about the time you arrived. Think hard, Diana. Exactly what did you hear?"

"Nothing." When she vigorously shook her head, the ache intensified. She stared at him, an appeal to stop the grilling, but he stared right back, his ebony eyes unflinching. His high, chiseled cheekbones were granite ledges reflecting the stony resolve of his Cherokee ancestors. She had almost forgotten what a relentless son-of-a-bitch Wayne Bearfoot could be.

"Believe me," she moaned. "All I remember is smelling the smoke...and the flowers."

"Smoke from the gun, recently fired, and I suspect those are your flowers over there..."

He gestured towards the wall behind the desk. Although she loathed seeing Havers' ruined body again, she eyed the extravagant mixed bouquet of hothouse blooms, imported from God knows where. They were tastefully displayed on a black lacquered Chinese sideboard. They smelled like a funeral, an odor now mixed with the metallic scent of blood.

"Take a look at this, Sheriff..." The rookie named Billy had dragged the revolver from the dead man's hand using a pencil hooked through the trigger guard. "Smith and Wesson 16-4, .32 Magnum."

"Damn it, son!" Wayne catapulted upright. "Put that thing down before you shoot yourself."

The kid sheepishly lowered the gun to the desk, then dropped his arms to his sides. "I didn't touch it."

She guessed the boy was in his early twenties, fresh out of the police academy. To her, he seemed like a pouting child caught with his hand in the cookie jar.

Wayne took hold of Billy's arm and guided him to the door. "Stand right here and stay out of trouble. Keep your ears cocked for the troops, they're on the way."

She assumed "the troops" were the backup team coming to secure the crime scene. *Good Lord.* Only an hour ago, she'd driven by Wayne's office and fantasized about arresting litterbug rednecks. It seemed a lifetime ago.

"How well did you know this fellow, Diana?" Wayne asked.

"Harold Havers? I hardly knew him at all. I met him once at a restaurant, but he'd been drinking that day, so I formed no opinion."

Wayne chuckled and winked. "Very civilized of you, Diana, and very true to form for Havers. Looks to me like he was also behaving true to form today." He took a clean handkerchief from his hip pocket and wrapped it around a bottle of J&B scotch sitting on the desk. He held it up to the window, where the green bottle caught the last rays of the dying sunset. "But the poor guy just barely cracked this one open. Can't be but one jigger missing."

Odd. If Diana were planning to kill herself, she'd get three sheets to the wind before pulling the trigger.

"Excuse me, Sheriff..." Billy spoke up from his post. "I know for a fact that Harry Havers was on the wagon."

Wayne frowned. "You know that for a *fact*, son? That surprises me. Did you know the victim?"

The boy flushed pink under his blond crew cut. "Well, sir, I didn't exactly know him..."

"Spit it out, Billy."

The deputy shifted uncomfortably. "I kinda knew his wife, sir."

"That so?" Wayne placed the scotch bottle back on the desk and crossed his arms. "Tell me about it."

"Hell, Sheriff, everybody knows Janelle. Her and me were drinking buddies down at The Sports Bar before she married that old man and got religion."

Wayne's dark eyebrows lifted. "You amaze me, Billy. How well did you know Janelle Havers?"

The kid smirked. "We hung out, you know. We'd meet up and leave one of our cars at The Sports Bar overnight, then come 'round and pick it up in the morning. Know what I mean?"

Diana knew what he meant. Coupling what Liz had said about Janelle with what Diana knew about The Sports Bar, Harold Havers' wife sounded like one hot lady.

"You a regular at The Sports Bar, Billy?" Wayne asked. "That's the new singles bar over at the bridge, am I right?"

"C'mon, give me a break, sir. You've been there." Billy's flush deepened to red.

"What makes you think Mr. Havers gave up drinking?"

"Janelle said so. She came to the tavern a few times after she got married, but all she drank was soda. Said she'd made her old man quit, too."

"Maybe he needed just one drink to do this?" Diana stole a quick peek at the body.

"False courage? You think so?" The sheriff bent close to the dead man's collar and sniffed. "Smells like that one shot of scotch ended up on his shirt."

What was left in her stomach churned at the thought of the faceless man with no mouth.

"If you're right that Havers stopped drinking, Billy, the forensics team up in Raleigh won't find liquor in his belly," Wayne said.

Diana squeezed her eyes shut. What was this about? Her would-be client had committed suicide, right?

"The phone is another problem," Wayne mumbled. "In my experience, a right-handed man would not place his telephone to the extreme left end of his desk."

"What makes you think he was right-handed?" She was curious in spite of herself.

"The gun was in his right hand. If you were going to kill yourself, would you shoot with the wrong hand?"

"I don't get it…?" Billy said.

"Think about it, son, and trust your instincts. See how his pens, his notepads, and all his other stuff is on the left? My guess is the killer knew him well enough to talk his way into the house, but not well enough to know that Havers was a lefty, or that he'd quit drinking.

"*Killer?*" Billy and Diana piped in unison.

Her brain raced. When she arrived, there'd been no sign of forced entry. Indeed, the front door was unlocked. It fell open to her touch.

"Havers let him in!" she exclaimed.

"Or maybe it was a flower delivery?" Billy pointed at the bouquet. "Harry lets the guy in, leads him back to his study, and the guy pops him?"

Wayne snorted. "Why would a delivery boy have a murderous grudge against Harold Havers?"

Murder was a far-fetched idea, but Diana couldn't rule it out. After all, if the wife, Janelle, was half the slut Liz had described, she could've had jealous lovers lurking behind every bush.

"So you think Mr. Havers' attacker shot him, placed the gun in his right hand, which was the wrong hand, and then doused him with scotch to make it look like a suicide?" she asked.

"It's one theory." Wayne shrugged.

"What if Mr. Havers had just answered the phone?" Diana said. "Do you think whoever called him might have heard the shot, or even heard the killer's voice?"

"It's possible. Even if Havers made the call and was interrupted by the killer, whoever was at the other end would have heard something," Wayne agreed. "On the other hand, if you heard someone blown away, wouldn't you call the police? Far as I know, you were the only one to report this, Diana."

"Maybe Havers was calling for help?" Billy offered excitedly. "He knows the guy's gonna shoot him, so he starts to dial 911, but the guy pulls the trigger…?"

"Or the *girl* pulls the trigger." Wayne moved to the window and watched two squad cars pull into the drive.

Diana couldn't tell if they were from the Iredell County Sheriff's office, Wayne's men, or if they were Mooresville city police.

"I sure would like to have a chat with Janelle Havers," Wayne said. "Where I can find her, Billy?"

"No way!" The kid bristled. "Janelle may be a little nuts, but she's not crazy. She claimed she loved Harry, and she'd never do something like this."

*"Never* is a long time, son." Wayne took Diana's elbow and led her out of the room. "When the troops work their way back here, Billy, tell them the lady and I stepped outside."

The rookie seemed nervous. "What do I do in the meantime?"

Wayne pointed a warning finger in Billy's direction.

"Yeah, I know—stand still and don't touch," the kid said.

Wayne gave him a thumbs up, then steered her out the back door to a patio overlooking the lake. "Sit down on that bench, Diana. Tuck your head between your knees if you feel the urge to pass out again."

"I'm just fine, thank you very much."

"Oh yeah? Let's see those hands."

Although it was absurd and slightly offensive, she held up her hands, wrists together. "Are you planning to handcuff me?"

Much to her surprise, he took both her hands into his own, turned them palms-up, and then sniffed her fingers.

"What are you doing?"

"Just checking. Just as I thought, no odor of gunpowder, so I'll have to rule you out as the prime suspect."

"Thanks a hell of a lot!" She was stricken with déjà vu. She'd first met Sheriff Bearfoot under disturbingly similar circumstances. Her very first client in North Carolina, an old codger named Jedidiah Porter, had been found floating dead in Lake Norman, and because she'd been the last person to see him alive, she'd been the prime suspect. Since then, Wayne and she had become friends, and it was Wayne who'd introduced her to Matthew.

"How is Trout, by the way?" Wayne smiled, seemingly reading her mind.

She squirmed under his knowing gaze. All the locals called Matthew Troutman *Trout,* and they all seemed to know about their intimate relationship. She knew Matthew was close-mouthed and discreet, so was she. Chalk the problem up to small town life.

"To tell you the truth, Wayne, I've been busy. I haven't seen much of Matthew lately."

"Too bad. You always work too hard, Diana, and you look tired."

No kidding. What did the man expect? She had just witnessed the aftermath of a gruesome murder. A fresh wave of nausea washed through her.

"Look, I'm sorry about all this," he said after a long silence. "It doesn't seem fair, you caught in the middle of this mess."

An understatement. Right now all she wanted was a cool shower, a glass of wine, and blessed, forgetful sleep.

"You live in Davidson, right?" he continued gently. "Then you must have known Harold Havers in a professional capacity."

She drew a blank.

"He's one of the town commissioners," Wayne continued. "I'd think you real estate types would be thick with all the politicos, doing zoning deals and the like…?"

She wearily shook her head. Liz had been prodding her to attend the town meetings, to hobnob with the movers and shakers, but so far she'd avoided that particular hornets' nest.

"Never mind. Let's try a different approach. Back up to when you drove in, Diana. Think hard. What did you see? Any other cars coming out while you were going in?"

Her brain worked backwards through the day. She recalled the road crews and the cement mixer, the truck of rednecks tossing French fries and beer cans, and finally, the white paneled van that almost hit her as she turned onto Crow's Nest Drive.

"Yes, I did see something…"

Wayne sat down beside her on the bench, urging her on.

She described the ladders clattering and the curly-haired fellow in a paint-splattered ball cap. "There was something familiar about the driver."

"Was he speeding?"

An image of the young man's face finally sharpened and came clear. She had a vision of Liz and this same man together. "Hold on, it's coming to me…" Her fingers reached out, as if to capture the memory. Now, instead of a reckless NASCAR driver, she felt the presence of a friend, a good friend. "Oh my God," she gasped. "It was *Danny*!"

"Danny?"

"Oh, you know him." She smiled. "It was Danny Capelli, Liz's old boyfriend, the one who helped us solve Jedidiah Porter's murder."

"Oh yeah, *that* Danny." Wayne's handsome face opened in a smile. "Nice guy."

While Wayne digested the new information, she heard voices echoing behind them as the investigators entered the room with Havers' corpse. The sun had finally fallen below the horizon and into the lake, leaving a sudden chill in the air.

"Come to think of it, I saw some tarps and paint cans down at Havers' boat house when I drove in," Wayne said, the smile vanishing from his face. "Danny's a professional painter, isn't he?"

The chill invaded her body. Everyone knew Danny was a painter. She should have kept her big mouth shut.

"If Danny was here..." Wayne said sadly, "then he was likely around when Havers died."

She wanted to bite her tongue off. "I could be wrong. Maybe it wasn't Danny, after all."

Wayne sighed. He lifted a small pad from his breast pocket and penciled a note. "This is serious, Diana. I'm sorry, but I'll have to ask Mr. Capelli a few questions."

An ambulance rounded a curve across the bay, heading in their direction. Its red cherry light was spinning in the blue twilight, but there was no siren, and it was moving slow. Tears stung her eyes as she recalled Newton's law: *a body at rest tends to remain at rest.*

No need to hurry for a dead man.

THREE

*Front page news...*

"Diana, how could you do this to me?" Liz wailed as she pushed through the door. "I saw it last night on the late news. Why didn't you call?"

Diana cinched the belt of her bathrobe tighter and moved out of the path of the red headed tornado. Liz was an aberration of nature as she spun across Diana's Persian carpet, toppling a stack of classical CD's and sweeping away a pile of mystery novels to make room for herself on the sofa. Today she wore a snug, emerald green cashmere sweater that showcased her large bosom and precisely matched her eyes. The jeans and sneaks indicated she was not on her way to meet a client, in which case she'd be in a pencil skirt and killer high heels.

"You go for a simple listing contract and end up in the middle of a murder investigation. Jesus, Diana, can't you stay out of trouble?"

Diana took a deep breath. "Hello to you, too, Liz. Anything else on your mind?"

"Are you kidding? What else is there? Harold Havers' death is front page news."

Last night's headache was still with her. Neither the shower, the wine, nor a few short hours of sleep had driven the demons away.

"Want some coffee, Liz?"

"I had my caffeine fix hours ago. Are you just now getting up? How come you aren't dressed yet?"

Diana treated her young friend to a look of cross-eyed incredulity. Much as she loved Liz, who exuded her own special brand of manic enthusiasm, right now Diana just wished she'd go away.

"C'mon, Diana? How awful was it?"

"On a scale of one to ten, I'd rate it about nine." She was tempted to go all the way to ten, but in all fairness, it could have been worse. Only Harold Havers' *head* had been blown away.

"You're holding out on me, Diana."

She wasn't in the mood for one of Liz's interrogations, but putting her off would require an act of God. Liz followed her into her bright, modern kitchenette, where Diana poured herself a cup of coffee and finished buttering something masquerading as a bagel.

"Want one?" she asked.

"A bagel? Yuck!"

Diana knew from experience that Liz's preferred breakfast included grits and red-eye gravy. To each his own. She added milk and sugar to her coffee, then told Liz what little she knew about Harold Havers' murder.

"I don't buy it." Liz compressed her full lips. Her green eyes snapped. "All this stuff about the bottle of scotch and whether or not Harry was right-handed sounds stupid to me. I'd bet money it was suicide."

Diana arranged her meager breakfast on a tray and headed for the patio. Liz trailed her through the living room, which was eclectically decorated with a mixture of antiques from Diana's former life along with several modern pieces she had purchased at the High Point furniture market. These new things were supposed to remind her that what she really needed was a fresh start.

As always, Liz ran a critical eye over her collection of modern art. She reached out and touched the ebony breasts of the African fertility sculpture. "I still don't get it. Why do you need all this crap?"

*"Crap, crap, crap!"* A strident voice squawked from the bedroom.

"Shut up, Perry!" Liz screamed at the voice. "I don't need your shit right now!"

Diana groaned aloud. By now Liz was accustomed to the obscenities uttered by Perry, Diana's African Grey parrot, whom she had inherited from an elderly client who used equally foul language. Question was, whose language was worse, Perry's, or Liz's?

"C'mon, Diana, you know I'm teasing about your art. I love it! But hey, can't you put some clothes on that African girl?"

It was a tired old joke. Liz had often complimented Diana's oddball sense of interior design, so this was just Liz, being Liz. In the beginning, her much younger partner had urged Diana to get out and date, to *get a life*, as she put it. And as much as she'd resented Liz's interference, her influence had helped Diana overcome her fears enough to begin a relationship with Matthew. For this, she'd be eternally grateful.

"What makes you think it was a suicide?" She asked once they had settled on deck chairs.

Beyond Diana's potted plants and a low brick patio wall, Lake Norman was a dazzling shade of electric blue, punctuated by white-capped waves and white sails. But the beauty was all but lost on her.

"Well, to begin with…" Liz dropped her voice to a whisper. "His wife, Janelle, the whore from hell, is enough to make any man kill himself." Liz proceeded to describe Janelle as a selfish, materialistic creature incapable of fidelity.

Her shrill tirade brought Diana's headache roaring back. "If what you say is true, maybe one of Janelle's lovers murdered Mr. Havers?"

"Or Janelle did it herself. That bitch is capable of anything."

Diana was tempted to tell Liz about Deputy Billy's testimony that Janelle had stopped drinking and gotten religion. Instead, she steered a more neutral course. "Tell me again, why did Mr. Havers decide to list his house? Did they have financial trouble?"

"Janelle *is* financial trouble. From what I hear, she forced Harry to build that big old castle. They were still putting on the finishing touches when she decided it wasn't big enough, or showy enough, or whatever hair got up her ass."

"How do you know all this?"

A sly smile brightened Liz's pretty face. "Danny told me."

Diana's heart lurched off beat. Just hours ago, she had inadvertently implicated Danny Capelli to Sheriff Bearfoot.

"How would Danny know all this?" Her heart continued to thud off rhythm.

"As you know, my Danny is a painter. He and his guys did Havers' trim, and now they're working on the boat house."

Diana felt sick. Since when had Danny become *my Danny*? Last she knew, the couples' off- again-on-again, relationship was off. They'd been childhood sweethearts and had sporadic affairs ever since, but Danny lacked the ambition to become as rich as Liz required.

"Are you two together again?" she asked.

Liz winked. "Not exactly together. Let's just say we've done a little heavy breathing at a distance, over the phone."

"What about the *Liz First Rule*?" Diana was well aware of her friend's credo: *Never get involved unless he's rich, on the road to getting richer, and owns a boat by the age of thirty.*

"Don't get me wrong, I'm still looking for Mr. Rich and Ready, but for now, you know how I feel about Danny."

Diana did know. From the first moment she'd seen them together, she'd known that Liz and Danny were a perfect couple. She had hoped that someday Liz would understand that, too. But now, as she struggled with guilt and tried to come up with the right words to explain how she'd unintentionally betrayed Danny, Liz's cell phone rang—granting Diana a reprieve.

"Hello?" Liz answered. 'What's up, Danny?"

As she listened, Liz first looked out to the water, and then cast increasingly agitated looks at Diana. Diana braced herself for trouble.

Liz's face turned sunburn pink as she cried, "Are you fuckin' kidding me? How could you, Danny?"

By the time Liz ended the call, Diana was ready to run for cover.

"I can't believe it!" Liz moaned. "Danny's down at the sheriff's office. He's a suspect in Harry Havers' murder."

Diana was way too big to hide under the deck chair.

"Jesus Christ, Diana, he said *you* put the cops onto him!"

Diana's tongue was swollen speechless.

"His fingerprints are all over the place, including the room where Harry was killed." Liz jumped to her feet. She toppled the table, dumping Diana's coffee cup into a potted mum. "And that's

not all…" she wailed in retreat. "That bitch, Janelle! Fuckin'
Danny was sleeping with her!"

The door slammed, Perry cursed, and Diana went in search
of a Tylenol overdose.

FOUR

## *The local pecking order...*

The heat wave persisted, along with drought. It parched the fairways leading to Rocky Creek Country Club, where the Davidson Garden Club was holding its October meeting. The entry doors were propped open when Diana arrived. Had the management chosen to pretend there was an autumn breeze, rather than run the air conditioning off-season?

"Diana, dear, I'm so pleased you could make it." Joanne Early Jones, president of The Club, bustled forward to greet her. "Your young partner, Liz, said you were dying to join our club. You should have spoken up sooner."

A fake smile was frozen on Joanne's face, and every instinct told Diana to cut and run. At the same time, she had to do penance. Poor Danny Capelli was in serious trouble, and while Sheriff Bearfoot had not yet arrested him, he was the prime suspect. Liz was as mad as a lobster dangling above the boiling pot, and since Diana had heated the water, Liz was owed her revenge. Committing Diana to membership in The Garden Club was the perfect punishment.

"This is delightful..." Joanne, whom everybody called Jo Jo, captured her elbow and guided her through the crowded clubroom where the social elite had gathered. "I understand you have a green thumb, Diana. Besides, getting to know these folks should be helpful to your real estate business."

If she hadn't known better, she'd swear Liz had coached Jo Jo on the importance of networking, a concept Diana purely loathed.

"I do enjoy gardening," she admitted. "But these days the only place I can indulge my passion is in a few pots on my patio." She badly missed having a yard of her own, a plot of ground where she could get down and dirty and dig until her bones ached.

"Well, then, you'll feel right at home tonight." Jo Jo beamed. "We're designing autumn hanging baskets to place at our Main Street merchants' doors."

Diana groaned inwardly. Decorative baskets were not her cup of tea.

"Follow me…"

Jo Jo was short and plump, a white-haired Mrs. Santa Claus who wobbled when she walked. She came from an old Davidson family, with old Davidson money, as did her husband, Gerald. The couple had been born in ancestral homes only one block apart. They had attended Davidson College, raised their children within the village limits, and now had retired to the prestigious Evergreen Adult Community, where they'd no doubt remain until death brought them full circle to the Davidson cemetery.

"Look who's here!" Jo Jo tapped a tall, statuesque woman on the shoulder. "You know Diana, don't you, Parker?"

"Good evening, Commissioner Jones." Mary Parker White turned and delivered the wry greeting to Jo Jo. "Of course, I know Diana." She winked. "We're old buddies, as a matter of fact."

Two emotions registered at once. First, Diana had forgotten that Jo Jo Jones was a commissioner, and second, the sudden presence of Parker was a welcome gift. She was close to Diana's age, forty-six, tall and willowy like Diana, but more importantly, they shared much the same background.

They hugged one another. Parker was also a Yankee transplant. Diana had grown up in suburban Philadelphia, but Parker had hailed from Wilmington, Delaware, which inched her closer to the Mason-Dixon Line. Plus, she had married Randall White, one of Davidson's own. These distinctions gave Parker a decided social edge over an outsider like Diana. Even so, they had met shortly after Diana moved to North Carolina and discovered they had much in common. At a time in her life when Diana had been thirsty for contact with the world she'd left behind, Parker had been her oasis in the desert—but then they had drifted apart.

"I didn't know you were in The Club," Parker quipped.

Diana recalled her friend's sarcastic edge, which often poked gentle fun at the Establishment. At the same time, she knew Parker had powerful social aspirations. While she'd never admit it, Parker wanted to score high in the local pecking order. Diana couldn't fathom why this was so important to Parker, but she understood the deep-seeded human need to fit in. Parker had spent her entire adult life trying to prove herself to an entrenched southern aristocracy, and now she wanted a payback.

Diana thought about that a moment. Ever since she'd moved to North Carolina, she'd been subtly aware of being "the other." As a northerner, she'd likely never be fully accepted by the generational natives as one of their own. The cultural differences between them, the historical memory of what had divided the north and south for so long, was an inbred fact, almost genetic in its power to divide. At least this was what her friends back in Philadelphia had conditioned her to believe. On the other hand, as Diana had learned to know her new southern friends, it seemed she might be suffering from reverse prejudice, an illness she should work hard to cure.

"I'm a new member." Diana smiled as she followed Parker and Jo Jo into the central gathering, where everyone was milling around two banquet tables. One was laden with refreshments, the other was adorned by various styles of hanging baskets, piles of autumn leaves, and dried flowers.

"This was our assignment." Jo Jo's eyes sparkled behind thick glasses. "Everyone brought a distinctive basket, as well as whatever fallen leaves or flowers they could gather from their own yards."

"I don't have a yard," Diana muttered. With a little luck, the teacher would excuse her from this project.

"No problem," Parker said. "Diana can collect those things in the park, can't she? It could be an extra credit project, provided she turns it in by the end of the week."

Had they actually been schoolgirls, Diana would have kicked Parker under the desk.

"Nonsense," Jo Jo said. "Diana can share the materials others have brought. We have plenty to go around. Good luck, dear…" She gave Diana a motherly pat on the arm, and then she was gone.

Parker rolled her eyes, which were almost as deep blue as Diana's. "Commissioner Jones is a tough cookie. Think she'll give you a gold star, Diana?"

Diana laughed as they moved towards the refreshment table. "I'll bet she's a good commissioner, though. Jo Jo likes a tight agenda."

"No shit." Parker snorted. "You should see her on the *Pretty Committee*."

Although Diana's knowledge of local politics was woefully lacking, even she had heard this derogative term applied to Davidson's Design Review Board. These were the folks who guarded the town's aesthetics by regulating signage, determining which colors were harmonious in public places, and what landscaping was least likely to offend the citizens' sensibilities. They forced developers, entrepreneurs, and new retailers to jump through hoops when they moved to town.

"Speaking of the *Pretty Committee*," Parker whispered. "Here comes its fearless leader now…"

A tall, elderly gentleman approached. In spite of the heat, he was fastidiously clad in a conservative three-piece suit, complete with silk pocket hankie, watch chain and bow tie. The man affected an aggressive stride, which seemed at odds with his frail, stooped shoulders. He was awkward like a giraffe that has bumped into one too many low-hung branches and then overcompensated with a determined walk.

"I'm sure you have met Commissioner Homer Locksley," Parker cooed.

Diana had seen him around town. His extreme height and full head of collar-length white hair were arresting features indeed.

"I've seen you reading the *TIMES* at the coffee shop," she told the man. "But we've never been introduced."

As Parker did the honors, Homer Locksley extended long fingers. His handshake was a bone-cruncher, his skin clammy to the touch.

"Please drop the *commissioner* nonsense," he said. "I don't know why Mrs. White insists upon introducing me that way. I'm a retired art professor, Mrs. Rittenhouse. Serving as a commissioner simply helps me fill the empty hours."

"That's right," Parker said. "Homer retired a decade ago, but the musty odor of the ivory tower still clings, does it not?"

Diana was accustomed to Parker's wry humor, but this last remark cut deep and bordered on the offensive. "Shall I call you Professor, then?"

"Oh Lordy no, that would be silly." He giggled nervously. "Please call me Homer."

"No doubt his parents named him after Winslow Homer." Parker smirked. "And that's why he went into art."

The old gentleman blushed furiously, but did not contradict Parker's comment. Instead, he turned his rheumy blue eyes on Diana. "Why does your name sound familiar?" He gulped at an iced drink containing a cut lime. "Oh, now I remember! You're the lady who found poor Harold Havers' body, aren't you?"

Diana nodded, guilty as charged.

"Drop it, Homer," Parker snapped. "I'm sure Diana doesn't want to discuss it. She came here to enjoy herself."

"Yes, but…" Homer moved away from Parker. "The thing is, Harold wasn't exactly a friend, but we did serve together on the Board for many years, so his death is extremely upsetting."

"Give it a rest, Homer," Parker hissed.

Diana looked from one to the other. In addition to the animosity Parker projected at Homer Locksley, she was also acting as a self-appointed guardian of Diana's feelings.

"I don't mind discussing it, Parker."

"Suit yourself, Diana. But excuse me if I don't stick around for the gruesome details."

Diana and Homer Locksley watched Parker stalk away. Apparently Parker was angry with both of them. Homer flushed red, confirming Diana's belief that there was bad blood between Parker and himself.

"Don't mind Parker," he said. "She knew Harold rather well, you see. He was her banker when she moved here, after her husband, Randy, died. I'm sure losing Harold is a great blow to her."

Diana tried to fit it all together. Although Parker was stingy with details about her personal life, as was Diana, Diana had managed to learn something about the tragic death of Parker's husband, Randall. He had been a Davidson graduate who then earned his medical degree at Duke, where he met Parker. The newlyweds had then moved to Winston- Salem, where Randall practiced at Wake Forest Baptist Medical Center.

Diana thought aloud. "Parker's husband died of a heart attack before her children were grown. Then Parker and her son moved back to the White family home here in Davidson, isn't that right?"

Homer shrugged and swallowed the rest of his drink. Apparently, he'd lost interest in the Mary Parker White story. "So what do you think, Mrs. Rittenhouse? Was Harold's sudden demise suicide?"

Suddenly she felt uncomfortable with this man. His manner seemed to reduce the gravity of violent death to juicy gossip. "Actually, Homer, I'm in no position to judge."

"I do hope it wasn't suicide," he said. "Jo Jo and I were discussing it earlier. Along with the other two commissioners, I'm afraid we were pushing Harold too hard."

Diana didn't know much about local affairs, except that a mayor and five commissioners governed Davidson. Again she felt a twinge of guilt at her lack of involvement.

"I know it seems silly," he continued, "but in order to sit on the Board, a commissioner must live in town. Our forefathers, in all their wisdom, believed one must live as a neighbor to those he governs in order to truly understand their concerns.

"Anyhow, when Havers built that architectural disaster out at The Point, he left the town of Davidson for Mooresville. Not to put too fine a point on it, but old Harold would have been out of a job come November. Nothing against the fellow, you understand, but one can't bend the rules."

Diana was fast developing an unreasonable dislike of Homer. For one thing, he spoke without a trace of southern accent. Instead, he had adopted pseudo-British speech patterns along with affected English mannerisms. All he lacked was a powdered white wig to pass judgment on the likes of Harold Havers.

"Our little civic duties were important to Harold," Homer continued. "Jo Jo and I were hoping it wasn't losing his job that pushed him over the edge."

"Perhaps he wouldn't have lost his job," she interrupted. For some reason she felt compelled to come to Havers' defense. "He was hoping to sell his house in Mooresville. Maybe his goal was to move back to Davidson and seek reelection."

"You don't say?" Homer pursed his lips and seemed displeased.

She made an excuse and broke away. Conversation with this man had made her feel acutely claustrophobic. She escaped to the refreshment table, where a cocktail bar had been set up to compliment the hors d'oeuvres. A beautiful black woman wearing a Hawaiian-style lei of autumn leaves around her neck was the designated bartender.

"I'll have rum and tonic like Homer Locksley was drinking." Diana smiled at the woman, whom she assumed was a waitress.

"Oh no, ma'am, Professor Locksley doesn't use alcohol. He was drinking Aquafina on the rocks."

Again Diana felt foolish and terribly out of place.

"Just because Homer prefers bottled water, doesn't mean you can't have a rum and tonic, Diana." Parker pushed in and poured Diana's drink herself. "Heaven forbid Homer Locksley should take a drink or smoke a cigarette. The man is Mr. Clean, except for one small flaw…"

Diana didn't want to hear more, but Parker lifted her hands and minced across the floor like a limp-wristed bunny. She held one hand out flat and waffled it back and forth.

"No one talks about it, but everyone knows." Parker rolled her eyes. "Every southern town has one…"

Diana glared daggers at her friend. The appalling homophobic attitude was so unlike Parker, that Diana was ashamed to be sharing the same room with the woman. For moments they stared at one another, until suddenly Parker's eyes misted with tears.

"Oh, dear, Diana, I am so sorry!" She pulled Diana away from the crowd. "What I said was horrible. Please forgive me, I didn't mean a word of it. Homer and I have been friends for years, and I couldn't care less how he conducts his private life."

Diana blinked as Parker transformed from a virulent bigot to a weeping child.

"It's the stress of losing Harold, but that's no excuse. I don't blame you for thinking the worst of me, Diana…"

Parker fled into the crowd, leaving Diana bewildered, conflicted, and certain of only one thing—this would be her first and last day of membership in The Garden Club. These people reminded her of the snobbish, ingrown cliques back in Main Line Philadelphia, where she'd also most certainly not fit in. So clearly these types were not indigenous only to the south.

Poor thing." Jo Jo materialized at her elbow. "Parker White is a nervous wreck, and who can blame her? Harold Havers lent her the money to save the *White Elephant,* but in the end she'll lose it."

Diana's mind raced to keep pace. She'd decided that Jo Jo Jones' resemblance to Mrs. Santa Claus was only skin deep, and like it or not, Diana was doomed to hear the latest gossip from this little creature.

"Of course Randall White's old family home *is* a white elephant. Who wants a Tara look-alike these days? Parker loves her old home place, but honestly, she can't afford it. We commissioners did what we could, but once she uses up Harold's loan, she'll have to sell."

Diana tried to move away, but Jo Jo pinned her.

"Really, Diana, think about it. Doesn't Davidson need a Harris Teeter downtown?"

What on earth did Parker's old plantation house have to do with a modern grocery store? Then she remembered a newspaper headline: *Board Approves Harris Teeter.* It seemed the White property on Main Street was the only viable location for such a store, so apparently Davidson had worked out a settlement with Parker and moved her, along with the house, onto a postage stamp-sized lot at the edge of town. The result for the gracious old home was aesthetic disaster, the gain for the town highly questionable. Although she didn't know the details of the settlement, it seemed Parker had gotten a raw deal.

"To tell you the truth, Commissioner Jones, it seems to me the White home could have been moved to a more appropriate site, maybe one of those large lots at the end of Main Street?"

Jo Jo's twinkling eyes frosted to an icy *how-dare-you* stare, and Diana realized that she'd overstepped her bounds.

"But what do I know?" she quickly amended.

---

"Never mind, dear." Jo Jo's smile was rigid. "We all feel bad for Parker, and we intend to make it up to her. Indeed, the mayor's wife is here tonight to make a very special presentation."

With these words, the plump president of The Garden Club lifted a small brass bell and vigorously tinkled for attention. Those assembled gathered around like obedient school children. The hot room steamed with anticipation, and everyone seemed privy to what was about to take place.

Everyone but Diana.

"Where is Mary Parker White?" Jo Jo stood on tiptoe, scanning the room. "Ah ha! Bring her on over here, Homer…"

The professor located Parker and corralled her into the circle of guests. A distinguished matron, with dyed black hair piled on her head and heavy strands of pearls around her neck, approached with a ribboned box in her hands. Diana recognized her from the society pages. She was Mrs. Connery, the mayor's wife.

The beautiful black woman wearing the Hawaiian lei stepped from behind the refreshments table and into a line, which included both Jo Jo and Homer Locksley. She handed the box to Parker. "Daddy couldn't be here today, and Commissioner Wadell is out of town, but they both approved this decision, so the entire Board is in agreement," she said.

Sensing Diana's confusion, a woman appeared at her elbow and whispered: "The black woman is Commissioner Lester B. Smith's daughter, Rhonda, and Commissioner Billy Wadell, the one away on business, is the one we call *Duck*. He's a big developer around town, so I imagine you already know him."

Diana did not know Duck nor the woman at her elbow, but appreciated the update. She was mortally ashamed for having assumed that Rhonda, the commissioner's daughter was a waitress.

"Go on and open it, Parker!" someone shouted.

Parker was ghostly pale. Her fingers fumbled with the bow as she opened the package. A hush fell on the room when she lifted out a varnished wooden gavel, and Parker's lips trembled as she read the inscription on the brass plaque: *"Honorary Commissioner, Town of Davidson."*

"Welcome to the Board, Parker!" The mayor's wife beamed. "Much as we regret the passing of poor Harold, life goes on."

"That's right, Parker," Homer Locksley added. "It's only temporary, of course, until next month's elections…"

"But we need you." Jo Jo smiled. "Next week we vote for a new Town Planner, and we require a fifth person to be the tie-breaker, if it comes to that."

"And God knows, you've earned it." Rhonda Smith lifted the colorful lei of autumn leaves from around her neck and placed it over Parker's head. "Do you accept the position?"

Tears welled up in Parker's eyes as she clasped the gavel to her breast. "Yes, oh yes!" She hyperventilated. "I can't begin to tell you—this is my lifelong dream."

FIVE

*Circumstantial evidence…*

"Sure, she deserves to be a commissioner," Liz said. She'd moved her desk to the extreme corner of their office, as far away as possible from Diana. "Mary Parker White is everywhere I go, and as you know, I attend all the functions."

Diana was terribly distracted as Liz rattled on about Parker's participation in all the community affairs, her perfect attendance record at town meetings, and the productive networking technique that had netted her an appointment to the Board.

"Obviously the woman craves power and recognition," Liz continued. "Like I always tell you, Diana, it pays to get in people's faces. That way they remember you when they're ready to buy or sell."

Diana closed her eyes and tilted back in her chair. As the late afternoon sun filtered through the tinted glass window of their office condo, warming her face, she realized she was emotionally and physically exhausted. Only five days ago she'd discovered Harold Havers' body, and the ensuing week had not been peaceful.

"Take our situation…" Liz was relentless. "Ever since you showed up in the news, our business is booming. Like they say, even bad publicity is better than no publicity. Am I right?"

Their phones had been ringing off the hooks with curiosity seekers, some of whom Liz had actually converted into live real estate leads.

"Get with the program, Diana. Now is the time to contact your old prospects and kick them into gear."

Diana tuned out the advice, but at least the topic was neutral. Lately her relationship with Liz had been strained. She'd stupidly told Wayne Bearfoot about Danny Capelli being at Harold Havers' house directly before the murder, so now she couldn't discuss the crime with Liz at all. The close bond they'd always shared wasn't broken, but it was badly frayed, and she desperately wanted to mend it.

"It wouldn't kill you to attend the town meetings, Diana. Now that your *best friend* is a commissioner, you might even enjoy it."

Diana detected a note of jealousy. In spite of their age difference, she had always considered Liz her new best friend. Even though Parker's background and interests more closely matched her own, Diana didn't really know the woman. Liz didn't have to compete for Diana's friendship, and she should know it.

"You win, I promise to attend the next town meeting," Diana vowed.

"Big deal. You already quit The Garden Club, so one town meeting only brings you back to square one."

Clearly Diana's stubborn, redheaded partner was out for blood. "I volunteered to work with the Community Players on *The King and I*. Doesn't that count?"

Liz swiveled and faced her for the first time that afternoon, her eyes wide with surprise. "I'm impressed."

Actually, working with the Community Players had been a trade-off. When she'd resigned from The Garden Club, Parker had been so upset she'd begged Diana to take over her duties as Properties Manager, a job Parker despised. Diana had felt so guilty, she couldn't say no. She already regretted her momentary lapse, but intended to make the best of it.

"Honestly, Diana, I am proud. Maybe there's hope for you yet."

Just then the doorbell chimed, and Diana prayed it was a potential customer. "You take it, Liz," she said, wanting to punt the lead.

"No way. It's your turn, Diana."

They were still arguing when a tall figure entered the anteroom. The man squinted as his eyes adjusted to the shade. He removed a straw fishing cap and ran fingers through his soft brown hair.

"It's Trout," Liz stage-whispered. "Should I get lost?"

Diana was so surprised she could hardly speak. Instead, she stared at Matthew's forehead, at the endearing sunburn line his cap made just above his eyebrows.

"Afternoon, ladies…" He ducked slightly as he entered their space, a reflex shared by many tall men who had bumped their heads on too many doorjambs. "Am I interrupting something?"

"I was just leaving…" Liz began shoveling papers into her briefcase.

"Not so fast, Liz." Matthew's powerful frame blocked her exit. "I haven't seen either of you girls in a coon's age. Besides, I think you'll want to hear what my old pal Wayne Bearfoot had to say about Harold Havers' murder investigation."

Although he was talking to both of them, Diana felt his intense brown gaze focused only on her. A sudden rush of heat disturbed her equilibrium.

"Diana's the one who found Harry," Liz said.

"Yeah, but your boyfriend's the one in trouble," Matthew countered.

Liz flushed. "C'mon, Trout, Danny's not my boyfriend. Not anymore."

"Then I guess you aren't interested."

Liz sighed, then heaved the briefcase back onto her desk and moved into the chair beside Diana. This was the closest they'd been all week. "Okay, I'll bite. What's up, Trout?"

Warmth traveled through Diana's body. Matthew was here, and Liz seemed to be calling a truce. Matthew and Liz had known each other forever. Like most locals, she shortened Matthew Troutman's name to *Trout*. She had visited *Trout's Place* for candy and ice cream when she was knee high to a grasshopper. He had watched Liz grow, and now he was waiting for her to grow up. At least that was Diana's take on their relationship.

"Mind if I perch here, Diana?" He winked.

He moved stacks of paperwork aside and sat on the edge of Diana's desk. Her knee burned where his left leg touched it.

"Now I don't mind telling you, Wayne has his nose to the ground like a Cherokee bloodhound, but he can't pin Danny down."

"What did he say about the gun?" Diana asked.

"It belonged to Havers, like they figured. He kept it in a table behind his desk.

An image slowly formed in her mind. She saw Havers' Chinese black lacquer table and an enormous bouquet of hothouse flowers. And yes, there had been a drawer.

"Were there fingerprints on the gun?" Liz wondered.

"Havers' prints were clear, along with residual prints that matched his wife, Janelle."

"I knew it!" Liz crowed. "I knew that bitch killed Harry, so how come the sheriff's still hassling Danny?"

Matthew lifted his hand, the rough, calloused hand of a workingman. "Slow down, Liz. It wasn't unusual to find both Harry's and Janelle's prints on the revolver. Sooner or later, every wife in America gets the urge to play with her husband's gun."

Matthew's remark got Liz giggling, which caused Matthew to blush beneath his dark tan.

"What I *meant* to say is statistics allow for both the victim's and the spouse's prints on the murder weapon. According to Wayne, it would be more suspicious if the wife's prints were not found."

"It's safe to assume the killer wore gloves, right?" Diana asked.

"I'm no expert." Matthew's handsome features opened in a smile. "You know me and guns, Diana."

His aversion to firearms was one of the many things she loved about him. Although Matthew's rugged, aggressively masculine persona conjured up images of rifle racks on pickup trucks, he had never owned a gun of any kind. A closeted pacifist, he wept at happy endings and would sooner throw a fish back in the lake than skin it for dinner.

"I still say Janelle did it." Liz scowled.

"Well, they always take a long hard look at the spouse," Matthew agreed. "But I hear Janelle has an airtight alibi. She was out of town all weekend helping her girlfriends set up a display at the furniture market in Highpoint."

"She's lying," Liz insisted.

"Her girlfriends were with her. Are they lying too?"

Liz's face fell. "Maybe she hired someone to kill him?"

"Yeah, it's possible…" Matthew's hand strayed to Diana's shoulder, and then he massaged the tension at the back of her neck.

"I hate to say it, but Wayne still sees Danny as his prime suspect. The boy had motive and opportunity."

"Danny wouldn't hurt anybody," Liz cried. "What's wrong with these cops? Don't they know Janelle slept with anything in pants? Why don't they go looking for those other guys and leave Danny alone?"

"But Diana didn't see any of those other guys at the scene. She saw only Danny."

The tension Matthew had eased between her shoulders hardened into a knot of guilt. "I told Wayne a hundred times Danny didn't do it," Diana said. "Maybe the killer was still around when I got there, or even worse, maybe he was hiding in the house."

Matthew shook his head. "Nope, Bearfoot claims the killer wasn't in the house or on the grounds. He and his deputy checked as soon as they arrived."

"What if he sneaked off while I was inside the house, before I found the body?" Diana interrupted. "He could've gotten away before the sheriff arrived."

"Look, I agree with you," he said. "Danny's a good man. Of course he didn't do it. Problem is, so much of the evidence points in his direction."

"Circumstantial evidence," Diana argued. "What about the other painters in Danny's crew? They had opportunity."

"Not according to Danny. He told Wayne he let his men off early, it being Saturday night. Then Danny stayed back alone to clean up. Wayne thinks Havers knew and trusted his killer, who got close enough to shoot him at point blank range. Yet the painters say Danny and Havers were friendly with one another, in spite of that thing with his wife."

When Matthew alluded to Danny's illicit affair with Janelle, Liz rose from her chair and turned her back. "So far

Danny's doing himself more harm than good. Why doesn't he defend himself?"

"Oh, he claims he's innocent." Matthew spoke gently. "He swears his relationship with Mrs. Havers ended weeks ago, and she backs him up on that point. At the time of the murder, Danny says he was making a racket, cleaning out buckets with a pressure washer, so he couldn't hear anything, not even a gunshot. But he does recall seeing a small white car leaving the house, a Honda Civic, *maybe*. Unfortunately, those vehicles are common as ticks on hounds, so it's not much of a lead. I think Wayne believes him, but the facts are hard to ignore."

Matthew rose and crossed to Liz. He brushed a strand of red hair from her forehead. "Danny always tells the truth, but sometimes honesty's not the best policy. He told Bearfoot he knew about the gun. He even knew where Havers kept it."

"The idiot!" Liz shrieked. "Why can't Danny keep his big mouth shut?"

"It gets worse…" Matthew gazed at his worn deck shoes. "It was like a joke between Danny and Janelle. Once, when they were alone in Havers' study, she told Danny that Harry would shoot him if he caught them together. She actually showed Danny the drawer where Havers kept his weapon."

"Danny *told* Bearfoot this?" Liz's green eyes expanded in tearful incredulity. "Does the man have a death wish?"

Liz stomped from the room, forgetting her briefcase and slamming the door.

"Sorry, Diana." He took both her hands and drew her to her feet. "I didn't set out to be the messenger of bad tidings."

"What's going to happen, Matthew?"

He slowly pulled her close. The thin fabric of his shirt pressed against her breasts. She felt the heat of his chest and the steady beating of his heart.

"I can't see the future," he whispered into her hair. "But I think it'll work out all right for Danny and Liz. But what about *us*...?" His hand traveled along her spine, easing her ever closer. "What about our vacation, Diana? Our trip to the beach?" His lips lingered at her temples. "Haven't we put it off long enough?"

Her heartbeat accelerated and she enjoyed the familiar melting at her core. They had put many things off far too long.

# SIX

## *Vicious gossip...*

Diana knocked again on her mother's closed door. No response. But like many residents at Shady Oaks Retirement Community, Vivian Whitaker never locked up when she left her room, so Diana let herself in. As always, she was overcome by bittersweet nostalgia. Two dressers, a secretary desk, and the nightstands with cherry glass lamps on either side of Mama's narrow bed transported her back to her childhood in Pennsylvania. And Mama's scent, White Shoulders cologne, was a visceral connection to her earliest memories.

As always, the room was too hot and too dark. Vivian ignored the air conditioning unit built into the wall beneath the window, claiming her old blood was already too cold. And she seldom opened the Venetian blinds to the little garden Diana had created especially for Mama's pleasure, complete with geraniums and a bird feeder. Viv claimed her old eyes were too sensitive to outdoor light.

Her mother's habits vexed Diana, but she'd never been able to reason with Vivian. In fact, Diana's father had always insisted that both Mama and she had stubborn streaks as wide as the barn door and deep as the well. Mother and Daughter were like oil and water—they'd never mix. And if those characterizations were true back then, they were doubly true now.

Yet Diana loved her mother dearly. She quietly closed the door and stepped back into the carpeted hallway. For many years now, the parent/child roles had been reversed, and caring for Mama had become an integral part of her life. Often Liz, and occasionally Matthew, had warned her not to obsess about Mama's condition, but she couldn't help herself.

Brittle diabetes and selective memory lapses were Mama's major complaints, and while the staff at Shady Oaks controlled her diabetes, her absent-mindedness was Diana's problem. Back in Pennsylvania, Mama had been living alone in the family homestead and had left a burner lit on the stove. She'd managed to burn the house clean to the ground.

Diana sighed and followed her nose down the hallway to the dining room. Fortunately, Mama hadn't been hurt in that fire, and luckily, the disaster had coincided with Diana's need to start a new life. Vivian had been born and raised in North Carolina, only one mile from Shady Oaks, so Diana had helped her mother pack her bags and brought her home.

Somehow the move back to the South had given Vivian a new lease on life, and Shady Oaks, a brand new retirement facility, had been the answer to Diana's prayers. Vivian's personality had expanded. She'd made new friends, and told everyone the story about the dashing Yankee farmer who'd stolen her heart, and then whisked her away to the land of snow. Unfortunately, she seemed to lavish her long dormant charm on everyone but Diana.

Anticipating Mama's wrath, she quickened her pace. They had agreed to eat dinner together every Friday night, and tardiness was unacceptable. As she rounded the corner into a gracious reception hall where the residents were assembling, she spotted a tall woman with a cane hobbling towards the menu board.

"Hi, Mama! Sorry I'm late."

Vivian rotated her body and lifted her heavy white eyebrows. Her eyes were as deep blue as Diana's, and her torso, once strong and athletic, now angled forward like a bent tree.

"This is not a restaurant, Diana," she grumbled. "These girls serve on a strict schedule. They can't be waiting around just to take your order."

"I realize that, Mother."

They linked arms and walked together, taking seats at Mama's assigned table. Mrs. Louise Turbyfil, Mama's current best friend, had already finished her rolls and salad.

"Oh, Diana!" Mrs. Turbyfil wiped her fingers and extended a bony hand. "We haven't seen you in ages."

Not true. Diana had visited last week. She glanced at the extended hand, which was exquisitely manicured and bore the largest diamond ring she'd ever seen. Each time Mrs. Turbyfil did this, Diana felt inclined to kiss that hand, as though Mrs. Turbyfil were royalty. Instead, she always took the hand into her own two hands for a friendly squeeze.

"We all heard about that murder you witnessed." Mama got right to the point over roast chicken and whipped potatoes. "Now tell us everything, all the gory details."

Diana was wildly hungry, as she always was when presented with Shady Oak's scrumptious home cooking. Yet she knew she'd never be allowed to enjoy one bite until she'd satisfied the ladies' curiosity.

Vivian and Mrs. Turbyfil were already eating dessert, and Diana was still on the main course when she turned the conversation away from murder and told them about her evening at The Garden Club.

"Mary Parker White, you say?" Mrs. Turbyfil's ears pricked. "I know that gal. My husband, God rest his soul, was her husband's supervisor at Wake Forest."

Diana's fork hovered above the fried okra. "Your husband was a physician, Mrs. Turbyfil?"

"My goodness, yes. Forty-three years of service before he retired. He was teaching part time at the university while he was Chief of Cardiology at Baptist. That was when young Randall White came on board."

Lou Turbyfil spoke with the gravelly voice of an ex-smoker as she warmed to her topic. Diana figured she could eat in peace while Lou carried the conversational ball.

"Now Randy was a good man, a hard worker, and everyone agreed he was a talented surgeon. Parker, however, was another kettle of fish. She never really fit in, you know? It wasn't just because she came from up north, more like she tried too hard. The woman was always pushing her way in. She nominated herself for Chairwoman of the Wives' Club, and even when she wasn't elected, she told us all what to do and when to do it."

"Let's be fair, Lou," Vivian interrupted. "I know how I felt when I moved to Pennsylvania—like I'd been stranded me in a foreign country."

"Yes, but that wasn't Parker's problem…" Mrs. Turbyfil's voice trailed off as she paused to finish her apple cobbler. "She was just plain pushy. And the White children were a worry, too. Such a pity, the way they turned out."

Diana's curiosity was peaked. It was one thing to launch a catty attack against Parker, quite another to malign her children. "Why were the children a problem?"

"I'm not one to talk out of turn…" Mrs. Turbyfil patted her lips and carefully folded her napkin. "But the girl, Cynthia White, was a terrible disappointment to her mother. She met some boy when she was an undergraduate at Wake Forest. The boy was from a good family, but something awful happened between them."

"I bet Parker's daughter got pregnant...," Vivian said, "and then had an abortion."

Diana gave her a swift kick under the table. "You know nothing about it, Mama."

"I can't say for sure what happened," Mrs. Turbyfil continued. "But Cindi dropped out of school and ran away from home. Adding insult to injury, she married a NASCAR driver. Can you *imagine*...?"

"Disgraceful." Viv agreed.

"Well, Parker had a nervous breakdown over it. At least that's what they say."

Their vicious gossip was revolting, nothing but hearsay. Diana left the table in disgust to get herself a sugar-free strawberry shortcake like her mother was eating, but when she returned, the slander was still hot and heavy.

"And that boy of theirs, Randall, Junior—I never saw a more pathetic little thing."

"What was *his* problem?" Vivian planted her elbows on the table and leaned closer to Lou.

"He was only a little fella when his daddy died," Mrs. Turbyfil whispered. "But even then you could see he wasn't right. He was so shy he'd throw up when company paid a visit. He didn't speak until he was almost three years old, and then he stuttered."

"Poor child!" Vivian gasped, then frowned in Diana's direction. "Why are you eating that shortcake? You don't need sugar-free, Diana. You are skin and bones as it is."

"I like it, Mother. It's almost as good as the real thing."

"No man will want you unless you put some meat on those bones." Mama hesitated, a devilish grin on her face. "By the way, how is Matthew?"

She refused to be dragged into a discussion of her love life, especially when she was still walking around in a physical and emotional daze. The brief encounter with Matthew in her office yesterday had unhinged her, even though an unwanted client had spoiled it by walking in mid-kiss.

"Yes, Diana, how is your handsome young man?" Mrs. Turbyfil probed.

All the ladies at Shady Oaks loved Matthew, who'd been kind enough to accompany Diana to dinner one time. Indeed, he'd also been seduced by the downhome southern cooking and would have joined Diana on a regular basis, if she'd been willing to share him with these nosey old biddies.

"Never mind, Lou, my daughter won't talk unless we change the subject. So, what would you like to discuss, Diana?"

Diana patted her lips and folded her napkin. "How about Bingo?"

SEVEN

## *Lester B. Smith*

Saturday nights were always the low point of his week. The pungent smell of fresh paint, along with the chemical stench of new carpet, turned his stomach, so he pushed the cold TV dinner aside and stared at the blank wall.

Although the shadows of twilight crept through the rooms, he didn't bother to turn on the lights. All the cozy floor lamps, along with the rest of the furniture from the old place, had been donated to Habitat for Humanity. This was his daughter's brilliant idea, her way of urging him to get on with his life. As if buying all new stuff could turn it around, or ease the loneliness, or bring back the dead.

This particular Saturday night was the worst so far. Although he hadn't taken a drink in years, he opened the cabinet under the kitchen sink and retrieved a bottle of Old Crow. Even at their real home, the house on Mill Street, he'd kept an unopened bottle under the sink. Everybody knew it—his mama, his wife, and the kids. They also knew he'd never drink one drop. But they were all gone now.

He took a paper cup from the roll and moved out to the back stoop, where the new neighbors wouldn't see him. It struck him that he was camping out here, living off paper plates and sleeping on a palette on the floor. And in spite of the children's urging, he couldn't find the heart to furnish the alien rooms.

He settled his bony haunches on a wooden step and gazed out across the darkening ruins beyond his newly seeded lawn, to where the old houses once stood. A backhoe was silhouetted against the sky, its giant claw tucked in for the night, its tires planted in the soil where the grape arbor once stood.

All gone.

His brown hand trembled as he sloshed amber liquid into the cup. It burned its way down his esophagus and spread fire through his belly. The others put him here in this award- winning bungalow, part of a project hailed throughout the state as the most progressive approach ever conceived to low-income housing.

All the commissioners had a hand in it. Homer Locksley, the art professor, had been the ringleader, the beacon light. The row of replicated 1920's bungalows became his raison d'etre, the tangible justification for an otherwise failed life. Homer's designs were the talk of the town, the nation, and ultimately Davidson received the governor's gold medal achievement award.

Harold Havers' banking connections had provided the funding, Duck Wadell's construction company had won the building bid, while Jo Jo Jones washed her plump hands of a lifetime of white guilt, avowing that the poor folk of Davidson deserved state-of-the-art housing.

No one bothered to ask the folks themselves how they felt about it, or if they wanted to move. For the first time in his career, Lester had voted against them all. He had begged and pleaded with them to reconsider. He had explained that the residents of Mill Street didn't want their homes destroyed. He'd told his fellow commissioners that one man's shanty is another man's palace, but would they listen?

They were surprised by his defiance. Hadn't he gone along with them all these years? Sometimes he felt like the token black man, who always got reelected because he could always be counted on to vote the right way. And suddenly he'd seen it in their eyes, the truth he'd carefully ignored: Lester really *was* Davidson's own Justice Thomas. All this time he had fooled only himself.

Pouring another drink, he longed to play the record backwards. When Harold Havers was murdered, his first impulse had been to celebrate the bastard's death. His second impulse was shame. How far had he strayed, and when had it begun?

The tips of his fingers were numb.

Everyone was gone.

Most of his lifelong neighbors had fled to the homes of relatives to live out their days, once their houses were destroyed. His son had moved up north a long time ago, without finishing high school, and Lester had always believed the shock of his leaving caused his wife's cancer and brought on her death back in 1985. His daughter, Rhonda, was a good girl, but she was divorced with two small children. Her job at Town Hall was all the extra work she could manage, so it was out of the question that Lester and his old mama could live with her.

His toes were numb as he climbed to his feet and headed for the carport.

And now Rhonda's grandma was dead.

Night after night the horror invaded his dreams. The old woman had survived segregation, raised six children, buried two husbands and a daughter, and held the family together for three generations. She hadn't complained when he told her about the move, but the light died in her eyes.

Lester and his mama had stood side by side when the volunteer firemen came that Saturday morning last year. It had been good practice for the men, burning down unwanted buildings, and their old homestead had screamed under the flames. Its bones crackled and popped and finally sighed into a smoking white heap.

And right then and there, Mama sank onto the grass, dead of a heart attack. Everyone agreed she died of a broken heart, and that the Davidson Commissioners had killed her.

Tears stung his eyes as he twisted the ignition. His old Chrysler LeBaron seldom fired up on the first try. He used the car infrequently. The third time was the charm, so he backed carefully out the driveway and headed towards Mooresville. It wouldn't look right if someone recognized him buying liquor at the local ABC.

The lights at Exit 30 disoriented Lester. There were so many new buildings now, even a big medical center, and nothing looked familiar. He understood he was slightly impaired. His vision was fuzzy as he pulled out onto Interstate 77. But then he noticed the headlights of the little white car that had been following him all the way from his home. And up ahead was the bridge crossing Lake Norman, so he drove very slowly.

The lights along the guardrail were a double string of white pearls. Far off on the dark waves, red and green running lights twinkled where boats were out for an evening cruise. It was all so beautiful and peaceful, like the highway to Heaven.

Except for the cars honking from behind. They wouldn't let up, honking and pressing his tail. Especially that little white one in his rear view mirror. It wanted to pass, but there was too much traffic in the fast lane. Finally its headlights moved out from behind him, fixing to squeeze in between two vehicles racing up from the rear. The white car made it and came alongside him, but the truck behind it was closing fast, its horn blaring. The driver in the white car began waving furiously and flashing his lights. He wanted to cut in front of Lester's Chrysler, but there wasn't room.

What could he do? He reckoned in seconds the little white car would be crushed, its driver the meat in a steel sandwich.

He glanced at the driver, couldn't tell if it was man or woman. It happened fast, like the decision was made far in advance, no need to question it. After all, he had no place else to go. He jerked the steering wheel hard right to make way for the white car. He heard the steel guardrail tear on impact and saw sparks, like fireworks in the night sky as he sailed into the air.

His neck lashed against his shoulder strap and pain tore like flames through his head. He felt the jolt and the sinking, and cold water lifting around his face to ease the burning pain.

He smiled and breathed deep of the baptism. All his dead relatives were standing around the river—Mama too—and they were so happy to welcome him home.

# EIGHT

## *An old fashioned pissing contest...*

Diana was drifting out at sea, where a blood red sunset stained the horizon, tinting the bouquet of clouds rose petal pink. It was a sinister beauty, somehow connected to violent death, and she was disoriented. All familiar landmarks had melted away, and she had misplaced her children. Clearly she was a disappointment to Amanda and Robby, who had evaporated in the surging tide while their mama slept. And far, far away, Westminster chimes called her home.

"Doorbell, doorbell!" The shrill squawking echoed in her brain.

"Shut up, Perry!" Her legs ached as she swung them off the sofa and touched bare feet to the carpet.

"Shut up, shut up, shut up!" Her African Grey parrot screamed.

"I'm coming!" Diana called. Whoever was ringing the doorbell was annoyingly persistent. She unlocked the deadbolt, but left the safety chain latched as she opened to the night.

Wayne Bearfoot's face materialized in the porch light. She blinked, shaking her head to clear the cobwebs. She hated falling asleep in daylight, and then waking up after dark. Whenever it happened, her internal time clock was disrupted.

"What's happening, Wayne?" She yawned, then noticed another man standing beside the sheriff.

"Sorry to bother you so late, Diana, but we need to ask a few questions." Wayne was all business in his starched tan uniform. His polished badge and gun caught the light.

The other man was small and wiry. His gray eyes darted in a pale face with sharp, wolf-like features. He was casually dressed in loose trousers and a patterned silk shirt, unbuttoned to expose his chest.

"Remember me, Mrs. Rittenhouse?" He winked. "We both grew up outside Philly, am I right?"

Suddenly it all came together. The brusque young man was a Davidson detective, imported from Camden, New Jersey. She'd met him several years ago after a break-in at her condo.

"Peter Sokolsky." He firmly shook her hand.

She looked from one to the other. The tall Cherokee Sheriff and the city cop were strange bedfellows, to say the least. "Why are you *both* here?"

Wayne rolled his eyes. "It's a matter of jurisdiction. Some poor guy drove off the bridge over yonder and got himself killed. Problem is, the accident occurred on the county line. I'm here for Iredell County, but Sokolsky thinks this is a Mecklenburg County matter."

"Actually, Mrs. Rittenhouse, *Tonto* can leave whenever he wants." Sokolsky scowled. "The victim was a Davidson man, so the ball's in my court."

Wayne stretched to his full, impressive height, his hawk eyes trained on the smaller man. "*Beretta* here fails to realize that death doesn't respect county lines. Like it, or not, we're stuck in this one together."

"I'm so sorry about the accident, but why question me?" As she began to wake up, her patience wore thin. Her feet ached, her head throbbed, and she'd spent the entire day tromping across both counties with clients from Ohio, who were unlikely to purchase any real estate until they checked every lake property in all fifty states.

"Did you see anything, Diana?" Wayne asked.

"Or maybe heard something?" Sokolsky shoved Wayne aside and took out a small black notebook.

"Saw nothing, heard nothing. I've been asleep the past few hours. But I'm really sorry about the man who drove off the bridge. That must have been horrifying."

"You go to bed kinda early, don't you, ma'am?" Sokolsky smirked.

Wayne elbowed the obnoxious man out of her face. "The detective means no disrespect. He's just tense after losing another Davidson dignitary."

The two were like a Shakespearean comedy routine, or, as Liz would put it: *they're just having an old-fashioned pissing contest.* She would have sent them both packing, but her curiosity was aroused. Pushing them aside, she walked into the parking lot for a better view of Lake Norman and the bridge. Traffic was backed up in both directions. An emergency floodlight illuminated a gaping hole in the guardrail.

"They hauled the car out an hour ago," Wayne said. "The victim hit his head during the crash. I'm just hoping he was dead before the water came up."

"The coroner will answer that," Sokolsky said. "Point is, how could it happen? Of all the places to run off the road, the unlucky bastard chose the one weak section of rail, the part being repaired."

"An eighteen-wheeler rammed it a month or so ago," Wayne explained.

"This guy was either drunk, or suicidal." Sokolsky rolled his eyes.

"Who was he?" she interrupted.

"Lester B. Smith, one of Davidson's commissioners," Sokolsky said.

"Another commissioner is dead?"

"Afraid so." Wayne sadly studied his hands. "Lester was a nice guy, too—black fellow. Long time ago we built a Habitat house together."

Suddenly Diana was uncommonly depressed. An image of the beautiful young black woman she'd met at The Garden Club materialized in vivid detail. The girl had been wearing a Hawaiian lei around her neck as she served refreshments. She recalled her name was Rhonda, and now her father was dead.

"I'm sorry I can't help, but surely someone saw something?"

"One of your neighbors, a college kid, saw the accident," Wayne answered. "He claims a small white car, maybe a Honda Civic, tried to pass Lester on the bridge. He said the white car was playing chicken with the oncoming traffic, almost like he knew Lester would give way to avoid causing someone else to crash."

"Are you saying someone deliberately forced him off the road?" She couldn't believe it.

Sokolsky growled. "I say the kid's story is bullshit. The boy was so high he couldn't see straight. He reeked of marijuana and stank of beer."

"Maybe we should arrest the kid?" Wayne winked at her.

"Maybe we should get busy and knock on some more doors," Sokolsky snapped.

"Go ahead, I'll catch you later…" Wayne turned to Diana as the ex-New Jersey detective walked briskly away. "I'm thinking Sokolsy will do better without me."

"I'm thinking you'll do better without him." She smiled. "And I'm really sorry to hear about Commissioner Smith."

"Yeah, me too." Wayne stared down at his boots. "Lester was a good man."

"Too much death, "she mumbled.

He wrapped a friendly arm around her shoulder and led her back to the porch. "How are you holding up, Diana? Matthew is worried about you."

She shrugged his arm away. She felt vulnerable and hated the feeling. Like in her dream, she seemed to be drifting helplessly out to sea. Ever since she'd seen Harold Havers' body, she'd dreamed of too many bloody sunsets. Her visions of lost children, the cloud like a bouquet of pink roses—these were side effects similar to PTSD.

"What about the flowers?" she suddenly said aloud.

"What flowers?"

"The big bouquet on Havers' table—did you check it out? My friend, Parker White, is a member of the flower club."

"So…?"

"So, when I told her about the bouquet at the murder scene, she suggested the police should call all the local florists."

"Did she, now?" Wayne chuckled. "Tell your friend to relax. We've been there, done that. We've called every florist in a fifty-mile radius. Nothing. Apparently, the flowers were a homemade gift."

Nonetheless, she thought, whoever assembled the arrangement had a professional touch and a woman's sensibility. It had already been established that Mrs. Janelle Havers was out of town the day of the murder. "Do you think Harold Havers had a girlfriend?"

A laugh rumbled up from his chest. "Is that your theory, Diana, or did you cook it up with your pal, Parker?"

"It's just a hunch."

"Don't you think Havers had enough on his platter—a young wife, financial responsibilities, and his job as a commissioner? In a word—no, I don't think Harold had a girlfriend."

She felt foolish. It was time to change the subject. "What about Lester B. Smith's death, Wayne? Do you think it was an accident?"

"In a word—yes." The corners of his dark eyes crinkled in thought. "On the other hand, from what I hear about the shenanigans of these Davidson politicians, I'd say they've made a lot of enemies. My guess…? Half the town has cause to murder the lot of them."

# NINE

## *Matthew*

Matthew was lounging on his favorite bench just outside Trout's Place. He'd left the door propped open so he could hear the phone, but didn't expect it to ring. Business was always slow on Wednesday, and in late October it was downright dead. The summer lake folks were long gone and the permanent residents were back to their busy lives, but he could still count on the dedicated fishermen. They pulled in as regular as clockwork, trailing boats and buying gas, bait and beer. He wished that customers would keep him busy for at least the next hour or so.

And if the phone rang, it might just be Diana. She said she'd drop by this afternoon, or call if she was running late. The thought of her made him smile. He closed his eyes and rested his head against the wall, the sun warming his face. He imagined her driving towards him on the Interstate, both hands on the wheel, her beautiful blue eyes intent on the road, her soft, short-cropped white hair ruffled by the wind rushing through an open window.

Like Matthew, Diana disliked air conditioning, cell phones, computers, and the noisy crush of modern life. They came from different worlds, but they were spiritual soul mates, and he thanked the lucky stars that brought them together. But were they really together?

He slumped lower on the bench and pondered the question. From the moment they'd met, the attraction was mutual, as powerful as a runaway freight train. Yet in the two years they'd known one another, they'd made love only a few times. Those times stood out as the emotional and physical highlights of his life.

He had loved his wife, Lynn, who'd died almost a decade ago, but sex with Diana was a whole different thing. Lynn, her personality and her lovemaking, was gentle, quiet, and submissive. Diana, on the other hand, was aggressive, expressive, and stunningly passionate. The first time they kissed, it took his breath away. Sharing her bed took him over body and soul. Through prolonged, unbearable tension to the exploding climax, sex with Diana lifted him out of himself, left him wired and soaring for days afterwards.

But who was this woman who'd come to him so late in his life? Diana was cultivated, worldly, reserved, and very private about her own needs. Like him, she had some reservations about sex outside marriage, so here they were—smitten like agonized teenagers, but hung up by old-fashioned, adult morality.

Diana was a tough, independent businesswoman. He was a professional widower, set in his country ways and content with his solo life...at least he used to be content. Were they were both so trapped in those roles that they couldn't change?

Lately that possibility had begun to terrify him. His need for Diana was a constant ache deep below his skin, but what if his skin was too thick to let it show? He'd offered her a chance to share his bed, but was he capable of offering more? He knew damned well she required more. So did he. God willing, he'd find the courage to let her know. Maybe that very afternoon.

A car pulled up to the fuel pumps, jarring Matthew from his reverie. At first he thought it was Diana, and his heart jolted in anticipation. But instead, an elderly man stepped from a brand new Ford 150 pickup.

"Hey, boss, you sleepin' on the job?" the man called.

It was Hoke Bodine, back from the funeral. Matthew rolled his head to work out the kinks in his neck and stretched as he climbed to his feet.

"Wasn't sleeping," Matthew grumbled. "How come you're here, Hoke? Didn't I give you the day off?"

"Yeah, but what can I do with what's left of this sorry day? Preacher took his good ole time at the church, and Sister Reva sung all fifty verses at the grave. Now I don't hardly have time to launch the boat and bait my hook, before I got to head home for supper."

"I hear you…" He stared at Hoke, who made a mighty fine picture in his Sunday best suit, with his new truck—all three black as midnight. He couldn't remember a time when he and Hoke weren't best friends, but on this particular afternoon he wished his buddy would go away.

"Where are all the customers?" He strolled up to Matthew's bench. "I brought me a change of clothes. Want me to go back to the garage and finish that tune-up on Mr. Johnson's Chevy?"

Matthew shook his head. "Forget it. But come inside and help me with something before you go…"

Hoke trailed him past the cash register, then past where they kept tobacco products locked up in a glass case on the back wall. Matthew was the only vendor, maybe in all of North Carolina, who refused to sell cigarettes or beer to minors, nor did he stock porno magazines. His odd behavior was less religious conviction, more personal distaste for the products, and everyone in a ten mile radius steered clear of Trout's Place if they were underage and wanted those items.

"It was a pretty funeral, all the same," Hoke muttered as they went down the snacks aisle. "Lester B. was an upstanding citizen. Near killed his daughter to lay him to rest."

"Never had the pleasure..." Matthew hadn't known Lester B. Smith, but he'd heard only good about the commissioner. "Shame about the accident. I never take the Interstate, unless I have to." Again he thought about Diana driving the Interstate to meet him, and the unease he'd been feeling all morning intensified.

"What you lookin' for back here, boss?" Hoke followed him into the dusty storeroom.

"Will you cut the *boss* stuff? Please?" It was a long-standing joke between them. In the twenty-odd years Hoke had worked for Matthew, he'd never let up. Hoke claimed Matthew was the only color-blind white man in the county, and calling Matthew *boss* was a guaranteed aggravation.

"Anything you say, boss." Hoke brushed dust from his black suit. "Nothin' back here but mice and spiders."

"Will you steady the ladder while I climb?" If memory served, Lynn's pink box was second from the left, top shelf. "Okay, let me hand this down...."

Hoke grabbed hold of the pink storage box and backed it out of the room, into the store. "Whew..." He brushed a cobweb from his face. "This here smells nasty. Should we open it outside?"

"It's musty, that's all." But the lugged the box into the sunlight and set it on the bench. "These things belonged to Lynn," he explained.

Hoke's memory stretched all the way back to Matthew and Lynn's courtship, their marriage, the birth of Ginny, Lynn's battle with cancer, and her death. Even after all those years, the hurt was still fresh, and the two seldom discussed Matthew's lost wife.

Matthew lifted a thick bolt of red Chinese silk from the box. He held it high and twisted it so the fabric unrolled in a long stream. "Yes, sir, this was what I was looking for."

Hoke gave him a look. "Lord, what you want with that?"

"I plan on giving it to Diana. She's coming 'round to pick it up this afternoon."

"Oh, *now* I get it." Hoke lifted his white eyebrows. "Miss Diana's coming, and that's why you want me to get lost."

"That's about the size of it." He handed Hoke the loose end of fabric. "Grab hold of that and roll it out. We need to shake it real good…"

Hoke grinned knowingly as he trotted across the parking lot. The patterned silk billowed between them like a red oriental cloud. It was complicated. Matthew knew Hoke was loyal to Lynn's memory, but he also adored Diana. Although he'd met her only once, the two had hit it off like chocolate sauce and vanilla ice cream. At every opportunity, he pestered Matthew to buy flowers and date Diana. No problem, because Matthew wanted to do those things, anyway. But it was the endless teasing and innuendo Matthew couldn't tolerate. His private time with Diana was just that—private.

By then the two men were at opposite ends of the parking lot. The carpet of silk flapped wildly in the wind as each held onto his end, squatting and shaking like crazed kabuki dancers.

"What on earth are you two doing?"

The teasing, female voice nearly scared him out of his skin. She'd coasted up behind them like a ghost ship in her big white Ford. By the time Matthew realized there was a witness to his folly, Diana had climbed out of her car. She was leaning against a fender, doubled up with laughter.

"Don't stop on my account," she howled. "Is this some kind of a new ballet?"

Neither Matthew nor Hoke was willing to drop the silk, which was now nicely aired. Instead, they soberly walked towards one another, folding it end over end like the flag at a military funeral.

"This is all your fault." Matthew grinned as he presented the folded offering to Diana. "It's the fabric I promised you—for the play."

"What play?" Hoke was still seemed sheepish about his performance.

"*The King and I,*" Matthew and Diana said in unison.

"Huh?"

"It's a musical about an English school marm who travels to Siam to teach the king's many children, but she ends up falling in love with the king," Diana explained. "Didn't you see the movie?"

"Nope." Hoke shrugged. "What are you going to do with Miss Lynn's material?"

Diana lifted her eyebrows.

"It belonged to my wife," Matthew quickly explained. "One of her crazy aunts was an interior designer for one of the furniture companies. This silk was left over, so she gave it to Lynn."

Diana was silent, absorbing it all. Matthew seldom mentioned Lynn's name in her presence.

"Obviously red Chinese silk isn't my style," he stammered. "Can you see me using it for curtains at the cottage?"

Diana smiled. "No way. From what I've seen of your house, flannel is a better fit." She turned to Hoke. "And to answer your question, Hoke, we'll use the silk to make costumes for all the little Siamese children. Won't they look cute?"

"Yes, ma'am."

"The Community Players talked Diana into being the props person. You won't actually sew the costumes, will you?" Matthew asked.

"Good God, I hope not. Anyone who expects me to thread a needle will be very disappointed."

Both men laughed.

Matthew's gaze lingered on Diana's face. Her eyes echoed the brilliant blue sky, and she held her head high, like a spirited filly. Her tall, slim body seemed relaxed in a casual, faded green cotton shirtwaist dress, and her shapely feet were clad, as always, in sensible sandals. Suddenly he desperately wanted to be alone with her.

"Hoke was just leaving," he told Diana.

"Say what?" Hoke's eyes sparked with mischief. "First the man puts me to work and I get my suit all dirty. Next he tries to pack me off without a thank you." Hoke dug into his pocket and brought out a dollar bill. "Take this, boss. Run inside and fetch a Cheerwine for the lady and me. I'm buying."

Matthew grumbled, but did Hoke's bidding. When he returned with three bottles of the sweet soda pop, Hoke was seated beside Diana on Matthew's favorite bench.

He pulled up a chair beside them. "Mind if I join you? I bought my own drink."

Hoke was telling Diana about Lester B. Smith's funeral.

"The police were sayin' that Lester B. was a drunk, that they found an empty bottle, and all. But I'm here to tell you that Lester B. hasn't had a drop in years. He was on the wagon. If he took alcohol that night, something mighty bad drove him to it."

Matthew tuned it out. Hoke had already told him the tale about how Commissioner Smith had lost his house, and then his old mama, but Diana was hearing it all for the first time. As expected, her empathetic reaction was immediate.

"Are you saying he had nothing to live for?"

"I reckon old Lester B. might've seen it that way," Hoke said. "But his daughter, Rhonda, sees it a whole different way. That girl has blood in her eye, and she blames Commissioner Homer Locksley for both her grandma's and her daddy's deaths. It was Locksley designed the new bungalows and put the Smiths out of their house. Rhonda says she's gonna kill him."

"That's enough, Hoke." Matthew took the unfinished soda from his friend's hand. "Diana doesn't want to hear that kind of talk. Besides, weren't you going to cook dinner for your wife tonight? You better get going."

Hoke's eyes shifted in confusion, then focused on Diana. "Sorry, ma'am. Didn't mean to trouble you about old Lester B., and Trout's right. I promised my wife, so I best be on my way."

Before Diana could protest, Hoke hurried to his new Ford and waved goodbye

She turned to Matthew. "Hoke can *cook*?"

"Sure. He can sew, too. Can we discuss something else, Diana?

"Wayne Bearfoot questioned me about Lester B. Smith's death."

"Yeah, he told me."

"He believes it was an accident."

"Sounds that way to me." Matthew agreed. "From what Hoke just said, the man was drinking and despondent. I suspect his reflexes failed him, or he made a wrong choice. C'mon, Diana, can we change the subject?"

"Do you and Sheriff Bearfoot communicate on a regular basis?" She wasn't about to be sidetracked.

"I reckon we do when you're involved."

"Did he say anything about Danny Capelli?"

"That's the good news." Matthew sighed. "The case against Danny is weak. The evidence is circumstantial, so Bearfoot's letting it drop. Besides, he has a new theory…"

Diana brightened. "That's wonderful news about Danny. Wait until I tell Liz! But what's Wayne's new theory?"

"He thinks Harold Havers had a girlfriend."

"But that was my theory!" She jumped from the bench and sat on the arm of Matthew's chair. "Didn't he give me any credit?"

"So you told him about the Trojans in Havers' pocket? Seems the birth control angle might be the key." He enjoyed the blush crawling up Diana's neck.

"N-no…" she stuttered. "I had no idea what Havers kept in his pockets, but what's your point? Lots of married men use protection."

Matthew felt heat crawling up his own neck. "Point is, Janelle Havers can't conceive children. She told Bearfoot that after she and Havers discovered she was infertile, they stopped using protection altogether. If the Trojans weren't needed for Janelle, then for who?"

"For *whom*…" Diana corrected him. "Now can we change the subject?"

He breathed a sigh of relief. "Let's go inside, okay? I want to show you something…"

By contrast, the temperature inside the store was cool, the lighting dim. His heart pounded as he led her back to his office.

"What is it, Matthew?" She reached out and touched his face. Her fingers were light as a bird's wing on his cheek.

He guided her into his arms and held her hand to his chest, so she could feel his pounding heart. He pulled her against his lower body, so she could feel his obvious need. And when he lifted her chin and kissed her sweet lips, he prayed to that mysterious power that had brought them together: *Please keep the customers away...for at least one hour.*

## TEN

## *Mind your own business...*

Diana drove through the downpour, smiling and humming to a Chopin impromptu playing on WDAV, the local classical radio station. Chopin finished, and Diana kept on smiling. Her good mood had not been inspired by her visit to Food Lion. Until she earned a few good commissions, she'd have to keep buying groceries at Food Lion, rather than Home Economist, her favorite health food store. If Liz and she didn't close a deal soon, they'd both be on involuntary diets.

She entered the Main Street business district and dutifully slowed to twenty-five miles per hour. Usually, the local police gave out speeding tickets like Halloween candy, but as she passed Davidson Town Hall, where an 8:00 PM Commissioners' Meeting was posted, the police seemed to be on high alert, buzzing around the hall. After all, tragedy had shaken her small town. Two of their five commissioners were suddenly and mysteriously dead.

Harold Haver's death still haunted her nightmares, jolting her awake in terror. The demise of Lester B. Smith had been far less personal, but still disturbing in its lack of resolution. Was Lester B.'s fatal plunge from the bridge accidental, or part of a wider plot?

She stopped smiling and checked her watch. It was 8:15. By now, the surviving commissioners, including her friend, Parker, would be assembled inside Town Hall. Did they question the gruesome coincidence of losing two from their ranks? Did they worry about their own safety?

She slowed from twenty-five to the now requisite twenty miles per hour. The Davidson Police Department was also housed in Town Hall, and as distracted as the officers likely were by the deaths, they'd still be intent on dispensing speeding tickets. An expensive moving violation was the last thing she needed.

She switched off the radio, and in the sudden silence, listened to the pelting rain and her growling stomach. She hadn't eaten since the packet of cheese crackers masquerading as lunch. Then she remembered the half-gallon of deluxe butter pecan ice cream stashed in the trunk with the other groceries. It was Matthew's favorite, and she desperately hoped he'd show up to share it with her that night. Suddenly she was smiling and humming again. Her hand strayed to the bolt of Chinese red silk beside her on the seat, its musty aroma transporting her back to yesterday afternoon in Matthew's store. Again she felt his lips on hers as he pulled her close. A sharp ache invaded her body, and she longed to prolong the sensation. Yesterday, if that blasted customer had not walked in at precisely the wrong moment....

She lifted her hand from the silk, returned it to the steering wheel, and took a deep breath. Somehow Matthew had actually made her consider making love on the floor of a convenience store, of all things! Such insanity was completely alien to her character.

Over the past two years, Matthew had been her haven in a world gone mad. They came from different worlds, yet he was her soul mate. And though she'd always considered herself a strong, independent woman, Matthew supported her where she was weak. He made her question her old ideal of absolute independence. In short, she really hoped he'd drop by for ice cream and keep her company over a late dinner. She hoped he'd laugh at her conspiracy theories, as he always did, allowing her to laugh at herself, a therapy she very much needed from time to time.

Diana hoped he'd come, but he'd never promised. In fact, he'd never even implied a visit tonight. The ice cream would not on its own conjure up Matthew's arrival. Silly woman! If she wanted him, she'd have to call him up and tell him so.

She turned right into the Davidson College Campus and steered towards the theater building, which the college generously allowed the Community Players to use for their productions. She parked as close as possible to the backstage door and decided now was as good a time as any. It would take only a minute to drop off the silk to the costume people, and then she'd be done with it.

Naturally, she'd forgotten her umbrella, so holding the bolt of silk above her head, she made a mad dash to the heavy oaken door behind the theater. She pushed her way into a dim hallway, stowed the silk on a metal folding chair, and then dried her hands on the lining of her jacket.

The space smelled vaguely like gym shoes, and the sound of children's laughter echoed from a brightly-lit room at the end of the corridor. The kids ranged from preschoolers to pre-teens, and were all assembled in a line according to height. Their hands were pressed together in prayerful peaks as they practiced bowing in unison. These were the little princes and princesses of Siam, rehearsing *The King and I.* They were the offspring of professors and town folk, and as Diana watched, she experienced a sharp pang of loss for the days when her own children appeared in amateur productions.

Enough of that. She ducked into the women's restroom and was drying her soaked crop of white hair with a paper towel when someone exited a toilet stall, slamming the door behind her. The tall, slim woman stomping towards the sinks startled Diana. She was obviously distraught, her face was flushed and her deep blue eyes were rimmed with red.

"Parker, what on earth are you doing here?"

"Don't ask." Parker White took a small plastic brush from her purse and dragged it viciously through her wet blunt cut.

"Aren't you supposed to be at the commissioner's meeting?" Diana considered wrapping her arms around her friend, but sensed that touching the angry woman might not be the best move. Parker had ceded her position as Properties Manager to Diana because of her honorary appointment to the Board of Commissioners, but if she wasn't even at the meeting, maybe Diana could wiggle out of it?

"Listen, Parker..." she began hopefully. "I see you've come to the rehearsal. Don't you want your old job back? I never wanted to be Properties Manager anyway, and..."

"Stop right there, Diana! You're not getting off that easily. I'm only here to settle a conflict, and then I'm leaving."

"What conflict?"

Parker finished applying her lipstick. Her trembling hand left a jagged red smear, not precisely where her lips would be. She lifted her eyebrows, a wry look in her bloodshot eyes.

"It was a crisis, actually." Parker snorted. "The children all wanted to dye their hair black, so they'd look authentically Siamese. But the mothers, God bless them, could not tolerate such disfigurement for their blond babies."

"So...?"

"So, I gave them a dozen boxes of black henna from the health food store. It'll wash out."

That was all well and good, but it didn't explain why she'd skipped the commissioner's meeting. Diana took a chance and laid her hand on Parker's shoulder. "What's really wrong? Do you want to talk about it?"

She roughly shrugged Diana's hand away and made a beeline for the door. "I adore you, Diana, but for once in your life, mind your own business!"

The words stung. She rarely shared her private emotions, but she had been known to poke her nose where it didn't belong. But Parker was a dear friend. Even Matthew had forgiven her for to meddling in the name of love.

She trailed Parker to the exit door, but kept her distance. She spied through the rain streaked window and watched her dash through the storm to where a shiny new Jaguar was parked, shedding water from its polished silver skin.

"Wow!" The fancy car took Diana by surprise.

She slid into the Jag after wiping stray droplets off the pristine leather seats. Last time they'd gone out together, Parker had been driving a nondescript little white car.

"She didn't *buy* that car, Miss Diana, she's only *leasing* it."

Diana spun around to face the short, plump woman who had materialized at her elbow. She recalled that the woman's name was Magdalena. She was Parker's former maid and moved with the stealth of an alley cat.

"Good Lord, Maggie, you frightened me!"

"Sorry." Maggie grinned, her deep brown eyes laughing. "But it's true. Mrs. White could easily afford to buy that Jag, but decided to lease it instead."

It made no sense. Diana knew that Parker had suffered severe financial setbacks. In the years since her husband's death, she'd used up the family fortune and was always whining about being poor. But if anyone had the inside track on Parker's money problems, it was Maggie. She'd worked for the White family for years, ever since she emigrated from Mexico.

Maggie folded thick arms across her ample bosom and leaned close, dropping her voice to a whisper. "Remember when Mrs. White fired me?"

Diana nodded. Several years back, when she'd first met Parker, she'd also met Maggie at a luncheon at Parker's big house. Back then the White mini-mansion was on Main Street, before the Town moved it to the ridiculously small plot behind the proposed new Harris Teeter. Soon after that luncheon and a string of financial reversals, Parker had been forced to dismiss Maggie. The loss had been tragic for Parker, but the whole community had worried about the Mexican woman's welfare.

Magdalena patted her heart and offered a shy smile. "You know I got married, right?"

Again Diana nodded, but the details had slipped her mind.

"My husband works part-time for Duck Wadell, the Davidson Commissioner? He's a big-shot developer around town…" She puffed up with pride.

Diana searched her fuzzy brain and remembered that Maggie had married a Hispanic man who worked as a gardener at the college. Apparently her husband was also moonlighting for this Duck person, whom Diana didn't know at all—except that Liz was currently courting him concerning a land deal of some sort. Liz claimed the deal could potentially save them from the poor house. But what did that have to do with Parker's new Jaguar?

"Anyway…" Maggie continued. "My husband told me that Mr. Duck bought Mrs. White's big old house. He paid way below market value for the place, but Mrs. White needed money so bad she had to sell…" The ex-maid paused to gloat. "So that money from Mr. Duck is how come she could afford that fancy new car."

Diana was stunned. No wonder Parker was upset. The *White Elephant*, as the town snidely described Parker's Tara, was Parker's last link to her husband's family and happier days. Diana knew how much that home had meant to her friend. It symbolized the status that had always eluded her in the closed, local society. That sort of status-seeking seemed silly to Diana, but Parker took it very seriously. A new Jaguar seemed a poor substitute. It would never replace Parker's larger ambitions.

"And that's not all..." Magdalena leaned closer. "Mrs. White is now living in a tiny apartment above the bookstore. Can you believe it? Poor thing."

Diana moved away. Once she had worried about Maggie along with the rest of the community, but now she found the woman's attitude distasteful. After all the years Parker had employed her and given her a home, Maggie now took obvious delight in her fall.

"Oh, I see you brought me the silk!" Maggie lifted the bolt off the metal chair and brushed away the raindrops staining its satiny surface. "My stepdaughter is in the play, you know. She's the Number One Princess, and I'm sewing the costumes." She sniffed the fabric and wrinkled her nose in disgust. "So we'll be working together, Miss Diana. Won't that be fun?"

Diana wasn't sure how much fun that would be, but she managed a smile. "At least Parker has been named to the Board of Commissioners. That's quite an honor, isn't it, Maggie?"

The woman shrugged. "Maybe so, but they didn't want her there tonight."

"Why not?"

"My husband told me all about it. He goes to each and every meeting, and today the Board is choosing the new Town Planner."

Diana knew next to nothing about local politics, but remembered overhearing a discussion at The Garden Club. After Parker had been awarded the commissioner's gavel, Jo-Jo Jones had mentioned the vote for Town Planner. She had specifically said that Parker was needed *to be the fifth person, the tiebreaker, if it comes to that.* Maggie and her civic-minded husband had gotten it wrong.

"You've made a mistake, Maggie. I know for a fact that the commissioners wanted Parker there tonight, of all nights."

"No mistake." Maggie turned her back and began walking down the hall, the silk cradled in her arms. "They told Mrs. White not to come because of her son, Randy. Since Randy is applying for the Town Planner position, they figured she couldn't make an impartial choice."

Somehow Diana had really fallen out of the loop. Parker hadn't told her about the house, the new car, or even her son. Had Diana become so aloof that even a good friend like Parker failed to confide?

She chased after Maggie. "Wait! Tell me more about Parker's son."

Maggie made a face. "Well, I've known Randy all his life, and he's always been a mess. I'd hoped he'd man-up once he finished college with his architecture degree, but I don't see any improvement." She shifted the heavy bolt arm to arm. "And Parker's girl, Cindi? Can't say much for her, either."

"Then maybe you shouldn't say anything at all!" Diana had heard enough. She refused to stand there and listen to petty gossip, so she headed for the door, leaving Maggie with her mouth hanging open.

The entire situation was extremely upsetting. Oblivious to the downpour, she rushed to Queen Vic, her faithful Ford Crown

Victoria. No fancy Jaguars for her, thank you very much. But if such a car helped soothe Parker's disappointments, maybe it was a good thing? She was so distracted, she stepped in a puddle and soaked her shoes. At the same time, she recalled the last evening she'd spent with Mama at Shady Oaks.

Over dinner, old Lou Turbyfill, had also gossiped about Parker's children. She'd described little Randy as a pathetic young boy who'd never gotten over his father's death, who would *throw up* whenever company came. Lou had been even harder on Cindi, the daughter who'd been jilted by a boy from a prominent Davidson family. According to Lou, Cindi had eventually eloped with a no-good born-again NASCAR driver and broken her mother's heart.

The malicious attacks against Parker's children angered Diana. Heaven knew, she'd endured enough interference trying to raise her own children, Robby and Amanda. Even Viv, their own grandmother, had predicted they'd come to no good.

She sighed as she peeled off her sodden jacket. What mother could judge her adult children: the decisions they made, or the quality of their lives? Certainly Diana's kids had their fair share of problems, and Diana tended to blame herself. If leasing an expensive Jaguar eased a mother's guilt, it was a small price to pay—cheaper than a shrink.

She opened the trunk, to stow her wet jacket. At the same time, she recalled how simple life had been back when her little ones were rehearsing for school plays. The bittersweet memory did little to lift her spirits.

Nor did the mess inside the trunk, where a half gallon of deluxe butter pecan—Matthew's ice cream—had melted into a sticky white puddle.

## ELEVEN

## *Standing room only...*

It turned out to be a long, lonesome weekend. Instead of sharing ice cream and romantic dinners with Matthew, Diana spent the solitary hours with Perry squawking obscenities at the rain. Over the years, her parrot had become intolerant of stormy weather. So that now, at the first rumble of thunder, he stalked across the hardwood floors and planted himself at the patio door overlooking the lake, cursing his fate and pecking at the glass.

In some perverse way, she empathized with the bird. After begging off work, leaving Liz to sit floor time, she had waited for Matthew to drop by. But as Saturday bled into Sunday, she realized he wasn't going to show. She'd received six phone calls from her mother. Like Perry, Mama was agitated by inclement weather. Viv blamed the rain for her arthritic aches and her low blood sugar. She complained that the Shady Oaks residents were restless and rude.

The seventh call had been from Matthew, who was upset because Hoke had called in sick, leaving him to mind the store.

Diana's wasted weekend.

Out of desperation and guilt, she'd finally agreed to accompany Liz to a Town Hall Meeting on Monday. But now, as they drove into town and looked for a parking space, Liz's incessant chatter was boring her to tears.

"Are you even listening to me?" Liz's red eyebrows dipped in a frown and her green eyes flashed. "Earth to Diana! You wanted to come tonight, but where the hell are you?"

Diana mumbled an apology and slowed to a crawl as a group of citizens carrying protest placards ambled across Main Street towards Town Hall. Diana hit the brakes. If she'd thought political demonstrations were a phenomenon of the big cities, she'd been badly mistaken. She knew Davidson College kids were sharp, liberal thinkers, but these weren't students in the street. They were ordinary, middle-aged townsfolk and they were riled up big-time. "What's all the fuss about?"

Liz rolled her eyes. "If you'd been listening, you wouldn't ask that stupid question. If you cared one iota about the work I've been doing, you'd know the answer."

A blush of shame crawled up Diana's neck. Ever since Harold Havers' murder, she'd been unable to concentrate. She'd allowed Liz to shoulder the lion's share of work, while she moped around waiting for someone to comfort her. In short, she'd behaved like a self-centered child and it was time to shape-up.

All the protest signs said *Stop the Land Grab!* She knew the so-called land grab was key to Liz's new real estate project.

"Tell me again?" She asked sheepishly.

"Promise you'll listen?"

"After I park…" Diana had to drive a block out of the way before finding one empty space at the old Methodist Church. They climbed out and opened their umbrellas. "Standing room only in Town Hall tonight," she mumbled. "Imagine that."

Liz explained her project as they walked, and this time Diana paid close attention. It seemed the mayor, along with the commissioners, had proposed annexing a large tract of acreage, mostly farmland, beyond the town limits. In return for city services and a voice in town politics, the landowners had to permanently set aside fifty percent of their land for open space, and then consider selling their acreage to authorized developers. The land to be annexed was called the extra territorial jurisdiction (ETJ). Residents living in the ETJ did not yet have voting or veto power in Davidson, so in effect, they had no say in their own destiny.

"So the landowners are pissed," Liz continued. "The annexation will mean big bucks for developers, but higher taxes for the people."

"And higher taxes will force the farmers to sell."

"Exactly." Liz licked her lips. "What's worse, is when investors realize they're only allowed to develop only *half* the land, with the other half dedicated green space, they'll figure they only have to pay the farmers *half* what the land is worth."

"So the farmers lose *half* their nest egg."

"That's about the size of it." Liz took Diana's arm and steered her through the crowd to the steps of Town Hall.

"That's not fair! No wonder everyone's up in arms." Diana thought the farmers were getting a very raw deal.

Liz tightened her grip. "Listen, you can't afford to be on their side, Diana. It's hazardous to your health."

"But it's wrong, Liz. I don't want any part of it."

"No, don't you dare say that! Let me introduce you to someone who can explain it better than me…"

Suddenly they were sharing space on the top step with an animated man who was shouting at the crowd. The stranger abruptly wrapped a powerful arm around both Liz and Diana, and then hustled them through the front door.

"My Grandma's tom cat was dumber than dirt…" He grinned. "But even old Tom had the good sense to come in from the rain."

Obviously this guy had some clout, because the gang of harried officials holding back the crowd ushered the three of them directly into the inner sanctum.

Their escort winked at Liz, then smiled at Diana. "You must be the other half of my dream team."

*Dream team?* Diana lowered her dripping umbrella and stared. He looked to be in his late thirties, with a ruddy complexion, crew cut blond hair, and small dark eyes that darted from side to side as he spoke.

"Meet Commissioner Billy Wadell," Liz said. "He'll set you straight."

"Everyone calls me *Duck*." He extended his hand.

Diana dried her fingers and shook his hand. She tried not to flinch from his bone-crushing grip. In her experience, men who gripped so hard were either trying to prove their masculinity, or prove they were forthright and trustworthy. Either way, they usually had a hidden agenda.

"I'm Diana Rittenhouse. Everyone calls me *Diana*."

As Duck laughed, a little too loudly, she recalled what she'd heard about him at The Garden Club: he was a long-time town commissioner. Maggie, Parker's former maid, had told her he'd recently purchased Parker's big old house at way below market value. And from Liz, she knew Duck was a major player in the local development game.

"What do you think of the sweet little deal me and Liz put together?" Duck asked.

*What deal?*

Liz came to the rescue. "She loves it, Duck. Once the ETJ is annexed, you'll do the land grabbing, we'll do the marketing, and we'll all get rich."

The jigsaw puzzle pieces fell into place. Wadell intended to buy as much land as he could from the tax-poor farmers, at half price, of course, and then Liz and she would market his developments as exclusive agents.

She glanced at the angry protestors being herded single-file into the hall. Each person was asked to leave his placard behind in the foyer before being ushered into the back of the small assembly room. Clearly only a few spectators would enjoy the luxury of sitting, while most would be left standing outside.

She studied Billy Wadell, who looked less like a duck, more like a muscular wrestler poured into an expensive business suit.

"I haven't had a chance to study the plan," Diana began, hoping to be diplomatic. "But I'm not sure I approve of your methods, Mr. Wadell."

Duck's pale eyebrows fluttered in surprise. "What's to study, Diana? Just skip to the bottom line."

Liz giggled nervously as she hooked her fingers through the strap of Diana's purse and tugged hard. "We better find a seat before they're all taken."

"Not a problem, ladies…" Duck bowed and swept his arm towards two chairs in the front row. "Those are reserved in your honor. My girls go first class."

*My girls?*

Once they were settled, Duck took his seat behind a long, curved walnut desk. He was the first commissioner in place, and a shiny brass nameplate mounted on the outer wall of the desk proclaimed that he was indeed Commissioner William Wadell.

As soon as he was out of earshot, Liz turned to Diana. "For God's sake, are you trying to blow this deal?"

"I want Mr. Wadell to understand that we won't be party to his underhanded shenanigans."

"His what?" Liz ran fingers through her mass of red hair, which was frizzing up from the rain. "Are you nuts? You've been missing in action ever since I began these negotiations, so who are you to judge?"

Liz was right, she had been MIA. "Look, I'm sorry. I promise to review everything first thing tomorrow morning." She brushed a stray lock off Liz's forehead. "Forgive me?"

"As long as you make the right decision…" Liz scowled and turned her attention to the front as the other commissioners wandered in.

Diana was determined to make it up to Liz, and attending this silly meeting was a good start. Afterwards, she'd take Liz out for drinks and dinner, someplace special and expensive. Even if she spent her last dime mending this rift, it was worth every penny.

That goal in mind, she fixed on the drama unfolding before her. She was determined to notice the details, and began by inspecting the brass nameplates. From left to right, the first plate was engraved with the mayor's name, and sure enough, Mayor Connery was in his place. His throne-like chair was positioned at a slightly higher elevation than the others, and at the moment, he was pointedly ignoring the unhappy buzz of the protestors by pretending to be engrossed in a thick document set before him.

Diana suspected that the commissioners, reading from left to right after the mayor, would be seated in descending order according to seniority. That would explain why plates one and two had been removed, leaving behind only sad shadows where Harold Havers and Lester B. Smith once sat.

The third seat was assigned to Homer Locksley, the retired art professor she'd met at the garden party, but Locksley had not yet arrived. Next was Joanne Early Jones, and Jo Jo was already holding court. She still looked like Mrs. Santa Claus as she patted her soft white hair with one plump hand and flirted with Duck.

Diana hoped Jo Jo had forgiven her for quitting The Garden Club, but before she could dwell on that worry, she was distracted by a secondary drama being enacted in the vestibule, just behind the meeting room. She heard angry shouting, a man and a woman engaged in a heated argument. From her unique vantage point, she recognized the tall, giraffe-like silhouette of Homer Locksley shaking a bony finger at Rhonda Smith, the daughter of the late Lester B.

It was impossible to hear their words, but Rhonda's body language emphasized her fury. Hands on hips, she stomped her foot and leaned towards Homer, eventually forcing his retreat. Suddenly, Diana recalled the day she'd gone to Matthew's to pick up the silk. Matthew's helper, Hoke, had been there. He had just returned from Lester B. Smith's funeral and made a comment about the bad blood between Locksley and Rhonda. What was it Hoke had said?

Just then Rhonda disappeared into the bowels of the building, and Homer Locksley shuffled to his place. He stowed a briefcase on the floor, hooked a gold-tipped cane over the edge of the desk, and dropped wearily into his seat.

Homer ignored Jo Jo's cheerful greeting and stared glassy-eyed into the unruly crowd. He was wearing a dapper three-piece suit, just as he had the day Diana met him at The Garden Club, and his face was an unhealthy blotch of red poking through his mane of shoulder-length white hair. She presumed his suit was too hot for the humid atmosphere, and she feared the combination of heat and passion were a recipe for apoplexy in such an elderly gentleman.

"I wish they'd turn on the air conditioning," she muttered.

"Dream on…" Liz grumbled. "Politicos are cheapskates. They like to see us sweat."

In Diana's experience, elected officials were all too willing to spend the taxpayers' dollars, especially when their own comfort was at issue. As she contemplated this, a sudden hush, followed by a curious buzz, rose from the audience as a new figure entered the room.

"Look, it's Parker," Diana whispered. "Doesn't she look beautiful?"

"She looks nervous," Liz said. "The people in the audience don't know her. They wonder what the hell she's doing up there."

"Don't worry, they'll introduce her." Should she be annoyed, or flattered, by Liz's unreasonable jealousy of Parker White? It seemed her friendship with Parker had sparked a competition, in which Liz felt compelled to vie for Diana's affection.

"Check it out..." Liz sneered. "Parker doesn't even know where to sit."

Fortunately, Mayor Connery patted the chair next to his, and Parker, with uncharacteristic clumsiness, wriggled into her seat. Perhaps she was nervous, after all. But she looked especially lovely in a simple black dress topped by a filmy over blouse patterned with autumn leaves. It seemed she wanted to make a good impression at her first Board Meeting, but the strain was taking its toll. Her forehead was creased with worry, and she kept twisting her wedding ring.

"We're still one commissioner short," Diana noted.

"Not for long." Liz nodded towards a distinguished matron with dyed black hair piled on her head and the signature strand of pearls around her neck. "Here comes the mayor's wife. How's that for nepotism?"

As Mrs. Connery approached the desk, Parker vacated her seat so that the mayor's wife could sit beside her husband. The ensuing ballet of musical chairs was as comic as an old time movie, but tragic for Parker, who managed to topple two chairs in the process.

The audience loved it. They clapped.

"Poor Parker!" Diana exclaimed.

"Klutz." Liz snickered.

When the laughter died down, Mayor Connery banged his gavel, and a plump young girl with thick glasses and an officious manner began passing out documents identical to the one the mayor had been reading. Each commissioner thanked the girl except Parker, who snatched the document and refused to make eye contact.

"That woman is the new Town Planner," Liz explained. "This is her first Board Meeting, too."

"Really? She's only a kid."

"Be careful, Diana," Liz giggled. "When you reach a certain age, you start thinking everyone looks like a kid... or so they say."

She ignored Liz's teasing and concentrated on Parker, who seemed ready to implode. No wonder she was upset. First she'd lost her house, and then this girl had been appointed Town Planner—instead of Parker's son, who'd also applied for the job. Talk about adding insult to injury! What good was an honorary appointment to the Board, when your fellow members rejected your own son?

As the meeting got under way, Diana vowed to be a better friend to Parker. In the beginning they'd enjoyed outings to the theater and concerts in Charlotte, but lately they'd drifted apart.

Next Rhonda Smith approached the desk, placing a water glass in front of each commissioner and a pitcher of water near the center of the table. At the same time, Duck Wadell rose from his seat and approached the bulletin board, causing a loud round of boos and cat calls from the audience.

"Jeez, I wouldn't want to be in his shoes," Liz said.

Duck picked up a pointer and tapped a large map of the ETJ, which was mounted on the bulletin board. "Think of all the benefits..." he began. "Once this land is annexed, the town will run water and sewer your way, and that's only the beginning..."

A group at the back of the room hissed at Duck's remarks. In turn, Duck lost his temper and passed the pointer to Homer Locksley. "Okay, if you don't believe me, listen to the professor. He's the expert, after all..."

She remembered that Homer was the Chairman of the Davidson Design Review Board, the *Pretty Committee*. He'd also received some sort of award for designing the low-income bungalows in town. What those credentials had to do with being an expert on the ETJ project, she could not fathom.

Nonetheless, Homer tugged loose the knot in his tie and wobbled to his feet. He was still glassy-eyed and red-faced as he ignored Duck's pointer in favor of his gold tipped cane, and then he haltingly approached the bulletin board. The audience continued to make rude noises as Homer took center stage. In turn, Homer faced them down in silence, his aristocratic white eyebrows twisted in a frown of professorial disdain.

"Get on with it, Locksley!" a rowdy man yelled.

Homer straightened his stooped shoulders and banged his cane on the floor. The harder he banged, the angrier the crowd became. The entire display was a shameful disgrace. Whether his position was right or wrong, the old man deserved respect. She watched in disbelief as Homer became more and more agitated. His face twitched, and as he began shouting back, spittle formed at the corner of his mouth and he gagged.

Suddenly, Homer dropped his cane. His tongue protruded as he gasped for breath, and in slow motion, he crumpled to the floor. His legs flailed and his arms jerked as he went into convulsions.

First the room was deadly silent, and then Jo Jo screamed. Mrs. Connery screamed too, setting the scene back into frantic motion.

"Jesus Christ, call 911!" the mayor shouted. "Homer's having a heart attack!"

Diana was paralyzed as dozens of cell phones appeared and former antagonists dialed for help, clogging the emergency lines in three counties. Duck Wadell dropped to his hands and knees. He stripped off his fancy suit coat and tucked it under Homer's head. He loosened Homer's tie. Jo Jo Jones was hysterical, while Mrs. Connery sobbed and clutched at her pearls.

Parker White appeared to be in shock. All the blood drained from her face, leaving her ghostly white before she lowered her head between her knees to avoid fainting.

Only Rhonda Smith seemed unmoved. She stood at the end of the desk as Homer Locksley thrashed on the floor. She stood tall, her arms crossed, her face as immobile as a beautiful ebony statue.

As the crowd circled, Diana began to pray. When Homer finally lay still, Duck began CPR, puffing through the old man's lips and pressing his chest. Time stood still, with every eye frozen on Duck's efforts until the paramedics arrived.

They gently pulled Duck aside, but Duck shrugged and shook his head. "Never mind, fellas. He's dead

TWELVE

## *Dropping like flies…*

Pandemonium broke loose. The Town Meeting was obviously over, but Mayor Connery kept banging his gavel as the audience stampeded towards the exits. The volunteer ushers tried in vain to organize the unruly retreat, while Duck Wadell held off a pack of ghoulish curiosity seekers pressing to get a look at the body.

Liz and Diana huddled together holding hands as the paramedics confirmed that Homer Locksley was indeed dead. Tears pressed behind Diana's eyes, while Liz cried openly.

"It's horrible! I never saw anyone die before!" She sobbed.

Diana squeezed Liz's hand and passed a motherly arm around her shoulders. Although Diana had witnessed death too many times, she knew no way to comfort her young friend. Lately the Grim Reaper was stalking Diana, leaving evidence of his violence at every turn.

"What do we do now?" Liz watched transfixed as the ambulance crew wheeled a stretcher through the crowd.

Good question. Obviously the surprise dinner Diana had planned was off. This was hardly the time for a festive reconciliation. She looked up at the desk, where the mayor had ceased banging his gavel in order to wrap his arms around his tearful wife. Jo Jo Jones was chirping like a demented magpie and pawing at Parker, who seemed frozen in shock. Rhonda Smith was stone cold calm as she began clearing away the water glasses.

"Hold it right there, Rhonda!" an authoritative voice boomed from across the room.

Startled, Rhonda put the pitcher down and stared at Detective Peter Sokolsky, who seemed to have materialized from thin air. But then Diana remembered the Davidson Police Department was located at the rear of Town Hall.

"What the hell took you so long, Peter?" Duck, who'd been unofficially in charge, seemed relieved to see reinforcements.

The detective from New Jersey was clad, as usual, in trendy loose trousers and a patterned silk shirt. He leaped to the desktop and waved his arms.

"Settle down, people!" he shouted. "Don't leave until I say so. We need to take your statements, do you hear?"

A collective groan rose from the crowd, and in exact opposition to Sokolsy's request, people rushed even faster to leave the building.

Liz moaned. "I can't stay, Diana. Danny is picking me up after the meeting. He's cooking me an Italian dinner at his place."

"What?"

Liz repeated the plans she and Danny had made. So much for *Diana's* surprise dinner. So much for the shock that had paralyzed Liz only moments before. Once and for all, Diana should learn her lesson and count on nothing.

"Are you actually dating Danny now?" She swallowed her disappointment. "Last I heard, you were just doing a little heavy breathing over the phone."

"Things change." Liz smiled slyly and began watching through the glass wall that overlooked the street.

She was hoping, no doubt, that Danny Capelli would arrive in his white panel van, a gallant knight come to rescue her from this madness. In truth, Diana was pleased to hear they were together again. Liz and Danny were made for one another, and if anyone could help Liz recover from the horror of what she'd just witnessed, that person was Danny.

Diana glanced at Detective Sokolsky, who was still shouting from the desktop. Every fiber in his wiry little body vibrated with rage as people continued to leave the hall. Diana had spoken to Sokolsky only days ago, when he and Sheriff Bearfoot had arrived at her condo to question her about the car accident that left Commissioner Lester B. Smith dead in Lake Norman.

Now Sokolsky was yelling to an enormous uniformed cop who stood nearby, apparently at a loss. "Get the lead out, Woods. Lock all the exits but the front door. If these people must leave, be sure to take names."

"Yes, sir!" The African American officer nodded his bald head, which was polished like fine mahogany, then began locking doors.

Diana leaned closer to Liz. "You better get going, or you'll be here all night. Peter Sokolsky means business."

"I hear you, but Woody is my buddy. He'll let me slip through." Liz caught the big policeman's eye and a smile passed between them. At the same moment, Danny Capelli's curly brown head appeared at the exit Woods was locking. Danny spotted Liz and wildly beckoned for her to come.

"This is your chance," Diana urged. "Get going before Sokolsky catches on."

Liz didn't need a second push. She extricated herself and impulsively kissed Diana's cheek. Again tears welled in her eyes. "I hate to leave you like this, Diana. Are you okay?"

"I'm just fine, so go."

She watched as Liz slithered towards the exit. Officer Woods hugged her, checked over his shoulder to be sure Sokolsky wasn't looking, and then allowed her to slip to freedom. Liz melted into Danny's embrace, and with a final glance in Diana's direction, she disappeared into the rain.

In the meantime, Sokolsky jumped off the commissioners' desk and faced the town officials. "Sorry to inconvenience you people, but I need to speak to you one at a time. Go to the mayor's office and wait for me there."

"See here, Sokolsky…" Duck Wadell bristled. "Maybe you get off playing bad cop, but the rest of us have better things to do."

Sokolsky fixed his steel gray wolf eyes on Duck. "If you have better things to do, Commissioner, then go do them. I'll put a big red mark beside your name and tell your constituents how you failed to cooperate with a murder investigation."

"*Murder investigation?*" All the commissioners gasped in unison.

Sokolsky opened a small black book and began taking notes. "In case you haven't noticed, you commissioners have been dropping like flies. Maybe we should take a closer look?"

Duck grumbled, but then he led Jo Jo, Parker and the Connerys towards Mayor Connery's office.

"You stay too, Rhonda," Sokolsky added. "And you, the new woman, please join them."

Rhonda Smith scowled, while the new Town Planner's eyes grew enormous behind her thick glasses. In the end, they all filed off to await Sokolsky's questions.

"What about the rest of us?" Diana spoke up.

"Ah, Mrs. Rittenhouse, we meet again." Peter Sokolsky's small, pointed teeth flashed white. He waved at the handful of spectators seated beside her in the front row. "You all stay put while I chat with Mrs. Rittenhouse. Okay?"

Sokolsky led her to a quiet corner. He fingered the gold chain at his throat, while she stared at the mass of black hair on his pale chest. The man habitually left his shirt unbuttoned half way to his waist.

"Well, Diana, what did you see here today?"

"Well, Peter, let me think about it." Sokolsky and Diana *hailed from the same neck of the woods,* as Matthew would say, but that didn't make Sokolsky her long lost pal. At the same time, she did want to help. After all, she'd been practicing her powers of observation in the moments leading to Homer's collapse, so she replayed the events in her mind and told what she remembered. Sokolsky took copious notes while chewing on the gold crucifix attached to the end of his neck chain.

Suddenly, the cross fell from his mouth. "Back up, Diana. Tell me again about the water."

She repeated how Rhonda had passed out the water glasses, and then the pitcher.

"Did you see anyone drink the water?"

Diana thought hard. "Yes, Homer Locksley."

Peter Sokolsky frowned. "Anyone else?"

Both Jo Jo and Duck had poured from the pitcher, but they hadn't yet taken a drink. At least I think that's what I saw..."

"Just Homer, then?"

She closed her eyes tight. "I'm just not sure…" Suddenly she felt a tightening in her throat. Any fool could see where Sokolsky was going with this. "Surely you don't think Mr. Locksley was poisoned?"

Now Peter was using the crucifix as a toothpick. He paused. "Did I say that?"

"If you did, then you're talking about a very imprecise murder weapon. Anyone could have drunk from that pitcher."

"Anyone but the poisoner, I should think." Sokolsky stared hard. "Rhonda Smith brought the water, right?"

"Yes."

"Do you know of any reason why Ms. Smith would want to hurt these folks?"

The tightness in her throat swelled to a painful lump as she vowed not to utter another word. Recently she'd opened her big mouth and implicated Danny for murder. She wouldn't make the same mistake twice.

Yet she remembered that after Lester B. Smith's funeral, Hoke told Matthew that Rhonda blamed Commissioner Locksley for her grandma's and her daddy's deaths. Locksley had designed the new bungalows that effectively evicted the Smiths from their family home. Rhonda had said she was going to kill him.

"What is it, Diana?" Sokolsky pressed.

"Nothing, Peter. That's all I know."

## THIRTEEN

## *Matthew*

By Friday night, Matthew needed a break. He corralled Hoke Bodine and asked him to mind the store for the weekend. He picked up the trousers and corduroy jacket he'd left at the cleaners, showered and shaved, and then left for his date with Diana.

Double date, actually, and while he'd have preferred a solo engagement with Diana, how could he say no to Liz? He'd known her since she was a little kid, since her parents used to drive up from Charlotte for a day at the lake, since she was a pint-sized, redheaded bundle of mischief begging for candy at his store.

Danny had become a good friend, too. He'd thanked Matthew for putting in a good word with Wayne Bearfoot and vouching for his character when Danny was under suspicion for Harold Haver's murder. If Danny and Liz wanted to thank them by treating them to dinner at Joanie's Fish Camp, then who was he to argue?

At least the weather was cooperating. As he drove north on Highway 16, towards the setting sun above Little Mountain, he was thankful the rain had finally stopped. Today, November first, an abundance of colored leaves still clung to the branches as fall stubbornly refused to give way to winter. This season always tugged at Matthew's heartstrings. He'd lost his wife, Lynn, in autumn, and even all these years later, November was hard. Only one person eased that pain, and as he switched on his left turn signal and turned into Joanie's parking lot, that person was waiting for him.

Diana stood at the edge of the driveway. Though the evening breeze was cold, she wore no jacket. She stood tall and expectant. Wind danced through her short white hair and ruffled the surface of the catfish pond beyond the parking lot. Matthew's heart skipped. She was like a proud filly, scenting the air in his headlights.

She spotted him the moment he turned off the lights, and her face opened in a smile. His heart skipped again as he strode to her side. He pulled her into his arms and held her close. For a moment, she said nothing, but tucked her cold nose under his chin and explored the warmth of his back with chilled fingers.

"You been waiting long?" he asked. She smelled of soap and lilacs.

"Liz and Danny are already inside," whispered against his chest. "It's crowded, so I asked them to save us a booth."

"You hungry?" He held her tighter. Her heartbeat was a captive bird against his ribs.

"*Very* hungry." Her hands traveled to his waist and hooked his belt. "How about you?"

Matthew gasped in surprise. "Absolutely," he managed before she offered her lips. Her kiss was deep and probing, stunning him with need. Diana was aggressive in love, a fact that belied her reserved demeanor. Matthew's mind never knew quite how to respond to Diana's take- charge approach, but his body had no trouble at all.

Right then and there, he silently vowed to take her home with him after dinner. She'd come with Liz and Danny, since it was convenient for them to drive together, but convenience be damned. Tonight the young couple could jolly well leave on their own, while he and Diana chose their own detours. At the very least, Matthew was determined to schedule their getaway vacation. They'd put it off way too long.

Reluctantly, he ended the kiss and urged Diana up the stairs to the noisy restaurant. Joanie's Fish Camp was popular, especially on Friday nights. The family-owned business was a local tradition, the perfect antidote to the glut of national chain restaurants sprouting like mushrooms around the lake. They offered a full complement of fresh water and seafood delights, along with hushpuppies, fries, and a great vinegar slaw—all at a fair price.

Matthew smiled as he spotted Liz and Danny waving at them from a booth. He steered Diana through the crowded space and slipped into the booth beside her.

"Well, you two took your sweet time getting here." Liz teased. "I saw you drive in, Trout. Did you get lost in the parking lot?"

"Something like that." Matthew grinned at Diana, who looked especially lovely in a soft blue denim shirt, rolled up at the sleeves. He knew nothing about fashion, but he liked the way the silver and turquoise necklace looked against her tan throat, how the color brought out her eyes. She wore jeans and sandals, both simple and elegant.

"We started without you. Hope you don't mind." Danny lifted a pitcher of beer and prepared to pour, but Matthew covered his glass.

"Thanks, but I'll order some sweet tea."

Liz laughed. "Didn't you know, Danny? Trout doesn't drink or smoke. He's the cleanest livin' man in the county."

Matthew laughed, too. Fact was, he'd never acquired a taste for alcohol and had long ago stopped apologizing for it. "Hey, help yourselves. Don't let me stop you."

"We won't…" Diana held out her glass for Danny to fill.

The waitress took their orders, and soon they were enjoying an extravagant meal. Comfort food, Matthew thought—calories and cholesterol to drive away the blues. Barely aware of the chatter at their table, he felt the tension drain from his body. He watched the warm glow of light on the knotty pine walls and communed with the stuffed bass mounted above their booth. Most of all, he liked the warm pressure of Diana's leg against his thigh.

"Hey, are you listening, Trout?" Danny's brown eyes caught his attention. "We're trying to make a toast here…" He lifted his beer. "Thanks to you, I'm a free man."

Matthew clinked his iced tea glass against the others. "C'mon, I can't take credit for that. Wayne never really believed you did it."

"Could have fooled me." Danny leaned across the table towards Diana. "Sheriff Bearfoot said you put in a good word too, Diana."

"That was the least she could do, since it was her fault you got arrested in the first place." Liz kicked Diana under the table, but her green eyes smiled.

Matthew wished he could steer the conversation away from Harold Haver's murder. He knew Diana was still shaken by the event, but luckily Liz seemed to have forgiven her for implicating Danny.

"Does Bearfoot have any new leads?" Liz asked as she took Danny's hand.

"He doesn't confide in me," Matthew said.

"Sure he does…" Liz pressed. "He's your best friend."

Matthew grumbled. "The case seems dead end in the water. Wayne still believes Havers was waiting for a woman that day, possibly having an affair. He thinks that woman brought the flowers, but the rendezvous ended in an argument."

"I still say his wife, Janelle, did it." Liz frowned.

Danny let go of Liz's hand. "Can we change the subject?"

Matthew's sentiments exactly. Everyone now knew that Danny had slept with Haver's wife. It was a sore subject, especially in the present company.

"Janelle has an alibi, and you know it, Liz." Diana, who'd been unusually silent all evening, finally spoke up. "She was at the High Point Market that day, and any number of witnesses can corroborate her story."

"Then who the fuck did it?" Liz snapped. "Nothing adds up. If it's true that Happy Harry had been *born again,* and given up drinking, and would never cheat on his wife—then who but Janelle had a motive?"

Matthew glanced at Danny. It seemed they both disagreed with Liz's fidelity theory. Didn't matter if Harry was born again and again, the male libido had a mind of its own.

"Besides..." Liz continued. "Harry had an appointment with Diana that evening to list his house. Why would he schedule a meeting with his lover at the same time?"

"Maybe he forgot I was coming," Diana ventured.

"Who wants dessert?" Danny interrupted, seemingly trying to steer them away from the uncomfortable topic.

"What does Bearfoot think, Trout?" Liz ran her fingers through her red hair.

Matthew stirred too much sugar into his tea. "Wayne hasn't given up, but he's stuck. No fingerprints, no witnesses, no more clues. Now, who else wants pie?"

"No, thanks." Diana pushed her plate of broiled catfish aside.

Matthew noted she'd hardly touched her food, and his sense of well-being evaporated. "You feeling all right?" he asked quietly.

"Just tired, I guess."

"She's still upset about Homer Locksley's death," Liz said. "Diana plans to attend his funeral, once they bring the body back. Ask me, she's a glutton for punishment."

Matthew was at a loss. He knew little about it, except that Diana and Liz had been at Town Hall when one of the commissioners died of an apparent heart attack. Surely Diana had been through enough traumas without putting herself through a funeral for a man she didn't know?

"Diana feels responsible for the world's problems," Liz continued. "You know how she is. She met the old guy one time, so now she owes him something." Liz spread her hands and rolled her eyes.

Danny leaned forward on his elbows. "The way I hear it, Homer Locksley's death was no accident. My pal, Woody…he's a cop in Davidson? He says they think Locksley was poisoned."

Diana groaned and buried her face in her hands.

Alarmed, Matthew wrapped his arm around her shoulders and lowered his face to her ear. "What's wrong?"

She shook her head.

Matthew glared at Danny.

"Look, it's not my fault, I'm just telling you what I heard." Danny's long frame slumped in the booth. "Woody says Locksley's death doesn't look like a heart attack. They figure someone slipped poison into the water pitcher, and Locksley got unlucky."

"That's absolutely ridiculous." Diana lifted her head. "I told Peter Sokolsky that night. If the pitcher was poisoned, everyone at the table could be dead."

"Maybe the killer wanted to take out all the commissioners and the mayor for good measure?" Liz wryly suggested. "You saw that mob, Diana. They were out for blood."

"Can we change the subject? Please?" Matthew had lost his appetite for pie. He took an angry gulp of his tea, but it was too damn sweet.

"Sorry, but there is one more thing..." Danny mumbled. "They sent Locksley's body up to Chapel Hill. The Medical Examiner and the Pathology team will sort it all out. They sent along the pitcher and glasses, too."

"What about the *bottle*?" Diana's eyes flashed.

Everyone stared. Even Diana seemed startled by her outburst. She took a deep breath, reached for Matthew's hand and held on tight.

"I just remembered..." she began slowly. "I saw Homer Locksley take a drink, but he didn't drink from a glass, he drank from a bottled water!"

"I didn't see that," Liz snorted.

"But it's true. I remember it clearly now. Mr. Locksley opened the briefcase beside his chair and took out a bottle of Aquafina, just like he drank at The Garden Club."

"Are you sure?" Liz demanded. "If Locksley drank his own water, then he wasn't poisoned at all. This whole investigation is a waste of time."

Matthew sensed a general easing of tensions around the table, yet Diana clung to his hand.

"You have an amazing memory, Diana," Danny said finally. "I'll mention the bottle to Woody."

"You do that, Danny." Matthew sighed. "Now, who wants coffee?"

FOURTEEN

*The stranger…*

The stranger sat at the back of the Chapel and listened as the organist played Samuel Barber's *Adagio for Strings,* one of Homer's favorites. The sad, measured notes of the dirge were so beautiful they tore at his heart, and he remembered how much Homer had admired Barber. Indeed, Homer had identified with Barber. Both men were artists—Homer a painter, Barber a composer. More than that, both men were gay in a time when homosexuality was both feared and despised. Although Barber was a Yankee, from the little village of West Chester, Pennsylvania, and Homer was Southern born and bred, both men knew the cruelty of small town life.

He bowed his head as the minister began his eulogy. Surely no one would notice him, and certainly no one would recognize him. He had changed utterly since his undergraduate days, and even if some of the professors gathered to pay their final respects noticed something familiar in his eyes, they'd never put it together.

Because like Homer, he did not belong. Never would. As an outcast, he'd achieved a certain invisibility in these ivy-covered walls of tradition, where men were men, with nothing in between. His years here had been a nightmare, and it was all Homer's fault.

Professor Homer Locksley, his teacher.

If only he hadn't been an art major. If only he'd never posed for life-drawing class. The day they met, the sun had filtered through the skylight and warmed his naked skin. Homer had seemed so much older. He was, in fact, vigorous and fit for a middle-aged guy. Homer's piercing blue eyes had lingered too long, causing him, the model, to respond with a sudden, self-conscious excitement he desperately wanted to hide. In that moment he'd knew for certain who he was, what he was, and Professor Locksley had known, too.

Too bad.

The minister intoned Locksley's name.

Homer Locksley, his mentor.

Folks might think it was wrong for an older man to take advantage, but the boy had wanted it that way. He shifted his slim haunches on the hard church pew and stretched his long legs. Sneaking back into the dorm after curfew, having tasted of the professor's sinful cognac and other forbidden joys, had only heightened the illicit pleasure. The stranger understood all that now, so why did he still hate the man, after all these years? He'd already been poised to 'come out' when Locksley found him. Locksley simply fired the starter gun.

As he looked around the familiar place, where stained glass still made dancing color patterns on his sleeve, he realized nothing had changed at his alma mater. The chapel still smelled of sweet flowers and musty paper. It still caused queasiness in the pit of his stomach.

The minister finished and the organist struck several decisive chords. At the same time, part of the congregation rose and solemnly approached the open casket. These were the tardy folks who didn't get a good look before the service started.

Did he dare? Part of him believed the custom of viewing the dead was barbaric. Surely the past was best remembered with all its rosy deceptions. Yet he was drawn to the body. Many times he had wished to see Homer dead, but part of him refused to believe in this death.

Taking a chance, he lowered his face and stepped into the viewing line. He avoided looking at anyone, lest he spark some connection to the ancient past, or worse still, betray his own guilt. Putting one foot in front of the other, he made it to the coffin.

When it came his turn, he took a deep breath and opened his eyes. An old man lay inside. His long white hair was combed out smooth against the pale blue silk. His cheeks were wrinkled parchment, touched by the blush of the makeup artist's brush. His lips, once plump as summer berries and sweet to kiss, were now a shrunken pouch of bitter regrets. Blessedly, his eyes were closed.

The stranger wiped away his shameful tears with the back of his hand, and at last he understood. This was not Homer after all. The whole funeral was a joke. Where had he gone?

Homer Locksley, his first love.

## FIFTEEN

## *Bobby sox and poodle skirt…*

Diana slipped quietly out the back of the church. She had no desire to view the body, let alone attend the burial. Besides, she knew very few of the mourners except Jo Jo Jones, who was seated with Mayor Connery and his wife. The other familiar faces belonged to people she didn't know by name. Fact was, after three years living in Davidson, she still wasn't part of the community.

Most of this was her fault. She was reserved by nature and valued her privacy too much. These were not ideal traits for a real estate agent, and she'd decided to reform. In this spirit, she'd invited Parker White to lunch this week, but Parker had declined, saying she had pressing family business in Winston-Salem.

That explained why Parker wasn't present at Homer Locksley's funeral. Diana felt that all of Locksley's fellow commissioners should have been there, but even Duck Wadell was missing. This was especially odd, since Liz and Diana were scheduled to meet Duck in a few minutes. It would be interesting to hear his excuse for not attending the funeral.

She paused in the vestibule to sign the guest registry, along with many others. It seemed those in attendance had been either very old, Homer's contemporaries, or young adults, the age of Diana's children. One of the younger ones was a handsome man seated beside her in the back pew, who looked to be several years out of college. Likely he had been one of the professor's former students, for he was obviously grieving for the man.

Squaring her shoulders, she took one last look at the beautiful Presbyterian chapel. Maybe she should join this church and cultivate new friendships? Yet, with Diana, religion was also a private matter. She preferred to commune with God while walking on a nature trail or watching a sunset—a hopeless recluse.

She carried this depressing thought, along with a lingering sadness from the funeral, across Main Street to the Soda Shop. On the way, she saw Parker White's new silver Jaguar parked in a remote corner of the municipal parking lot. Its ostentatious splendor was all but concealed by a stand of evergreen shrubs.

*Sneaky little rat!* She bet Parker had never left town after all. If that were the case, she'd gone to great lengths to avoid this funeral. Likely she was avoiding Diana, too. She pictured Parker holed up in her apartment above the bookstore, peeking out from behind closed curtains as the dutiful friends of the deceased filed out of the church.

Diana considered confronting the woman. If she hadn't had this meeting, she would have stormed Parker's apartment and demanded an explanation, along with a civilized cup of tea, of course. As it was, she calmly entered the Soda Shop and stepped backwards in time.

Long a campus hangout, the small grill resembled something from *Happy Days*. Diana half expected Ronny Howard and the Fonz to drop coins in a jukebox and bebop across the floor. Instead, Liz waved her to a table.

"Hey, how come you didn't wear your bobby sox and poodle skirt?" Diana teased.

Liz gave her a blank stare. "What about you? You look like you just came from a funeral." She frowned at Diana's dark suit.

Liz knew very well she had just come from Locksley's service, but Diana refused to rise to the bait. Instead, she pulled out a chair, sat down, and was amazed to see that Liz had ordered an enormous, sloppy hamburger. It was three in the afternoon, that never-never hour between lunch and dinner, a bizarre time to eat a meal. Yet ketchup clung to Liz's fingertips like bloody fingernail polish, and her stack of greasy fries was almost obscene.

"What can I get for you?" A middle-aged waitress appeared.

"Iced tea?"

After much urging from the waitress and a minor argument with Liz, Diana got her way and was served tea, no food.

"Did the funeral make you lose your appetite?" Liz licked her fingers clean and dried them with a napkin. "I understand. Was it awful?"

"It was very moving, actually. Where is Mr. Wadell?"

"Late, as usual. Wasn't he at the service?"

"Nope."

"That's weird. He should have been there."

Diana agreed, but it was no big deal. All she wanted now was to finish this meeting, go home, kick off her shoes, pour a glass of white wine, and then call Matthew. They'd spent all of last weekend together, and she was still walking around in a fog of contentment. In truth, contentment was way too mild to describe how good she felt.

But she dragged her mind from thoughts of Matthew, and turned to Liz. "Listen, what should I say to Duck?"

"Good question. The whole ETJ deal is on hold until they elect new commissioners, and the emergency elections should have been held last week."

Diana understood the problem. Even with Parker more or less certain to be elected permanently, the town was still short two commissioners. Viable candidates would eventually come forward, but they also deserved time to campaign.

"As far as the annexation is concerned," Liz continued. "Of course Duck will vote *yes,* and he says Jo Jo's vote is also in the bag. No one knows where Parker White stands on the issue…" Liz made a face. "And we can only hope that whoever gets elected has his head screwed on right."

Of course, Liz hoped the new commissioners would favor the *land grab.* Diana still had severe reservations about the fairness of this concept and suspected the farmers were getting a raw deal. She had avoided an in-depth study of Liz's scheme simply because she hadn't wanted to argue with Liz. The truce between them was still too fragile.

"Today, just listen to Duck and pretend to agree, Diana. Smile, and I'll do all the talking, okay?"

"No problem." With a little luck, neither Duck nor Liz would guess that she hadn't done her homework. "By the way, how's Danny?"

"He's awesome!" Liz's eyes lit up.

Apparently Matthew and Diana were not the only couple who'd enjoyed a special weekend after the catfish dinner. "So, what have you two been up to?" Diana asked.

"Well for one thing, Danny's been playing detective with his buddy, Rodney Woods. You read about Locksley's autopsy in the paper, right?"

Diana blinked like an idiot. All week she'd been so distracted thinking about Matthew and the romantic vacation to Wilmington they'd planned, she had completely tuned out the news.

"You knew about the poison, right?" Liz seemed incredulous. "You just came from the man's funeral, and you didn't know?"

Diana was definitely slipping. Had she been sane, the mystery of Homer Locksley's demise would have been foremost in her mind.

"Well, let me tell you what the papers *did not* say..." Liz warmed to her subject. "Danny got it firsthand from Woody, you know?" She took a deep breath. "The poison was called sodium fluoroacetate. It's a fine white powder that you can't smell or taste. Someone mixed it with water and injected it into Homer's bottled water."

"The bottled water I told you about?"

"Yeah, but according to Woody, his boss, Peter Sokolsky, had spotted the Aquafina bottle right away. He'd sent it off to the lab along with the other stuff."

Diana felt sick.

"The killer put the poison into a hypodermic needle and injected it under the plastic bottle cap. Danny said a few drops will kill a horse."

"So Mr. Locksley's death was deliberate?"

Liz scoffed. "They use this sodium fluoroacetate to kill rodents and other pests around the farm, but even the government has banned it because it's so dangerous. You bet your sweet ass someone intended to kill him."

"So how did the murderer get his hands on the poison?"

"You mean, how did the *murderess* get *her* hands on the poison?" Liz gloated "They're looking at Rhonda Smith on suspicion of murder."

Diana was shocked, although the theory made some sense. Had Rhonda openly made death threats against Homer? If she'd been half as vocal generally as she'd been with Hoke Bodine, no wonder the police were looking at her.

"It seems Homer Locksley designed the new low-income housing bungalows at the edge of town, and then cast the deciding vote which caused some folks' old family homes to be destroyed," Liz continued.

"Rhonda's grandma and her daddy, Commissioner Lester B. Smith, were both displaced by Homer's vote. Their old house was burned, and they were forced to move into one of the bungalows. The shock caused Grandma to die of a heart attack, and shortly after that, Lester B., who hadn't used alcohol in years, got drunk and drove his car into Lake Norman. They say Rhonda blamed Homer for both deaths. Plus, she had motive and opportunity..."

"How do you mean?" Diana cut in.

"Lester B. was an addicted gardener. His old neighbors claim he kept lots of farm poisons in his garage. Before they burned the place, Rhonda saved his gardening tools and maybe the poison, too."

"They know all this for a fact?" This story made her uncommonly sad.

"They haven't found the poison anywhere in Rhonda's apartment, so it's still a theory," Liz admitted. "But there's more. Rhonda is diabetic, so she's a whiz at injecting insulin. Needless to say, she knew how to use a syringe. Plus, having worked at Town Hall for years, she knew Homer's habits. She even knew his preference in bottled water, so she could have prepared the lethal bottle ahead of time and switched it out with the one in his briefcase. Put it all together, and you've got your killer."

Diana was not convinced, plus she hated the idea. Damning as all the evidence was, it was still circumstantial. Any number of citizens bore grudges against the commissioners, including the angry farmers at Town Hall, who, by the way, were more likely to possess deadly animal poisons.

"Have they actually arrested Rhonda?" Diana asked.

"No, but they put her on suspension at Town Hall, so she has no job. It's too bad, since she's divorced with two small children. Woody thinks they'll arrest her soon."

Now Diana felt worse. She averted her gaze from the remains of Liz's bloody hamburger and looked out the window, where she saw Duck Wadell arriving, just in the nick of time. He leveraged his athletic frame from the driver's seat of a black, late-model Mercedes Sport, and then opened the passenger door.

A stunning woman, with mile-long legs extending from a leather miniskirt, climbed out with Duck's help. Once on her feet, she was, in fact, as short as a child. Her long legs seemed inadequate support for the huge bosom under her skin-tight red sweater, and by the way Duck's hand lingered under one of her breasts, Diana had no doubt as to the nature of their relationship.

"Oh, shit!" Liz gasped. "What the hell is *she* doing here?"

"Who is she?" Diana continued to stare as Duck led the woman in their direction.

"Janelle Havers, Happy Harold's merry widow!" Liz hissed. "What a dick! Clearly Duck is sleeping with that slut, but I can't believe he had the nerve to bring her to this meeting!"

Diana had no preconceived prejudice against Janelle. In fact, she was frankly curious to meet this femme fatale who always reduced Liz to a frothing maniac. Sure enough, Liz's face flamed red as she gripped the edge of the table.

"Swear to God, I can't do this, Diana." Suddenly Liz jumped to her feet. "Make some excuse, will you? I'll owe you big time…"

Before she knew what was happening, Liz escaped through the back door. She left Diana with the lunch bill, a real estate dossier about which she knew next to nothing, and considerable egg on her face.

SIXTEEN

## *Nothing in common…*

"Where the hell is Liz?" Duck Wadell demanded. Having introduced Janelle Havers, he lost no time getting right down to business.

"I'm afraid she had to leave," Diana said.

"You're kidding, right? Jeez, I'm not that late." He eyed the dossier on the table. "What now? Do we do this thing without her?"

Diana shrugged. "To tell you the truth, Mr. Wadell, I don't know anything about this project. Talking to me without Liz would be a waste of time."

He scowled and crossed his arms. "At least you're honest, Diana. We wouldn't want to waste anyone's time, now would we?"

Her face burned. Liz had put her in an awkward position. She was embarrassed, angry, and at a loss how to deal with any of it. "I am so sorry… should we reschedule?"

"Excellent suggestion…." Wadell took possession of Janelle's arm. "Have Liz give me a call."

He began leading Janelle towards the door, but she broke loose. "Go on without me, darlin'," she drawled. "I'll sit a spell and chat with Diana."

"Aren't you coming over to my place?" he whined.

"Well, sure I am, darlin'. But I'm a big girl, and I reckon I can get there under my own steam." Janelle smiled.

Duck seemed nonplussed. Clearly his plans for love in the afternoon had gone seriously astray. He obviously understood what Diana had quickly sensed—it was pointless to argue with Janelle Havers.

"Catch you later, then." He sighed and left the Soda Shop.

For an uncomfortable moment, the two women sat across the table from one another in silent appraisal. Diana was grateful for this respite. It gave her a chance to collect her thoughts.

"Can I buy you a soda, or something?" she said at last.

"No, thank you, ma'am," Janelle answered shyly. "I really do want to talk to you, but if it's all the same, I'd rather talk outside?"

"Yes, of course, that's fine..." Diana signaled the waitress and quickly paid for her tea and Liz's hamburger. All the while, her mind raced. What could Janelle possibly want? They were complete strangers, with nothing in common.

Yet Janelle followed on Diana's heels as they stepped into the chilly November afternoon. Once outside, Janelle led her into a little park between storefronts. The grassy alcove fronted the village post office, and several wooden benches were placed along the sidewalk. Janelle chose a bench in a patch of weak sunlight, where the bare branches of an enormous crape myrtle cast deep shadows on the lawn.

They sat side by side.

Diana's dark wool suit provided some protection against the cold, but Janelle's arms, which were bare beyond the short sleeves of her red sweater, were covered with goose bumps. Her small hands fluttered nervously in the lap of her leather miniskirt, and Diana was struck by her child-like vulnerability. Whatever troubled this woman, she was clearly reluctant to begin the conversation. In the meantime, Diana had come to realize there was only one topic where they shared common ground.

She cleared her throat. "Do you want to talk to me about your husband?" Diana began gently.

Janelle startled, and then she stiffened. When she lifted her eyes, they were an astonishing shade of lilac and wide with surprise. "Why would I want to talk about him?"

"Harold Havers..." Diana said. "I was the one who found him, don't you remember?"

"Oh, God, yeah!"

Janelle's mouth was painted bright red. As it gaped open, Diana noticed a tiny fleck of lipstick clinging to her perfect white teeth. For some reason, the imperfection tugged at Diana's maternal heartstrings.

"Now I get it..." Janelle continued. "You were the one who found my Harry dead."

Diana longed to take it back, because obviously this wasn't the topic Janelle had wanted to pursue. "I'm so sorry..." was all she could think to say. The sun went under a cloud. Across Main Street, Homer Locksley's hearse pulled away from the Presbyterian Church.

"It's okay to talk about him," Janelle said. "I miss him a lot, but Harry was as good as dead to me a long time ago."

Diana was taken aback by the woman's voice, flat and void of feeling. When she searched Janelle's eyes, she saw worry lines artfully hidden beneath heavy makeup.

"It's no big secret." Janelle stared at her. "Everyone knew my marriage to Harry was a huge mistake."

Diana had no desire to become this woman's motherly confessor. Indeed, the closer she looked, the more she understood that Janelle was anything but a child. The harsh light revealed she had aged beyond her years, so her aura of vulnerability was merely an illusion. Perhaps this revelation emboldened Diana to continue.

"I am sure it was difficult. Mr. Havers was a good bit older, wasn't he, Janelle?"

"What the hell does that have to do with the price of eggs?" she snapped. "How come everyone assumes it was *me* who cheated on *him*? It was the other way around, damn it! I wasn't enough for Harry. He was sleeping with some other woman before the honeymoon was even over."

Diana was speechless. Surely this was nonsense. Although she had known Harold Havers only slightly, he was no one's vision of a ladies' man. Anyone with eyes in her head and a brain in her skull could easily imagine Janelle was too much for him to handle in bed, or in any other circumstance.

"You don't believe me, do you?" Janelle pouted. "But it's true. First off, Harry was upset when he found out I couldn't have his babies, and then he got mad when I made him stop drinking. Oh, he pretended to go along with it. He came to church with me and claimed he was saved, but underneath he was sorry he ever married me."

Diana averted her eyes and squirmed on the hard bench. This was more than she needed to hear. And yet, she recalled the night of the murder, when Wayne Bearfoot's young deputy vowed that Harold Havens had found religion and stopped drinking. He'd also said that Janelle loved her husband and would never hurt him. Bizarre as it all seemed, there was a grain of truth in Janelle's story.

"What makes you think your husband was having an affair?"

"A woman knows these things. What's worse, he was sleeping with some older woman. I could smell her on him."

Diana was appalled, but her curiosity was peaked. "That's ridiculous, Janelle. How could you possibly know she was *older*?"

"Her perfume, of course. On nights when Harry came home late, after claiming he was meeting some client at the bank, he stank of *White Shoulders*." Janelle wrinkled her nose in disgust. "Only old ladies wear that scent. Isn't that right, ma'am?"

"Please don't call me ma'am." This was really too much. Diana was way too young to be a ma'am, and way too young to be harboring motherly feelings for Janelle. Yet the girl had a point. *White Shoulders* was Diana's mother's perfume of choice, a definite favorite of the geriatric crowd.

"Sorry, Diana. I didn't mean to lay all this on you. I don't know what the hell I'm talking about half the time."

The woman was clearly in distress. Two sad streams of mascara ran from the corners of her odd lilac eyes. Her black hair, straight from the dye bottle, was tangled from the wind.

"Look, Janelle, why did you want to talk to me today?"

She pulled a shredded tissue from her purse and blew her nose. "I came along to talk to Liz, not to you. But I know you guys are good friends, so when she wasn't here, I hoped you'd tell her something for me…"

Diana sighed and braced herself, quickly guessing where all this was leading.

"I bet Liz *was* here, but she took off when she saw me coming. Isn't that right, Diana?"

Diana nodded.

"Yeah, I knew it. She hates me." Janelle blew her nose again. "I never meant it to happen between Danny Capelli and me. I knew all along he was Liz's boyfriend, but I was so lonesome. Like I said, Harry locked me out of his life, and all of a sudden, Danny was there, painting our house."

"I understand, Janelle."

"No one really understands, let alone Danny." Janelle sobbed. "He was always in love with Liz, from way back when we were all kids together in Charlotte. He knew it, and I knew it, but at the time he was with me, Liz was treating him like a piece of shit. Know what I mean?"

Everything Janelle said was true, but Diana hated being man in the middle. "What do you want me to do, Janelle?"

"Tell Liz I'm sorry, okay?" She grasped Diana's wrist with frigid fingers.

"Sure, I'll tell her."

Janelle took a moment to compose herself. She loosened her grip on Diana's wrist, and then held her hand. In spite of all the hateful gossip Diana had heard about Janelle, she realized she liked the woman. Janelle was raw and coarse, but brutally honest. She also sensed Janelle would make a good friend, and she'd tell Liz so.

"Thanks for everything, Diana." Janelle grinned. "But there is one more thing…"

"Yes?"

"Do you have a car?"

"Of course."

Would you give me a lift over to Duck's house?"

## SEVENTEEN

## *Duck Wadell*

Duck Wadell knew his lover would come, but when? Janelle was a resourceful creature. Likely she'd beg a ride off the Rittenhouse woman, who'd either take her home so Janelle could get her own car, or better yet, bring her directly to his house. If she came direct, it was a good sign. It meant Janelle was willing to trust him to take her home after dinner, or take her home after breakfast tomorrow morning.

The thought of Janelle spending the night caused a familiar tightening in his chest. God knows he was trying to bed the woman, but in spite of her reputation, she was making him jump through all the hoops. He'd been courting her like a schoolboy, with expensive dinners, first-run movies, even flowers. Folks who saw them together assumed he was getting some action, when in fact he was getting nothing but cold showers.

He unlocked the roadside door of his rustic log home and turned on all the lights. As always, first sight of the open, spacious interior, with exposed beams and heart of pine floors, filled him with pride. The custom-designed home, on two secluded acres, with his own private peninsula, had cost a small fortune. That was okay. He could afford it. Once the ETJ project went through, he could afford this and then some.

Any woman should be impressed, even Janelle. Sure, the place Harold Havers built for her was also on the lake, but it was an architectural monstrosity, a pretentious, tasteless, starter castle compared to Duck's place. Surely she could appreciate the difference?

He shucked off his jacket, removed his tie, and hung them both on a hanger in the closet. He tugged his collar open, took a deep breath. Anticipating Janelle's first visit, he'd hired cleaners to spiff up the joint, and the girls had done a great job. He hardly recognized the place with all the magazines put away and all the ashtrays clean.

Someone had created an autumn arrangement of dried flowers, gourds, and a pumpkin on the hearth. When Duck turned on the gas logs and settled beside Janelle on the couch, she'd take it all in and understand that in spite of his rough exterior, he was a man of refinement, with much to offer.

He wandered through the great room to where the glass window wall had been polished spotless. His pricey new deck boat rocked gently at the dock, and the water was deep blue. Off to the west, the sun had begun its descent down through the sky and the sunset promised to be a beauty. Winter sunsets were always the best. Something about the cold clear air, the way light passed through the clouds, produced the gaudy pink, red, and gold effects. Romantic. Women liked such things, and Janelle would be no exception.

He had set the gas grill up on the deck, and it was ready to go. Duck's skills as a chef were severely limited, but he broiled a mean steak. It was too cold to eat outside, though.

He walked back to the kitchen, checked inside the fridge where two thick rib eyes were marinating. The salad stuff was ready, and the red wine was breathing. So far, so good. He lifted two wine glasses from the cupboard, set out plates on the table. Since this was a special occasion, he located the colorful cloth napkins his second wife had bought in Mexico, but he gave up trying to fold them right.

Finally, he opened the box of steak knives he won at the Mercedes Dealer's Grand Opening and tested the blades. They were high quality, razor sharp. Duck smiled with satisfaction. He loved getting stuff for free. But how should he position them? Right or left of the plate? Frustrated, he tossed a knife on each napkin and headed for the bedroom.

The master suite was obscenely large, dominated by the king-size bed set dead center. Per his instructions, the cleaning crew had changed the sheets, and as he sat on the side of the bed, he debated whether or not to turn down the covers. Too obvious? As he imagined Janelle entering the room, the tightness in his chest increased.

He pictured her in the leather miniskirt and tight red sweater she'd worn today. Would she remove her clothes while he watched, or let him help? He groaned as he bent over to push off his loafers. He could almost see her long legs emerging from her pantyhose, and the womanly curve of her hips. He imagined how her heavy breasts would fall as the sweater came over her head, and how he'd hold one breast in each hand, gauging the weight, watching her nipples harden as he coaxed them with his rough thumbs.

*Jesus Christ!* His erection was sudden and unexpected. Duck stood up and peeled off his shirt. He crossed to the mirror, saw the front of his trousers peaked like a tent, stared approvingly at his well-muscled chest and decided the hours of agony in the gym were worth the effort. Not bad for a guy pushing fifty. Janelle would soon understand what a man like Duck could give her, compared to an old geezer like Harold Havers. On his best days,

Duck doubted Harry could get it up. Even an overdose of Viagra would never elevate poor Harry to Duck's league.

And yet, Harry had been Duck's best friend. The thought caused his passion to wilt as he moved into the bathroom. He slipped the gold Rolex off his wrist and saw it was 4:30, almost an hour since he'd left Janelle at the Soda Shop. Did he have time to shower?

He glanced into the mirror mounted on the medicine cabinet, where the fluorescent lighting was far less forgiving than the natural glow in the bedroom. Here Duck looked older than fifty. His pale, bloodshot eyes were couched in puffy folds, while his chin had softened and begun to sag. A crop of blond bristles grew like fungus on his jaw. A shave was definitely in order.

He splashed his face, lathered, and reached for his razor. Harry had been a good pal. They'd done countless deals together, working side by side like a harnessed team. They'd helped one another get rich, not always operating within the legal mainstream, but they'd always understood one another. Duck missed old Harry more than he was willing to admit. No one deserved to die that way, and Duck suspected one of their mutual enemies must have done the evil deed. But who? The same bastard might also harbor a grudge against him, so he'd been watching his back. And at some gut-deep level, Duck felt guilty about Harry's death.

The razor slipped and nicked the mole near his right ear, drawing blood. He cursed, and then chuckled. His fair skin was dotted with imperfections earned from years of courting the hot Carolina sun, and his dermatologist would give him hell over this one. He wadded a bit of toilet tissue, pressed in onto the cut, and then his thoughts returned to Harry.

Of course he felt guilty. He'd spent the better part of the past month trying to get into Janelle's pants. Fucking your best friend's widow was a sure-fire guilt trip, yet lately Billy *Duck* Wadell had decided he was too much alone. Two failed marriages and a string of meaningless affairs had left him numb. Even the money didn't help.

He glanced again at his watch and decided to go for the shower. He reached behind the curtain and got the water heating up while he pulled off his pants. Naked, he was still a fine figure of manhood. His stomach was flat, his legs short, but strong, and, he noted with some satisfaction, he had another hard-on.

It was then he heard the footsteps in the kitchen.

Shit! He should have skipped the damned shower. On the other hand, there was something erotic, if not romantic, about Janelle discovering him in the buff. He had deliberately left the door unlocked—a subconscious move designed for just this result?

He pretended to be oblivious to the advancing footfalls as they moved across the bedroom carpet. He whistled off-key and hurriedly picked the blob of toilet tissue off his face. He smiled because the bleeding had stopped.

He expected Janelle to call out before she entered, but he suspected that modesty was not one of her hang-ups. But when the door was flung open with such force it shattered the tiled wall, he was truly stunned.

"What the hell are *you* doing here?" This was definitely not the person he wanted to see. His stomach lurched with fear as he dropped his gaze from the ice-cold eyes filled with hatred, to the glinting knife.

His free steak knife!

Duck could not resist or scream before the sharp blade sliced between his ribs, then angled upwards to pierce his heart. He felt the lifeblood pumping from his body as his lips formed the words he could not speak. The pain was a flash fire in his chest, it scorched his veins and seared the nerve endings at the farthest reach of his consciousness as he crumpled to the cold tile floor.

He heard a buzz, like distant singing in his ears, and then there was nothing.

EIGHTEEN

## *The late night news...*

Diana had not resented dropping Janelle at Ducks, since she was heading north to Mama's anyway. In fact, she'd continued to think about Janelle all through dinner with Mama. Afterwards, when Vivian and their tablemate, Lou Turbyfil, decided to watch TV in the Bistro rather than accompany Diana back to Mama's room, she was grateful for the chance to be alone.

Plus, she'd been assigned a task of major importance—the seasonal switching-out of Mama's wardrobe. That job would fill the long hours between dinner and the eleven o'clock news, when Diana could leave without appearing too eager, so she got busy packing up the light-weight tops and other summer clothing. She'd then take those clothes home with her and store them until next spring.

She thought about Mama as she sorted, putting cotton jackets in one bag—shirts, dresses, and shoes in others. Alone in her mother's room, surrounded by a few select pieces of antique furniture from their family home in Pennsylvania, she realized how very much she loved her mother. Once upon a time Vivian would not have tolerated foolish television, but at this very moment she'd be glued to *Wheel of Fortune,* to be followed by *Jeopardy.* Like many residents at Shady Oaks, Viv had become a game show addict.

As she folded Mama's summer nightgowns, the scent of White Shoulders floated from the drawer, reminding her of the odd conversation she'd had with Janelle that afternoon. The woman had insisted that her murdered husband, Harold Havers, had been having an affair with an *old woman* who favored this perfume.

Diana giggled at the idea. One thing was certain—Harold's amorous old woman was *not* Vivian Whitaker. Mother had given up on men when Diana's father died. Since then, she'd contented herself with critiquing Diana's romantic decisions. Mama had never liked Robert Rittenhouse, Diana's ex. In spite of Robert's extreme good looks, his old money, and his success as a Philadelphia lawyer, Mama never trusted him. God, she had sure called that one right!

Diana had almost given up on men herself—until Matthew. And miraculously, Mama adored Matthew. After meeting him only once, Viv couldn't say anything bad about the man, and Diana didn't need Mama to tell her what she already knew: Matthew was Diana's miracle.

"Aren't you finished yet?" Mama's voice startled her.

She glanced at her watch as first Mama, then Lou Turbyfil in her wheelchair, pushed through the door. Clearly she'd lost track of time, and the game shows were over.

"Nothing good on TV?" she asked them.

Both elderly women scowled.

"Two stupid shows about Frosty the Snowman," Mama said.

"Yes, the first one was narrated by Jimmy Durante, the newer one by John Goodman." Lou snarled. "You'd think the networks could find a better way to waste our time."

"You two sound like the Grinch who stole Christmas," Diana mumbled.

"Lou has a surprise for us, Diana." Mama passed a critical eye over the bags Diana had filled. "But she won't tell *me* anything."

"Nope, I wanted to tell you both at once." Lou dug deep into her purse and came out with three tickets. "These are for *The King and I*, performed by the Davidson Community Players…" She paused for effect. "But, of course, you know all about the play, don't you, Diana?"

"Where on earth did you get those tickets?" Diana's jaw dropped.

"An old friend brought them by," Lou said mysteriously. "She's a new friend of yours, Diana."

"I know all about that play." Storm clouds gathered in Mama's eyes. "Diana's in charge of properties, aren't you, dear?"

Diana realized she was in hot water. Whatever Good Samaritan had been selling tickets at Shady Oaks had done her no favors.

"My old friend Parker White sold me the tickets," Lou explained. "Parker understands that just because folks live in a retirement community, doesn't mean they're brain-dead. She appreciates the fact that we still enjoy culture."

"Parker White…why does that name sound familiar?" Mama asked.

"We were talking about Parker last time Diana was here. Don't you remember, Vivian? Parker's husband and my husband were both physicians at Wake Forest."

"That's right, she's that Yankee woman with the horrible children." Mama frowned.

Diana wanted to hide under the bed. Somehow Parker's name kept cropping up in the most unusual circumstances. She thought Parker had washed her hands of *The King and I*, so what was she doing at Shady Oaks, stirring up trouble?

"Why didn't *you* think to bring us tickets, Diana?" Mama examined the little rectangular billet in her hand. "It says the play opens on a Friday night. That means you could have taken us on your regular visiting day without going out of your way. But maybe you don't care about us? Maybe you think we are brain-dead?"

"You never liked musicals, Mother."

"Who says? Parker White may not be a good mother, but I bet she's a better daughter than some…"

Mama's accusation hung in the hot little room as Lou picked up the ball.

"Parker's not too happy about her daughter, I can tell you that." Lou leaned forward in her wheelchair. "She didn't want to talk about Cindi, but I have my ways…"

"Isn't Cindi the girl who dropped out of school when she got pregnant, or some such thing?" Mama's nose twitched at the scent of gossip."

"Now I don't know for a fact she got pregnant, "Lou confessed. "But I do know she married a NASCAR driver named Ray Martinez. It broke Parker's heart."

Diana closed her ears and checked her watch. It was only ten o'clock, time for the reruns of *Diagnosis Murder*, Mother's absolute favorite.

"When Parker sold me these tickets, she was very upset." Lou pressed on. "It seems Cindi and her husband were in town, and they tried to call Parker. Can you imagine such a thing? Mother and daughter don't speak to one another for years—then, out of the blue, Cindi tries to make contact?"

"What's wrong with that?" Diana believed life was too short for these long-standing feuds. Both Mama and Lou stared at her, like she were crazy.

"Cindi and Ray live like gypsies, don't you know?" Lou said. "They drift from town to town following the race circuit, and what's worse, they're both into that *born again* nonsense. No wonder Parker is ashamed."

Mama nodded in agreement. "So, did Parker ever talk to the girl?"

"Good heavens, no! Cindi left a message on Parker's answering machine. Said she and Ray were staying in nearby Rockingham for some race next week, but certainly Parker did not call them."

Diana had heard enough, so she turned on the television just as Dr. Sloan was discovering a corpse in the hospital supply cabinet. Lou and Mama were instantly riveted to the screen, and Parker's problems were abandoned as Dick Van Dyke did his thing.

Breathing a sigh of relief, Diana continued to pack bags and count commercials until the magic moment when she could depart. Her trips back and forth to Queen Vic, bearing the clothing sacks like a packhorse, went largely unnoticed. Unless, heaven forbid, she left the door ajar, allowing a draft to reach the older ladies. When this happened, Mama hit the mute button and screamed her displeasure. Her reaction brought out the devil in her, so each time she made a trip, she deliberately left the door a little wider ajar.

Even this simple pleasure did little to speed up time. When the jaunty music came on TV, signaling the late night news, she was truly desperate to flee, but she sat for a moment on the edge of Mama's bed and glared at the perky little newscaster who'd taken her sweet time getting there.

Diana was preparing to say her goodbyes, when she noticed something familiar on the screen as the camera panned in on the entrance to a rustic cabin surrounded by woods. The driveway was clogged with police cars. Red cherry lights spun atop each vehicle, while some sort of human drama was being played out in the headlights.

"What's all this?" Lou Turbyfil squinted for a better look. "Did that sheriff say Iredell County?"

"Yes, he said the murder happened at Lake Norman!" Mama turned up the volume.

As Diana's eyes adjusted to the grainy image, she recognized Duck Wadell's house, and the walls of Mama's small room closed in around her. She spotted Wayne Bearfoot standing beside his squad car. He was questioning a tearful Janelle Havers, who clung to him for support. Diana saw mascara streaks on Janelle's ruined face and bloody smears on her bare arms. And absurdly, she noticed the young woman was still wearing the red sweater and leather miniskirt, the same outfit she'd had on when they were together several hours ago.

*Commissioner William Wadell was widely respected throughout the community. He is the fourth Davidson commissioner to die in less than one month. Authorities report Mr. Wadell died from a knife wound to the heart..."*

The news was an assault, stunning and violent. As Wayne approached the camera to speak, all Diana could see was a talking head describing a 911 call that came too late. Suddenly, she felt faint.

"Did you know that man Wadell, Diana?" her mother demanded.

But Diana couldn't speak as the paramedics carried a black body bag from the house to a silently waiting ambulance.

"You seem to know something." Lou pressed

Diana was dizzy. If she didn't escape right then, they'd never let her go. "I don't know him." She lied.

Before the women could react, Diana ran out the door. She unlocked her car, climbed inside, and lowered her head to the steering wheel until the dizziness passed. Willing her mind to numbness, she drove on automatic pilot, into the night.

## NINETEEN

## *A guilty schoolgirl...*

The sun came up as usual Saturday morning, in spite of the dark spirits that had haunted Diana during the night. It burned through the sky, causing the white mini blinds to glow like shimmering squares of parchment in the paneled walls. It warmed her face as she stretched her bare legs down through the cool sheets and wiggled her cold toes against Matthew's hairy leg.

He stirred in his sleep, but didn't wake up even when she brushed the tousled brown bangs off his face and watched the rapid eye movement under his closed lids. She hoped he was having a sweet dream, because God knew she didn't want to transfer her nightmares into his peace. Matthew's love had saved her last night, chasing the demons away as she succumbed to his passion and sank into blessed oblivion.

Thank you, Matthew. She lifted onto one elbow and continued to explore his face. Years of working in the Carolina sun had bronzed his skin to the texture of soft leather and etched laugh lines at the corners of his eyes. Morning whiskers grew like frost on the craggy ridge of his jaw and around his expressive mouth. Diana smiled as she pictured him with a beard and moustache. They would be white, in stark contrast to his tan skin and dark hair. Interesting. Maybe she'd convince him to grow a beard and moustache someday.

He'd certainly been a good sport about being waked up late last night by the rantings of a mad woman. After leaving Mama's place, she'd gotten off at Matthew's exit and driven straight to his cottage. Her need to see him was a visceral longing she couldn't control, and she'd kept him up until the wee hours of morning talking about Duck's murder. She'd wanted him to hold her, make love to her, and tell her everything would be all right.

Like a child. No, like a woman desperately in love. Problem was, Diana understood death. She knew how suddenly, without warning, it could take away a loved one for all time. Last night she'd needed reassurance that Matthew was safe, that she was safe, and that they were both really alive. She'd needed him inside her, where she could hold him forever.

She turned over, hooked her leg around him and kissed him softly on the lips. In sleep he looked as innocent as a child. She'd told him that once and he'd laughed. He'd said, "I look innocent, because I am innocent. I'm pure of heart and mind." Not quite, but in some respects, in spite of his physique and virile persona, Matthew was innocent. Compared to other humans she'd known, he was open and honest, with no hidden agenda. What you saw, was what you got, and she liked what she saw very, very much.

She also liked how Matthew made love to her. She kissed him again, but this time she parted his lips with her tongue. She reached under the covers and took hold of him. As her kiss deepened, he stirred and came to life in her hand. In the ways of love, he was far from innocent, and he was no child.

He didn't open his eyes, but a smile played at the corners of his mouth as his strong hands gently guided her into position above him. He slowly spread her thighs with his knees, pinning her in a very dangerous place indeed. He whispered her name and kissed her throat as their need took on an urgent life of its own. Her body ached for him all over again, as though last night's lovemaking had served only to create an unquenchable thirst. She longed to drink of him deeply, fully, until she could hold no more.

As they began moving together as one, a slow rhythm calculated to prolong the sweet agony, she sensed a disturbance at the corner of her consciousness. It began as a distant, unwelcome distraction—a sound out of place. She tried to push it away, but it grew louder—the crunch of tires on gravel.

"Did you hear that?" She panted into Matthew's ear.

His heart raced against her chest and he struggled to comprehend. At the same time, his dog, Ursie, began to bark and a car door slammed. A sudden, unreasonable fear invaded Diana when she rolled off Matthew. She couldn't breathe, and her body clenched up in loss and protest.

"What is it?" Matthew's dark eyes were glazed with passion.

"Someone's here. A car just drove up right outside our window."

He groaned and leveraged himself upright, like a drowning man breaking surface. He blinked against the light.

"What should we do?" she gasped. Her panic was way out of proportion, heightened, perhaps, by the cruel interruption. She hated herself for reacting like a guilty schoolgirl, but for both their sakes, she didn't want to be caught in Matthew's bed.

His heart continued to race as he reached across her and snagged his watch from the bedside table. "Too early for a social call," he growled. "But I guess I better take a look."

She longed to pull him down and drag the covers over both their heads, but Matthew wasn't one to hide or retreat. As he lurched out of bed and stretched to his full, impressive height, his powerful, aroused body was a thing of beauty. Under different circumstances, she'd have gloried in just watching him, but as things were, she felt cheated and frightened at the same time.

She held her breath as he padded barefoot across the hardwood floor and lifted the blinds. At the same time, Ursie stopped barking. Apparently, the dog knew their visitor.

"Well, I'll be..." Matthew muttered. "It's our old pal, Wayne Bearfoot. Damned if he's not the early bird. Or, by the sorry looks of him, I'd bet good money he never went to bed."

The panic lodged at the base of her throat finally broke loose. "Oh, please don't tell him I'm here, Matthew!"

He smiled and winked. "I reckon he's already noticed your car. He's parked right beside it."

"I won't talk to him!" She felt like she was pleading for her life, or, at very least, a modicum of dignity.

Matthew returned and sat on the edge of the bed. He kissed her forehead and held her hand. "After what you told me last night, how you were the one who dropped Janelle Havers at Wadell's house, I suspect Wayne's looking to talk to *you*, not *me*."

He was right. Likely Wayne had tried to call her at her condo, but then he'd put two and two together. Her car was a dead giveaway. You'd think a person could find a little privacy at Matthew's remote lake property, but Bearfoot had a nose like a bloodhound. Her panic gave way to anger.

"Tell him to leave, Matthew."

He sighed and nuzzled under her chin. "Hey, I know how you feel. I'm getting too old for this, uh, what do they say...*coitus interruptus*?"

She giggled in spite of herself. She'd never expected Matthew to come up with that term, but then, he was full of surprises. She gently pulled his face away and held it between her hands.

"I still won't talk to him." She smiled. "Tell him I'm taking a shower."

He arched his eyebrows. "You want me to lie to the sheriff?"

"It won't be a lie." Before he could stop her, she scrambled out of bed and scampered to the bathroom door.

"Should I invite him in for breakfast?" he teased.

"Don't you dare!" She grabbed a towel off the back of the door and threw it at him. "Get rid of him. Tell him to call me at home this afternoon."

"Yes, ma'am. Anything else?" He stood at attention, delivered a mock salute.

She stared at his nakedness until he began to blush. "Yeah, Matthew, put on your pants before you answer the door."

## TWENTY

### *Can't change the world...*

Matthew's shower stall included a high window that let in light and opened to his wooded side yard. By the time she finished shampooing and rinsing, she thought she heard an engine jump to life, but just to be sure, she wiped a little peek hole on the steamy glass and had a look. Sure enough, Wayne Bearfoot's patrol car was easing out of the drive, so she breathed a sigh of relief.

*Silly woman.* Her skin tingled as she rubbed herself with one of Matthew's big luxurious towels. Perhaps she should've taken a cold shower, because her body still vibrated with need. The good soaping hadn't erased his warm, or the masculine scent from her memory. His texture was imprinted on her brain, and she ached to call him back to bed. Instead, she wrapped herself in a soft terrycloth bathrobe, which was handily hooked behind the door, rolled up the way-too-long sleeves, and headed towards the amazing smells issuing from the kitchen.

"Good morning, Sunshine." Matthew grinned from his post at the stove. "Hungry?"

She was definitely hungry, and Matthew looked good enough to eat. In his haste to get dressed, he'd pulled on a pair of faded jeans with holes at the knees. His ancient flannel shirt of brown plaids was buttoned crooked, his tousled hair sported a cowlick, and his big feet were bare. She'd never thought feet were especially sexy, but Matthew's looked so tan and sturdy planted on the cold floor, that she began to rethink that hypothesis.

"What?" He caught her staring, and in turn, his gaze moved to her bare feet. "Want to borrow my slippers?"

No way would his size twelve slippers fit her feet, but her toes were cold. "Maybe a pair of socks?"

"You got it..." He handed her the spatula. "Take over, please..."

As she stepped to the skillet, her stomach growled with delight at the concoction Matthew was cooking. By the time he returned and helped her don a pair of woolen socks, then seated her at the table, her mouth was watering like Pavlov's dog.

Morning sun poured into the kitchen as he delivered her breakfast on a plain white plate. The omelet was light—fragrant with exotic cheeses, filled with chunks of ripe tomato and tender ham. Fresh chives were scattered across the top, and when she picked up a fork, cut off a mouthful, and bit in, she tasted heat, texture, and something zingy on her tongue.

"Uhmm..." she moaned. "You'll make some woman a good catch."

"Think so?" He pinned her with his warm brown eyes. "I am available, you know."

She looked away and swallowed a long drink of ice water. They'd entered dangerous territory, and as needy as she was at that moment, she was way too vulnerable to continue.

"Did your mama teach you to cook like this?" She changed the subject.

For a moment he was silent, but she felt the burn of his gaze.

"Nope, my daddy taught me to cook. Folks called him Trout too, and he always claimed the way to a woman's heart was through her stomach."

Yes, that was one way, she silently agreed. But as a familiar heat gathered in a place considerably lower than her stomach, she decided Matthew's impressive culinary skills were the least of his seductive charms. He lifted an insulated white coffee pitcher and topped off her cup. Then he served her another slice of toast, which he had brushed with olive oil, herbs, and a hint of cheese. When he finished eating, he carried his plate to the sink and began cleaning up after himself with the practiced efficiency of a man accustomed to living alone.

In the meantime, Diana continued to gobble like a starved, third-world street urchin. Couldn't help herself. She licked her fingers and picked up the crumbs, and when every morsel was gone, she gathered up her dishes and joined him at the sink.

"What did Sheriff Bearfoot want?" She lowered her plate into the sudsy dishpan.

"Like I figured, he wanted to ask you about Duck Wadell's death."

The conversation was inevitable. They had to discuss this most recent murder, but suddenly all the warmth washed out of her, like the water down his drain.

"But I don't know anything, Matthew. Didn't you tell Wayne that all I did was drop Janelle off?"

"Sure, I told him." He sounded deflated. "I told him everything you told me, but he still wants to talk to you."

The sun ducked under a cloud, leaving the kitchen dark. Matthew reached up and turned on a fluorescent lamp, which bathed them both in a cold blue hue.

"I bet they think Janelle did it." She had no confidence in most so-called lawmen. So far, Bearfoot had fingered Danny for Harold Haver's murder, and he'd been wrong. Then Peter

Sokolsky had blamed Rhonda Smith for poisoning Homer Locksley, and Diana's instincts told her he was wrong, too.

He handed her a dishtowel. "No, as a matter of fact, Wayne's convinced Janelle is innocent. He's worried about her."

So was Diana.

"Janelle was in shock when the police arrived," Matthew continued. "And once things calmed down, Wayne took her to Lake Norman Medical Center. They sedated her."

Tears stung her eyes. She turned away and began stacking cups and plates in the cupboard. Life was so unfair. She could only imagine the horror Janelle must have felt when she found Duck's body. Sedatives were a temporary fix, to be sure, but after experiencing two violent deaths—first her husband, then her lover—Janelle was a likely candidate for a psychiatrist's couch.

"What will she do now?" Diana wondered.

"Well, I know what she *will not* do." Matthew dried his hands, sat back down at the kitchen table. "Wayne said Janelle has decided she can't keep living in Harold Haver's house. She's lonely in that big, empty place, and scared all the time."

His words transported her back to her own moment of terror in Haver's house. She recalled the castle-like den, with its baronial furniture and the sweet scent of flowers, and a chill shot up the back of her neck.

"But where will she go?" she asked.

"She's moving back to Charlotte to live with her mother."

Janelle had come full circle, then. A bone-deep sorrow invaded Diana. Having come so far from her poor urban roots, having won and lost a wealthy husband, having lost a second chance at happiness with a new lover, Janelle must feel defeated indeed.

"It's all so damn sad." She sank into the chair across from Matthew. "What's happening to our world?"

"You want the long, or the short answer?" He reached across the table and held her hand. "Either way, you're asking the wrong guy."

She looked up at him. His eyes were kind and his hand steadied her.

"I can't answer your question, Diana. All I know is it's not your fault. Somehow you need to step away from all this."

"Are you saying I can't change the world?" She attempted a smile.

Matthew grinned back. "I'm saying you always try to take on the world's problems, at great risk to your own health."

"Is this a lecture?"

"Yeah, maybe it is." He rose from his chair and stood behind her. His large hands began massaging the tension lodged in her shoulders. "I know you, Diana. You have this knack for getting plumb in the middle of downright dangerous situations. You thrive on it."

"Do I look like I'm thriving on all this?"

"No, but I bet you have some theories…?"

She leaned into him and closed her eyes. Theories? She hadn't really thought about it, not in any concrete way. But now that he'd mentioned it, she did see some troubling connections between these murders. She needed to reason it through and ask a few questions.

"Ah ha, I knew it!" He whispered into her hair. "Your silence gives you away, my dear. So I'm asking you right now—stay out of it. Promise?"

She tilted her head back against his chest and crossed her fingers as he kissed her.

## TWENTY-ONE

# *Acute claustrophobia...*

As soon as she got home from Matthew's, Diana fed Perry and cleaned his cage, ignored Bearfoot's multiple messages on her answering machine, and went to bed for a long nap.

When she woke up, her head was still a fog of post-love languor, and she decided a long jog might clear the cobwebs. She slipped into her jeans, her ancient Bryn Mawr College sweatshirt, and laced up her running shoes. And although every muscle ached from her unaccustomed acrobatics with Matthew, she embraced the pain as a sweet reminder and carried it with her into the winter afternoon.

Diana's condominium complex was built on a little thumb of land poking into Lake Norman. Interstate 77 ran between this thumb and the village of Davidson, and they were connected to the town by an overpass. As she jogged across the bridge, with traffic speeding in endless chains beneath her feet, her lungs filled with cold air and exhaust fumes—not the most pleasant leg of her run.

She slowed to a panting walk and admired the artful landscaping that graced the portal to the town. Off to the left, she spotted the roof of the new office condo Liz and she had purchased, while to her right, the new medical center loomed, its plate glass windows reflecting the weak light. Here the very old and the very new lived cheek by jowl, like vinyl on an antique loveseat.

Did this schizophrenia produce a strange energy that drew people to this part of the south? Here the natives clung to the trappings of the past with fanatic reverence and elevated the old original families to the status of royalty. And here the allure of modernity, and the money it attracted, were equally revered. This mindset allowed whole communities of charming, turn-of-the-century bungalows to be sacrificed in favor of a Wal-Mart.

But in Davidson, the commissioners were almost reactionary. They rejected chain stores in favor of small family business, and when new construction was approved, it had to match the brick college buildings and the historic storefronts.

As Diana thought about the commissioners, four now dead, she slowed to a crawl and gazed into the public park, where ducks floated on the still surface of a tiny pond and a gang of children, ecstatic to be free on a Saturday afternoon, kicked a ball around the playground.

She leaned against a quaint traffic sign: *Slow...Duck's Crossing,* and again asked herself: *what was happening here?* That morning Matthew had asked if she had any theories, and his question had been rolling around in her mind like a marble in a maze.

She moved down the block and turned right on Main Street, passing the Presbyterian Church, where only yesterday she'd attended Homer Locksley's funeral. It was déjà vu. She saw the bench where she'd sat with Janelle Havers and discussed Duck Wadell. Now he was dead, too.

Did she have any theories? She was hot from the exercise, yet a chill shot up her spine. It snaked across her shoulders and down her arms, and she suddenly understood the real reason she had walked into town. Her ideas were as nebulous as shadow and light, but she'd come this far. Did she have the guts to confront Parker White?

Parker's silver Jaguar was still parked in the city lot, and she recalled the eerie feeling she'd had yesterday—that Parker was watching from behind the closed curtains of her apartment above the book store. But as Diana reached her door, her courage failed and she went into Hometown Books instead.

She pretended to be engrossed in the titles by local authors, while reviewing the reasons why she wanted to talk to Parker. Parker's name kept cropping up. Harold Havers had been Parker's banker. He'd loaned her the money to keep afloat—at least for a little while. Duck Wadell had paid her less than market value for her house, the so-called *White Elephant.*

She couldn't get a grip on Parker's relationship to Homer Locksley, but Parker had been extremely rude to him at The Garden Club. Collectively, the commissioners had caused Parker's family home to be moved to the obscenely small lot behind the proposed Harris Teeter, and they had all rejected her son's bid to become Town Planner.

What did it all mean? In any small town overlapping relationships were inevitable, and everyone was privy to everyone else's business, so likely these coincidences were meaningless. On the other hand, Parker was supposedly her friend. If Diana had questions, surely Parker would be happy to answer, so why was she so nervous?

The two women who owned Hometown Books had asked several times if they could help her find anything, so she decided to actually buy something. She chose a mystery by Patricia Cornwell, who had graduated from Davidson College. She paid with the twenty- dollar bill she kept in her jeans for emergencies— then it was time to pursue her own mystery.

She stepped boldly back into the winter day and approached Parker's entrance. The door at street level was unlocked, so she took the stairs two at a time and rapped loudly on the only door at the top of the dark hall. And then she waited. Her behavior offended her number one social rule: always call first. Likely Parker wasn't even home. Just when she was about to let herself off the hook and flee, she heard slippers shuffling across the floor inside. A deadbolt shifted in the lock, and the door creaked open.

"Diana, what on earth...?" At four in the afternoon, Parker still wore a nightgown and robe.

Her appearance threw Diana off balance. "Uh...I was downstairs buying a book." Like an idiot, she held the mystery novel up to Parker's nose. For a moment Parker just stared. Her blue eyes, so much like Diana's, were underhung by deep shadows and ringed with red. Clearly she was having a bad day, and likely Diana was the low point.

"I suppose you want to come in?" Her voice was not welcoming.

"I was jogging, you see. Can you spare me a glass of water?"

The silly excuse stuck in her throat, but Parker opened the door and Diana followed her into a tiny apartment. The lighting was dim and gloomy, and the space smelled like an over-ripe cat box. As her eyes adjusted, she recognized some of the antique furniture from Parker's former home. It looked cramped in the small space, giving the impression of an over-crowded warehouse, and while she sympathized with Parker's need to salvage pieces from her past, she should have abandoned these massive reminders.

"It's a mess, isn't it? How the mighty have fallen, eh, Diana? I'm overwhelmed by all this stuff. I can't seem to get it together."

"Well, you just moved, didn't you?" Diana countered cheerfully. "It takes time to get the feel of a new place."

"Does it?"

Diana was grinning like a jackass and felt like a boorish intruder. What had she been thinking? Parker was her friend, and she desperately wanted to comfort her. "Can I help you unpack some of these things?"

"Will you adopt two cats?" Parker said. "Before they had their own yard and a garden shed all to themselves. Here they're in jail."

"Sorry, I have a parrot," Diana answered too quickly.

Parker gave her a wry look. "Never mind. You said you were thirsty. Shall I fix us a pot of tea?"

"Yes, thank you, I'd love that."

As Parker moved into the cluttered galley kitchen, Diana's guilt soared. Maybe the cats felt like they were in jail, but Parker shared their cell. Already Diana was succumbing to acute claustrophobia. She wandered to where an old mantelpiece had been placed against the wall to replicate a fireplace. Three family photographs were prominently displayed on the mantel.

The first, in an ornate gold frame, was a wedding photo of a radiant young Parker and her handsome groom, Dr. Randall White. The second and largest photo featured a gorgeous young man in his graduation cap and gown. He was movie-star handsome, with dark, haunted eyes and strong, regular features.

"Is this your son?" Diana called out.

Parker puffed with pride as she hurried back to the living room with a silver tray, two dainty cups, and pot of steaming tea. "Yes, that's Randy, the day he graduated from Davidson."

Diana looked more closely at the photo and remembered what her mother's friend, old Lou Turbyfil, had said about Parker's son. She had described him as a pathetic little thing, scared of his own shadow. The fellow in this photo bore no resemblance to that child.

"He's very handsome." Diana smiled.

"Yes, he's a heart-breaker." Parker beamed.

As Diana replaced the photo on its ledge, she looked again. She sensed something familiar about Randy White, yet she was sure they'd never met. She picked up the third photo. This one was a group portrait with Randall, Parker, young Randy, and part of a fourth person, who had been clumsily torn out of the picture. Diana was absolutely certain that the wayward Cindi, married to a NASCAR driver, was the excluded party.

She couldn't resist. "Don't you have a daughter, Parker?"

"I don't want to talk about it." Parker abruptly lowered the tea service onto an unopened cardboard box. Her mouth had flattened to a thin, cruel line.

Diana took her at her word, and did not press the issue. An uncomfortable silence stretched between them, and as Parker leaned over to pour Diana's tea, Diana smelled alcohol on her breath.

"Are you sure you're okay, Parker?" She took a small sip of the bitter liquid.

Parker clumsily set the pot down, sloshing hot tea onto the cardboard box. "Do I look okay?" she snapped. "You heard about Duck Wadell, right? How should I feel?"

"Are you worried about your own safety?"

"Because I'm a temporary commissioner? Of course not," she snorted. "I've only been to one Board Meeting. I haven't had time to make murderous enemies, but if I were Jo Jo Jones, I'd watch my back."

Her outburst startled Diana. It was a weird combination of anger, denial, and what sounded like a veiled threat against Jo Jo. The string of killings had upset the whole town, but Parker seemed totally unhinged. Diana watched her closely, but saw no trace of the refined, self-possessed woman she'd once known. Stress and fear can do terrible things, but she never expected they could reduce Parker to daytime drinking.

Suddenly Parker's close proximity was unnerving. "May I use your bathroom?" Diana asked.

Parker looked perturbed. "I guess so. It's through my bedroom, the door on the left."

Maybe it was a combination of physical fatigue mixed with the cat box stench, but Diana's temples throbbed and her stomach was queasy. The sight of Parker's disheveled, unmade bed, with two dirty cats on the pillow and an empty Vodka bottle on the floor, did not improve her condition.

She pushed into the bathroom, which was no bigger than a small closet, and opened the medicine cabinet in search of aspirin. Instead, she found a veritable pharmacy of prescription drugs, including Thorazine, Stelazine, and Haldol. She didn't know much about medicine, but even Diana knew these drugs were antianxiety or antidepressant agents, and she prayed Parker was not drinking and drugging at the same time.

Finally she located a bottle of Tylenol and helped herself to two. She took a long drink of water and braced herself with both hands on the cold sink. She was definitely feeling woozy, and as she closed her eyes, hoping the feeling would pass, she suddenly thought of her mother. Mama's presence filled the small space. Diana could smell her! No, that odor wasn't Mama, it was Mama's perfume—White Shoulders.

Her heart raced and her eyes popped open as she remembered Janelle's exact words: *On nights when Harry came home late, after claiming he was meeting some client at the bank, he stank of White Shoulders...*

Harold Havers and Parker White? Ridiculous. The man was her banker, not her lover. Diana broke out in a sweat. She followed her nose to the plastic clothes hamper and popped its lid. Sure enough, Parker's underwear reeked of the perfume. Funny, from all their outings together, she had never known Parker to use that scent. Was it reserved it for her romantic trysts?

"What are you doing, Diana?" Suddenly Parker's tall frame filled the doorway. Her face was white as flour dough and her eyes were dagger blue.

How could she explain snooping in Parker's clothes hamper? Diana could think of no plausible explanation, so she didn't even try. "Sorry, I'll be right out..." she mumbled.

"Your tea is getting cold." Parker's voice was dry ice.

Parker continued to stare. Diana's heart tried to beat its way out of her chest. Finally, she got her vocal chords working. "I'm not feeling well, Parker," she gasped. "I'm afraid I'll have to take a rain check on that tea."

After an eternity, Parker inched aside, allowing Diana to escape to the bedroom, the living room, and finally the front door. All the while, Parker followed wordlessly, her arms folded across her chest.

Diana twisted the doorknob and backed into the hallway. "Sorry to run off like this..." She wiggled her fingers in a clumsy goodbye. "I'll call you later, all right?"

Without looking back, she fled down the stairs and escaped into daylight. She leaned against the wall of the building and took deep gulps of frigid air.

TWENTY-TWO

## *Liz*

Liz was worried. Diana had told her about her unannounced visit to Parker White's apartment, and Liz was more convinced than ever that her friend had taken leave of her senses. Their current expedition to the Mecklenburg Hall of Records was more proof of Diana's fragile sanity.

Liz led her down the long, sterile hallway. "You're crazy, Diana. What if that tea was poisoned? Maybe that's why you felt so sick? Remember what happened to poor Homer Locksley."

"Don't be silly, Liz. I'm here, aren't I?"

"Yeah, but that's only dumb luck. Maybe that drink of water you took in the bathroom diluted it? What if you'd finished all the tea left in the cup?"

"Will you cut it out?" Diana picked up her pace and easily passed Liz.

Diana's long legs could out-distance a Marathon runner, but sooner or later Diana would get lost. She didn't know her way around the county records.

Sure enough, Diana stopped in her tracks. "Okay, so where's the Recorder of Deeds?"

Liz snickered and took the lead. They entered a big, open office where a handful of Monday morning functionaries were grumpily nursing their coffees. She approached the receptionist. "Where are the Davidson deeds?"

The woman guided them to a computer and explained how to access the town's real estate transactions. Liz chuckled at the look of pained confusion on Diana's face. She was more comfortable with the massive, old-fashioned deed books than computerized files. "You know we could have done this research on a laptop from the comfort of our office," Liz said.

Diana scowled. "Give me a break Liz. I'm a hands-on kind of gal and need to see and touch the files."

She had begged Liz to come along as her technical advisor, even though, in Liz's estimation, the effort was a wild goose chase. "Okay, what are we looking for?" Liz sighed.

"All transactions in the past five years."

They wanted to trace the liens against Parker White's big house, including the recent sale to Duck Wadell. Liz typed in the relative information, and then motioned to Diana. "Hey, pull up a chair. You can watch over my shoulder."

Once Diana was settled, looking disgruntled in her subordinate role, Liz picked up where they'd left off. "Parker's husband was a doctor, right? I'll bet he taught her to use a hypodermic needle, so she could have injected the poison into Locksley's bottle."

Diana held up her hand. "Enough with the conspiracy theories, Liz. Parker had no reason to hurt Locksley. Besides, where would she get that rodent poison?"

"Maybe Parker had a grudge against Locksley? She had a garden shed at the old house, right? She could have found the poison there."

"Please shut the f___ up!" Diana snapped. "What do you have against Parker? If you're jealous, forget it. We came here about Harold Havers, remember?"

Was she jealous? Maybe. But Diana was too wrapped up in her loyalty to Parker to see the sinister possibilities. On the other hand, Liz still thought her old rival, Janelle, had killed Havers. If Liz was jealous, it was because Diana had spent time with Janelle. What's worse, Diana had claimed she actually liked Janelle. She'd even tried to convince Liz to give the woman a second chance.

"Okay, let's dig us some dirt and prove that Parker is guilty…" Liz began scrolling through the real estate transactions.

"Or prove her innocence," Diana grumbled.

*Whatever.* Liz sighed and concentrated on the screen. Diana's theory about Parker's perfume, White Shoulders, was downright silly. Any number of old biddies wore the scent, and if Diana took that tidbit to Bearfoot, he'd crack his ribs laughing.

Unfortunately, Liz had nothing better to do than help Diana snoop. Now that Duck was dead, leaving only Jo Jo and Parker on the Board, the ETJ project was on hold. So were all those juicy commissions she'd been spending in her dreams. Once the commissioners were replaced through the lengthy election process, without Duck at the helm, it was unlikely that the new group would support such a contentious issue. In other words, she and Diana would still be fighting for their financial survival.

"Look, here's something…" Liz pointed at an entry from three years ago. "Harold Havers entered a lien against Parker's property. Looks like he gave her a *personal* loan."

"That's strange." Diana leaned forward. "Havers was the head honcho at Wells Fargo. Why not make the loan through the bank?"

"And take a look at the tax value," Liz added. "Parker's property was assessed at $925,000 before they moved it off Main Street. I wonder if Happy Harry expected any special perks for giving Parker that loan. After all, Parker had been a widow for a long time, and every woman needs affection. Right, Diana…?" Liz gave her friend a lascivious wink.

Diana kicked Liz under the table. "I don't see her with a man like Havers."

"Why not? Maybe he had some hidden charms? Got himself a young wife, didn't he? Or maybe Parker's motives were like Janelle's? They saw a million reasons to love him, and they were all in Harry's bank account."

Diana gave her a sour look.

Liz paused on the next transaction. "Last year the town of Davidson purchased Parker's land in order to build a Harris Teeter. The Addendum says they paid her $725,000, gave her the lot where the house now stands, and covered all her moving expenses. That's $200,000 less than the assessed value!"

"Yes, and the tax valuation generated after the move dropped the value to $625,000, a net loss of $300,000 for Parker! What a rotten deal. The town's payment was an insult!" Diana exclaimed.

"Was Parker insulted enough to kill?" Liz pushed back her chair and stretched.

Diana shook her head. "No one in her right mind would kill four people for $300,000."

"*Right mind?* You said it first, Diana. In Charlotte, a grade school kid killed his playmate for lunch money."

Why was Diana defending Parker? They'd come to the Hall of Records looking for motives, but now Diana was in denial over the facts and seemed defeated.

"It wasn't fair," Diana conceded. "I see why Parker has a cabinet full of antidepressants, but that doesn't make her a murderer."

Liz shut down the computer and turned to Diana. "No, but it gives us 300,000 reasons why she might be…"

## TWENTY-THREE

## *Matthew*

Jeeter had been Matthew's best childhood friend, but when he died suddenly in Gainesville, Florida, he was reluctant to attend the funeral. He didn't want to leave, even for a few days, because he was worried about Diana.

He huddled under the portico, sheltering from the icy drizzle that had begun at dawn, and rang Diana's doorbell. His suitcase was packed and stashed behind the seat in his truck, but he was still emotionally conflicted. Ready to go, but willing to be swayed.

"Get in here, Matthew!" Diana abruptly opened the door and dragged him into the foyer. "You're soaked to the bone."

She hugged him, then reached under his dripping raincoat and, getting her sweatshirt all wet.

"Hey!" He laughed and shrugged out of his coat.

"Hey, yourself." She grinned. "Leave your shoes at the door, will you?"

As she walked away, looking sexier than any woman had a right to in old running pants and tattered slippers, he pushed off his loafers and padded after her in his stockings. By the time his feet hit the kitchen linoleum, he smelled freshly brewed coffee.

"I bought cinnamon buns at the bakery." She was already pouring his cup. "Do you want two, or three?"

He saw she'd purchased a half dozen. "Three, thanks." He pulled his favorite chair up to the table and sat down.

"Three for the road, then." She sat across from him.

He'd called her late last night and told her about Jeeter's death. She'd convinced him to go to Florida and not worry about her, but she'd also been worried about him driving on icy roads. Seemed like there was plenty of worry to go around.

"Can't you fly, Matthew? It's safer, and you'll be there in less than two hours."

The security at Charlotte-Douglas International Airport was formidable, and he'd go nuts waiting in all the lines. "You know me, I'd rather drive."

"You'd rather drive during an ice storm?" She rolled her eyes, then poured extra milk into her steaming coffee.

They'd reached an impasse, so he steered the subject back to Parker White. Diana had described her suspicions, or rather Liz's suspicions. Privately Matthew thought the theories were pure nonsense.

"So you two think Parker might have been involved with Havers?"

"Maybe. But was she actually attracted to him, or was the sex payback for the loan he'd given her?" Diana nibbled thoughtfully at the edges of her cinnamon bun.

"Very romantic. What do you figure went wrong the day Havers died?"

"Maybe she went there to rekindle the affair. Maybe she brought him flowers."

"Well, we know he was ready and willing." He chuckled. "They found a condom in his pocket, remember?" Diana blushed, and he felt heat crawling up his own neck. "So why would she kill him?"

Diana slowly shook her head. "Maybe she wanted to negotiate another loan, and he said no. Or maybe he rejected her advances…"

"And maybe Parker just happened to know where Havers kept his gun and blew him away."

"She might have known. Even Danny knew where the gun was kept." She frowned. "Or maybe Havers took the gun out of the drawer to defend himself?"

"That's a boatload of maybes, Diana, and they found no fingerprints. If she wore gloves, then the murder was premeditated, not the crime of passion you've described. And what about Parker's famous perfume? Did you smell *White Shoulders* at the scene of the crime?"

Suddenly Diana looked weary and defeated, and he wished he'd kept his big mouth shut. His only goal had been to convince her to back away from the whole sorry mess.

"All I smelled were the flowers," she admitted. "We're back at square one."

He reached across the table and took her hand. "You sound disappointed. I thought Parker was your friend?"

"She is."

He watched her closely. She seemed at a loss. Even Wayne Bearfoot was worried about Diana. She had avoided his phone calls, and when he'd finally gotten her on the line, she'd been edgy and evasive. Wayne had told him she'd had nothing to contribute regarding Duck's murder, but he'd suspected she had some screwy theory about Havers' death.

"I spoke to Wayne…" Matthew began carefully. "They found no fingerprints at Duck Wadell's, either. But Duck was a powerful man, and the way he died…" He cleared his throat, wishing he'd never opened that can of worms. "Well, he didn't think a *woman* would be strong enough to stab him that way."

"Right..." Diana scoffed. "Men always underestimate the strength of a woman scorned—or wronged. I told you how Duck cheated Parker out of $300,000."

Matthew squeezed her hand. "Yeah, you did. So you think poor Parker killed Duck, too? Lordy, if that's how you feel about your friends, then your enemies are doomed."

She yanked her fingers free of his grasp. "You think I'm crazy, and maybe I am. But don't worry about it, Matthew. Just go to your friend's funeral and forget it."

"So now you *want* me to go?" Evidently she'd rather see him driving on ice than punching holes in her theories. "Just for the record, Wayne told me Wadell had some serious enemies. Many of those enemies were building contractors Duck cheated folks, and two guys in particular, twin brothers from Charlotte, are meaner than the Mafia. Wayne's giving them a closer look."

She balled up her napkin and tossed it at him. "Give me a break. Mafia in North Carolina? What do you call them, the Mayberry Mob?"

He laughed, relieved the tension between them had dissipated. Diana was a feisty critter, with a sharp wit and the tongue to match. These were only a few of the many things he loved about her.

"It's not like *I want* to go to Florida..." he mumbled. What he did want, above all, was to follow Diana into her bedroom and join her in her big, king-size bed. They'd never made love, seldom even kissed, in the sanctity of her condominium, and the idea filled him with a sudden, intense need. He searched her eyes and fancied he saw his hunger reflected there.

"God, I wish you didn't have to go," she said. "But Jeeter was your best friend, and I think you'd always regret missing his funeral."

Hearing Jeeter's name brought him down hard. They had been inseparable from kindergarten through high school, right up until Jeeter enlisted and went to Afghanistan. But when he returned from the war, Jeeter had changed. He was mean, withdrawn, and unable to relate to any of his old friends. When he left to make a new start in Florida, Matthew lost touch…until recently. Suffering terminal cancer, Jeeter had begun calling wanting to reconnect and talk about what he called his *black hole.*

"You're right. Of course, I'll go." He pushed the third bun aside uneaten. He stood up, stretched, and checked his watch. Already ten o'clock. He needed to hit the road, and Diana was overdue at her office.

She wrapped her arm around his waist and walked him to the door. Funny thing about black holes—hard as you try to forget, they're always there, lying just below the surface of civility. The dark side of human nature had its own seductive allure, and lately Diana had been walking the thin skin above the abyss, treading too heavily.

He wished to God she would leave these murders alone. He stepped into his loafers and allowed Diana to help him into his coat. Her fingers were cool. She smelled fresh from the shower. He was suddenly scared to death to leave her alone.

"Now don't get into trouble while I'm gone…" He pulled her close and held her tight.

"Now don't get yourself into trouble on the icy roads." She smiled.

When she lifted her face, he kissed her long and deep, trying to convey how very much he would miss her. When their finally lips parted, he knew he was making a terrible mistake.

"I'll be home for Thanksgiving," he said. "We'll eat some turkey together."

"Only if you do the cooking." She playfully pushed him away. "Now get going, Matthew, before I change my mind."

"Goodbye, then..." He backed out the door, into the drizzle.

"Goodbye, asshole!" the damn parrot hollered at his back.

And for once, Matthew agreed with the bird..

TWENTY-FOUR

*Stone the stranger…*

Danny Capelli sat directly behind Diana in the back seat, leaning into her headrest and barking directions into her ear. He was as excited as a toddler on a sugar high, but Liz, seated beside Diana up front, was less enthusiastic about their mission.

"I hate the races," she said as Diana navigated through Mooresville's Lakeside Park. "My brothers used to drag me to Lowes Speedway, and all that noise gave me a headache."

"You girls don't get it," Danny said. "It's all about the danger. Those NASCAR drivers live on the edge."

Liz looked cross-eyed at Diana. "It's a *guy thing.* Turn left here, Diana."

Motor sport suppliers and famous race shops were nestled in the manicured lawns on both sides of the road. Although Mooresville was dubbed Race City U.S.A., Diana had never investigated this part of town, which was NASCAR Mecca. All she knew about the topic was that Dale Earnhardt had died in a crash, leaving fans in perpetual mourning.

"Jeff Gordon, Rusty Wallace…" Danny intoned a litany of racecar drivers. "I wonder if we'll see any of those famous guys at the ceremony."

Diana drove into the crowded parking lot of a low-slung brick building called The North Carolina Auto Racing Hall of Fame. She turned off Queen Vic's engine.

"As long as Ray Martinez is here, I don't care who else shows up," she said. NASCAR had thus far failed to capture her interest. Maybe Liz was right: it was a *guy thing.*

"Don't worry, Racin' Ray will be here," Danny assured her as they climbed from the car. "After all, he's the guest of honor."

Diana felt out of her element as she followed them into a small gift shop and paid the modest fee for all three admissions. After all, this outing was her idea. She had spotted the news item in the local paper: *Martinez Wins Snap-On Gold Wrench Award,* whatever that meant, and she'd recognized the name immediately. Martinez was the husband of Cindi, Parker's wayward daughter, and Diana couldn't pass up this opportunity to meet her.

"Racin' Ray won at the Rock," Danny whispered with reverence as they entered the museum.

"What rock?" Diana asked.

"That's what they call the Carolina Speedway down in Rockingham," Liz explained. "Martinez won the Pop Secret 400 a couple of weeks back, and Danny says it's a very big deal."

Old Lou Turbyfil, Mama's friend, had told them that Parker's daughter and her racing hubby lived like gypsies, and that recently Cindi had tried to contact Parker from nearby Rockingham. Parker had never returned her daughter's call.

As they moved into the main showroom, Diana wondered if she could use her friendship with Parker as an entrée with Cindi. But if Cindi was half as hostile towards her mother as Parker was towards her daughter, it would be a tricky maneuver.

"Man, this is awesome!" Danny's eyes stretched wide to behold the sparkling hubcaps on thirty-some polished racecars and 1960's muscle cars filling the room.

In spite of the large crowd milling around in after-church clothes, the noise seemed oddly muffled in the cavernous space, which more closely resembled a warehouse than a museum. The lighting was dim, with spotlights illuminating famous cars as well as the uniforms and helmets worn by prominent drivers. At one end of the room, a space had been partitioned off for the Goodyear Theater, which apparently featured a continuously running film chronicling the history of NASCAR racing. The muted squeal of tires and screaming brakes issued from the theater, while a group of children fought for a turn to ride in a racecar simulator. The simulator gave young drivers a chance to experience the thrill of the track, courtesy of computer technology.

"Too bad Matthew couldn't be here," Liz said.

Diana agreed. Matthew had called from Florida. He had phoned from his motel room after attending his friend's funeral, and while he'd tried to put a brave face on it, she'd heard the sorrow in his voice. No matter how warm and sunny the weather, how inviting the heated pool, he seemed depressed.

He claimed he missed her, and God knew she missed him, too. But she'd already decided not to upset him further by mentioning her plan to visit the Auto Racing Hall of Fame. He might misconstrue the visit as *looking for trouble*, and she'd promised not to do that. But how could she get into trouble while surrounded by so many good Christian folk? Obviously these people were dressed in their Sunday best. They'd likely left the pews, gone out to dinner, and then come here to the festivities. What harm could she possible come to?

She realized they had already lost Danny, who was across the room, his nose pressed to a trophy case.

Liz nudged her arm. "Hey, that's Ray over there. See the guy in the jump suit?"

Sure enough, surrounded by an enthusiastic group of men in coats and ties, stood a small dark man in a racing outfit. Those uniforms, like the cars themselves, always looked like traveling billboards to Diana. Covered from head to toe with gaudy advertisements, the uniforms were commercialism mutated out of control. But Racin' Ray Martinez seemed happy enough as he grinned with startlingly white teeth, framed by a cropped black moustache. He raised an engraved trophy high above his head. Evidently the award ceremony had just taken place.

"He's so small," Liz noted. "Maybe they have to be tiny to crawl into the racecars?"

Liz's speculations didn't interest Diana. She had focused on the plump blond woman clinging to Ray's arm. Cindi was tall like her mother, but lacked Parker's cool, regal grace. She had the same hair, but it was clumsily cut and teased into an old-fashioned style. Parker wouldn't be caught dead in the peacock blue sweater set her daughter wore, nor would she laugh so loud. Simply put, Cindi possessed none of her mother's sophistication. But when Diana looked into Cindi's deep blue eyes, she saw Parker's genes.

"Who's the kid?" Liz nodded at the little girl attached to Cindi's arm.

Obviously the lovely child was Asian, possibly Korean, and she carried neither Parker's nor Cindi's genes. "I assume she's adopted," Diana said.

"Let's go talk to them." Liz urged Diana forward.

But Diana held back. "Please, Liz, I'd like to talk to Cindi alone. I'm sorry, but this will be hard enough without two of us ganging up on her."

A hurt look flashed across Liz's green eyes, but then she turned towards the racecar simulator. "Do they let adults ride that thing?"

"Get in line and find out? Maybe they'll let you ride, since you're tiny enough to crawl in."

Liz laughed and stepped into the queue.

And Diana headed across the room. As she neared the Martinez family, she began to feel ill-at- ease. This NASCAR culture seemed like a lifestyle totally foreign to her own. How should she talk to these people? Did she even speak the same language? When she came up beside Racin' Ray, he grinned and handed her an unsolicited, autographed photo.

"Thank you very much, Mr. Martinez," she mumbled. "But I came here to talk with your wife." Both Ray and Cindi seemed surprised. Likely neither was accustomed to Cindi sharing the limelight.

"You sure you want to talk to me?" she said.

"Absolutely." Diana smiled encouragingly and reached for Cindi's hand. "I'm Diana Rittenhouse, a friend of your mother's."

Cindi jerked her hand away, her eyes enormous with surprise. "A friend of *my mother's...?*"

"That's right..." Diana tried to keep her tone soothing. By then Ray was scowling, too. Was it her imagination, or were all the fans closing ranks, a crowd circling to stone the stranger.

"If Mother sent you, I have nothing to say." Cindi turned her back on Diana.

TWENTY-FIVE

*Two sides to every story...*

Feeling rejected, Diana retreated from the Martinez family as the adoring fans closed the circle around them. She drifted back across the room to where a much younger crowd, mostly children, were cheering and clapping for Liz in the racecar simulator. She was setting a cyberspace track record, speeding through the computerized maze in record time and avoiding all the pitfalls popping up on the screen.

"Go girl!" Danny beamed with pride. He looped his arm around Diana's waist and pulled her closer to the action. "Isn't Liz awesome? She's the best driver around."

"She's not as good as my daddy," a tiny voice protested.

Diana peered down into the dark, angled eyes of Cindi's beautiful daughter. Somehow the child had escaped her family and followed her. Her rosebud lips formed a perfect pout, exquisitely painted on her porcelain doll face.

Diana said. "Your daddy's a champion, isn't he?"

She nodded shyly and touched the shiny hood of Liz's car. "Can I ride with that lady?"

"Why don't we ask her, once this ride is over?" Diana noticed the machine took quarters and began fishing through her purse.

"Come here, Maya!" Suddenly Cindi materialized at Diana's side. "You're not supposed to talk to strangers."

"But she's not a stranger." The precocious child took Diana's hand. "She said she's a friend of Grandma's."

Cindi flushed crimson and gave Diana an exasperated look. "Maya has big ears. She's never met her grandma, but she sure knows how to work a situation to her advantage."

"I'm sorry…" The sad fact of this engaging child not knowing her own grandma flustered Diana. "That's my friend, Liz, driving the car. I'm sure she'd love to take Maya along for the next ride."

"Can I, Mama? Please?" Maya tugged at Cindi's skirt.

Cindi exhaled in frustration. She glanced at Liz, then back at Diana. "Are you sure your friend won't mind?"

"Heck, no, I'd enjoy having a co-pilot." Liz had big ears, too. "Danny, lift that kid into the car." Before Cindi could object, Danny swung Maya off her feet and plopped her onto Liz's lap.

"But *I'm* paying…" Cindi pulled a handful of quarters from a little beaded bag and gave them to Liz. "Thanks, ma'am, but don't let my girl drive you crazy."

"No problem," Liz said as she and her small companion began racing on a brand new screen.

Cindi turned to Diana. "Look, I'm sorry I was rude before, but hearing about my mother makes me nuts. I didn't mean to take it out on you, Diana."

Diana was surprised that Cindi even remembered her name. "I understand, but I'd still like to talk to you. Can we find a quiet spot?"

Cindi led her behind the Goodyear Theater, and they exited the back of the building through a metal service door. Cindi lifted an empty soda can from a dumpster and wedged it in the door, so they could get back inside. Then she waved Diana into one of two white plastic chairs set on the small concrete patio, and she sat in the other.

"So, what's up?" Cindi took a pack of menthol cigarettes from her beaded bag and lit up. "Want one?" She held out the pack.

"No thanks." Diana had quit smoking several years ago, but like most addictions, cigarettes still tempted her. The sweet smell of Cindi's smoke made her lungs contract with need.

"Ray hates it when I smoke," she confessed. "It goes against the Teachings. The body is supposed to be God's temple, but mine's not perfect yet."

"Neither is mine." Diana thought about the two bottles of wine she'd consumed since Matthew left for Florida.

"Well, nobody's perfect." Cindi sighed. "I inherited my bad habits from my dear mother. What's she doing these days, drugs or alcohol?"

Diana was tempted to say *both*, but held her tongue. "I am worried about your mother," was all she was willing to say.

"So what else is new?" Cindi blew a perfect smoke ring. "Long as I can remember, everyone worries about Mother. First it was Daddy, then my brother, but no one worries more than Mother herself. Selfish bitch."

Cindi's hatred was palpable in the frigid air. Diana shivered and told her about the murders of the Davidson commissioners.

"Yeah, I watch TV. What's all that got to do with Mother?"

"Parker is now a Davidson commissioner. Didn't you know?"

Cindi blinked in disbelief. "No way! Mother's into politics? Jesus, who'd believe it? But they say all politicians are lying crooks, so I guess she fits right in."

Cindi's red hot anger was shocking. After all, Diana had a daughter, too. Certainly Mandy and she had had their fair share of squabbles, but Parker must have seriously abused this child to inspire such vitriol. At the same time, Cindi was a very atypical born-again Christian, one who smoked and cursed. Was she to blame for their alienation? Either way, she wasn't there to offer family counseling, so she asked Cindi what she knew about Harold Havers and Duck Wadell.

"I've never heard of those men." She stubbed out her cigarette and ground it into the concrete with her high heel. "If you're thinking Mother has a love life, you're on the wrong track. She's too selfish to love anyone but herself—and money. And far as her finances are concerned, I bet she's doo-doo deep in debt."

Cindi lit another cigarette, while Diana regrouped. It seemed the girl knew nothing about Parker's current life, so if she'd expected answers, she was sniffing in the wrong hole, as Matthew was fond of saying.

"Those two men were Davidson commissioners," she explained. "They, along with a third, recently died under suspicious circumstances. That leaves only two commissioners left alive—your mother, and Joanne Early Jones."

Cindi's shoulders stiffened and her blue eyes, so much like Parker's, registered shock. "She's working with Jo Jo?  I'm surprised Mother hasn't killed her yet."

Now Diana was shocked. "You know Jo Jo?"

"Fuck yeah, I know her!" Cindi spat out the words. "I hate that bitch as much as Mother does. Hating Jo Jo's the one thing we always agreed on."

"But why?"

Cindi's eyes narrowed as she sized Diana up. Diana wondered how high she would register on the trust scale. When the long silence finally ended, Diana guessed she'd passed the test.

"It happened a million years ago, but Jo Jo started all the trouble…" Cindi began. "I was a freshman at Wake Forest. Daddy was a surgeon who taught at the university's medical school. Jo Jo's husband was a lawyer, and he also taught at the school. Long before that, when both men were undergrads at Davidson College, Daddy beat Mr. Jones out of a prestigious scholarship, and that started the family feud."

Diana couldn't believe her ears. This sounded like the Hatfields and McCoys all over again. She had observed Parker and Jo Jo together at The Garden Club and had seen no animosity then. "Surely all that is past history…?"

"Think so?" Cindi hissed. "Stupid little me didn't care about the feud, so what did I do? I fell in love with the Jones' son, Jarrett, who was also a freshman. We fucked like rabbits, and I got pregnant."

Cindi's words felt like bullets from an assault weapon. "Then what happened?"

"Can't you guess?" Cindi moaned. "Jo Jo already hated my parents. She despised Daddy for winning that scholarship and thought Mother was a Yankee-Come-Lately without proper breeding or social status. In other words, Parker's tramp daughter wasn't good enough for Jo Jo's boy."

"I am so sorry." Cindi's story had the tragic ring of truth. She recalled how old Lou Turbyfil had described Parker as a young faculty wife at Wake Forest: *She never really fit…she was always pushing her way in…she tried too hard.* For the first time, she understood Parker's obsessive need to conquer those social barriers.

"Your poor mother. What did she do?"

"Don't you dare side with her!" Cindi snapped. "She was worse than Jo Jo. Once the Joneses decided I wasn't good enough for their son, they gave Jarrett the money to buy me an abortion. I was scared to death, and so was Jarrett. We didn't want to lose the baby. We wanted to run off and get married, but by then, Mother was furious. She said if I wasn't good enough for Jarrett, then he wasn't good enough for me. Jo Jo yanked Jarrett out of school and sent him to finish at Davidson College. My own father arranged for the termination, and my parents forced me to have the procedure."

Suddenly Cindi's eyes filled with tears. She stomped out her second cigarette and pretended to have smoke in her eyes. "Years later, after I married Ray, we found out I couldn't have babies. I always figured that abortion ruined me. Then we adopted Maya."

What could Diana say?

"After the abortion, I dropped out of school and ran away from home. I never called Mama again, not until last month, but I sent her two Christmas cards—one after I married Ray and joined the church, and one with a picture of Maya when she was a baby. Know what she said?"

Diana shook her head.

"Mother said, 'That child is not my granddaughter. Please do not mention her again.'"

After hearing Cindi's story, Diana was ready to strangle Parker with her own two hands. "What about your brother? I bet he loves Maya."

Cindi shrugged. "Not really. Randy lives in his own little world, and he always takes Mama's side. Last I heard he was hanging out like a beach bum down on the Carolina coast— Wilmington, I think. He's as crazy as she is, and he's a drug addict, too."

Diana was speechless. Certainly there were always two sides to every story. For instance, Cindi was a religious person. Maybe her idea of a 'drug addict' was different from Diana's. Parker may have hated Jo Jo once upon a time, but surely that hatred had faded over the years. One aspect of the feud was alive and well, however, and that was the rift between Cindi and Parker.

"Don't get me wrong, Diana…" Cindi wiped her eyes with the sleeve of her sweater. "It all turned out great for me. I have Ray and Maya, and I love them so very much. My old boyfriend, Jarrett, is married with kids and we're still friends. So I'm fine most of the time, until someone like you comes along."

"Sorry…" Diana mumbled. Once again she'd put her two cents in where it didn't belong. She had an uncanny ability to gain people's trust, and then make them miserable. Thank God Matthew would be home soon to distract her from her misadventures.

# TWENTY-SIX

*Dead wrong...*

Matthew came home for Thanksgiving, but wasn't willing to cook for Diana. He told her he was tired after the long drive from Florida and down in the dumps after Jeeter's funeral. He wanted to get out among people having fun, someplace festive and noisy with laughter, and decided Milly's Cafeteria in Statesville was just the ticket.

Diana assumed most restaurants would be dreary and deserted on such a traditional family holiday. Not so. They circled three times before finding a parking space, and then waited in line outside. At least it was a beautiful, sunny afternoon, completely different from the cold gray Thanksgivings she remembered from Pennsylvania. As they stood hand in hand, a gentle breeze ruffled Matthew's soft hair and his face was ruddy with sunburn from his stay in Florida. His brown eyes were smiling, but after complimenting Diana on her new red dress, he'd been unusually silent.

She understood. The rituals of death, from the funeral to the delayed shock of losing someone you love, had a numbing effect on everyone. Jeeter had been the first of Matthew's contemporaries to die, and the implications were chilling to middle-aged mortals like Matthew and Diana.

As they moved into the building and took their place in another long line, Diana felt a little melancholy, too. She'd been hoping for a more intimate reunion dinner, just the two of them at

Matthew's and maybe a sleepover. Plus, she felt guilty about being in Statesville and not eating with her mother at the Oaks. She'd urged Mama to come out to eat with them, but Mama wouldn't do it—two stubborn souls in gridlock. In the end, they had compromised. After finishing their meal, Matthew and she would take Mama out for dessert: frozen yogurt, Mama's favorite.

"Danny Capelli dropped by the store." Matthew arched his eyebrows. "He said y'all went to the NASCAR museum. Since when were you interested in racing, Diana?"

She shrugged, pretending nonchalance. "It was something to do, wasn't it?

Matthew seemed unconvinced as they inched closer to the buffet. She hoped Danny hadn't told Matthew she'd been on a murder-related fact-finding mission. Total avoidance was the best policy, so she quickly changed the subject:

"Hmm… that smells good. Are you getting turkey, Matthew?"

"What else? By the time we get there, I'll be hungry enough to sample everything."

As they took their trays and silverware, her mouth watered uncontrollably. The buffet offered six varieties of meat and fish and every vegetable known to man. It was a weight watcher's nightmare, and the cakes and pies were downright sinful. Yet they filled their plates to brimming, approached the cashier, where Matthew snatched the bill, and then searched the crowded dining room for a table for two. Just as they began to despair, a familiar voice called out…

"Hey, Trout! Over here… by the window."

Sheriff Wayne Bearfoot's chiseled features soared like a hawk above the scuttling waiters as he beckoned from across the room, and Diana's spirits drooped. Now she'd have to share

Matthew, but from the wide grin on Matthew's face, she realized that this was exactly the festive distraction he'd been hoping for.

"Do you mind sitting with them?" he asked.

"No, it'll be fun."

As they approached the table, Diana saw that Bearfoot was not alone. A brunette with wide, expressive black eyes smiled shyly and seemed to be debating whether or not she should stand up to greet them. Moving her enormous bulk was likely a major undertaking, because the young woman appeared to be nine months pregnant.

Wayne placed a firm hand on her shoulder, making the decision for her. "Meet my wife, Marianne. As you can see, our baby is due any minute. We decided she shouldn't have to cook the Thanksgiving meal in her condition."

"Good call..." Diana winked at Marianne. "We all need a break now and then, don't we?"

Marianne nodded as Matthew gave Diana a wry look. Okay, so Diana wasn't exactly famous for slaving over the kitchen stove. If anything, Matthew was more deserving of the Betty Crocker Award, but hey, women had to stick together.

Matthew and Marianne were already old pals, but once he'd introduced Diana and they'd taken their seats, the four began chatting like old friends. Diana couldn't take her eyes off Bearfoot, who looked entirely different in a casual corduroy jacket and chinos. Instead of the starched and formidable sheriff, she saw a regular guy called Wayne, husband and father of two young sons.

"Where are the boys today?" Matthew asked.

"With their grandparents," Marianne said. "It seems they prefer dinner at McDonalds, then a live turkey race at the YMCA. Can you believe it?"

Her words made Diana remember holiday meals with her own two kids, when being stuck with their parents was often a fate worse than death. "Yeah, I believe it," she muttered.

She glanced at Matthew, who had relaxed in the congenial atmosphere, and then she experienced an acute tug of regret and longing. She felt the warm pressure of his knee against her leg under the table and wondered yet again how much happier she would have been if Matthew, not Robert Rittenhouse, had been her husband. But as she finished the last bite and pushed her plate away, she knew there was no turning back the clock.

"Whew, I'm stuffed." Marianne puffed through her lips and patted her tummy. "I really, *really* need to visit the little girls' room, and then I'd like to take a walk."

"I'll go with you…" Diana offered.

"Nope, you and Wayne stay put while I do the honors." Matthew jumped to his feet.

Diana knew Matthew was always restless after a big meal and he liked to stretch his legs, but his departure left her alone with Wayne. She and the sheriff watched in silence as Marianne waddled into the restroom and Matthew paced outside the door. When Marianne reappeared, Matthew took her elbow and guided her through the lobby and outside to the sunny afternoon. Only then did Wayne turn to her. He took a deep breath and pinned her with his eyes.

"So, Diana…" He smiled. "Are you steering clear of trouble these days, or are you still up to your eyeballs in the murder investigations?"

Her cheeks burned. Wayne didn't know the half of it, but he likely suspected the worst. Ever since he'd rescued her that evening at Harold Havers' house, right after the murder, he'd figured she'd be engaged in amateur sleuthing. Unfortunately, she'd told Matthew about her visit to the Hall of Records and confided her theories about Parker's involvement with the deaths of both Havers and Duck Wadell. Fortunately, she hadn't told Matthew her reason for visiting the NASCAR museum or about her talk with Cindi, so at least that conversation remained private.

"What has Matthew been telling you?" At some level, she resented the fact that Matthew and Bearfoot were so close.

"Trout hasn't told me a damn thing. What's up, Diana?"

Wayne's surprise seemed sincere, so she exhaled in relief. So far her theories remained her secret, so they weren't subject to his derision.

"I've been far too busy to worry about the murders, Wayne. Solving crime is your thing."

He chuckled, finished his pecan pie, and then filled his glass with iced tea. "Matter of fact, I have solved one of the murders, Diana." He daubed at his mouth with a napkin, prolonging the suspense. "But I guess you're not interested...?"

She bit her tongue and waited. Two could play that game.

"Tomorrow it'll be in all the papers, and I've already told Janelle Havers the good news." He yawned.

"You know who killed Harold Havers?"

"Nope, but I know who killed Duck Wadell."

Diana stirred too much sugar into her coffee, then dropped her spoon. Any second Wayne would tell her that he'd arrested Parker White. But the sheriff hesitated and squirmed uncomfortably on his chair.

"To be perfectly honest, *I* didn't solve that case," he grumbled. "Credit goes to that hotshot detective from Davidson, Peter Sokolsky."

Diana had witnessed the animosity between the Cherokee sheriff and the brusque New Jersey cop the night when they'd both appeared on her doorstep to question her about the death of Commissioner Lester B. Smith, who had just driven his car into Lake Norman. She understood why Wayne hated to credit Sokolsky with solving the crime, but she wanted details, and she wanted them now.

"Well?"

"It was sound police work," Wayne admitted. "Janelle had told me the only thing missing from the murder scene was Duck's gold Rolex watch. Seems the guy never took it off his wrist, unless he was taking a shower. And he was about to take a shower when he was stabbed. But the watch was missing. So when I told Peter Sokolsky, he contacted all the pawnshops in the area. He even had a snitch working both sides of the *fence,* pardon the pun, and that's how he nailed the killer."

She held her breath. She could picture Parker killing in passion, or for revenge, but she couldn't imagine Parker stooping to common thievery.

"Anyhow, that's how Sokolsky caught the guy." Wayne shook his head. "It's a sad story, really."

*Guy?* Her jaw dropped open. "I don't understand?"

"The fellow's name is Job Little, and the name suits him. He's the middle-aged son of one of the farmers in the ETJ. Duck and the others intended to annex his daddy's land. Anyhow, Job's mentally challenged, with the mind of maybe a ten-year-old, and like Job in the Bible, he's had trouble all his life. When his old daddy started crying about how Duck was set on stealing their land, Job didn't understand. He picked up on his father's rage and believed he was duty-bound to defend the old man.

"In fact, considering his capabilities, or lack thereof, the way poor Job planned the murder indicates premeditation. His daddy had pointed Duck out to him at the Town Meeting, the same one you attended, Diana, the one where Homer Locksley died. After that, Job took to stalking Duck. He had finally passed the driver's test, so Job had a license. He followed Duck out of town that day, after you all met at the Soda Shop."

Wayne paused and stared at her, but Diana was too stunned to respond. She remembered Matthew telling her about two twin brothers from Charlotte, building contractors whom Duck had cheated. She'd joked and called them the *Mayberry Mob*. If not Parker White, she could have imagined gangsters killing Duck, but not some unlucky soul like Job.

"Anyway…" Wayne continued. "Job was smart enough to wear gloves, but not smart enough to resist stealing the watch. Poor slob might have gotten away with it if he'd only resisted temptation. When the Davidson cops arrested him, he blurted out his confession. Said he'd never planned to hurt Duck, but the knife was just lying there. Clearly Job knew he'd done something wrong, but didn't understand the consequences. Even in jail, his only concern is the dog."

"What *dog*?"

"Job took the money from the pawnshop, made a donation, and rescued a racing greyhound. Then he bought dog food, a fancy collar, and enough fencing material to enclose a big pasture. Sadly, Job's elderly father can't keep the animal, so I picked her up and dropped her at the Animal Emergency Clinic in Troutman. They'll take her back to the pound tomorrow."

Wayne was right. This was a sad story. "What will happen to Job?"

"Peter Sokolsky's out for blood, looking for Murder One. I hope the judge and jury will take a good long look at Job and put him in a home for the mentally handicapped, where he'll get some help along with the punishment."

Diana hoped so, too. Anyway you looked at it, the result was tragic. While she was relieved to see Parker in the clear, she was horribly embarrassed to have harbored suspicions against her in the first place. Fact was, she'd been dead wrong, and Matthew had been right all along. Now she should butt out and mind her own business.

"Here they come…" Wayne nodded towards Matthew and Marianne, who were laughing like teenagers. They had linked arms and were flushed from the walk in fresh air. "They make a handsome couple, don't they?" Wayne teased.

"Heaven forbid!" Diana snorted. "Matthew doesn't want more babies. He's been there, done that." But what did she know? In truth, she had no idea how Matthew felt about starting a second family. She did know he'd be a loving father, and she experienced another tug of regret. If Matthew wanted babies, her personal biological clock had basically stopped ticking, so he needed to find himself a younger woman.

She put that unhappy thought aside as they said their goodbyes. Matthew left a big tip, paid the bill, and before Diana knew it, they were standing outside the restaurant, where the line of prospective diners was only nominally shorter than it had been when they arrived. They groaned in unison and held their over-full stomachs.

"We'd better go pick up your mama," Matthew said. "But I'm telling you right now, I'm not eating one bite of frozen yogurt."

Her sentiments exactly. "I'm glad we didn't ask for a *doggie bag*."

As soon as those words left her mouth, an impossible, extravagant, insane notion invaded her brain. "Hey, Matthew, do you think Mama will be up for an adventure…?"

## TWENTY-SEVEN

*Amazing Grace…*

"Don't even think about it, Diana." Matthew leaned against the concrete block wall, slowly shaking his head.

"Isn't she the sweetest little thing you ever did see?" Mama hunched over and extended her half-eaten cup of sugar- free yogurt through the wire mesh of the kennel. Mama didn't need to convince Diana. She was already in love, kneeling on the dirty linoleum floor in her new red dress, her nose pressed to the cage.

When they'd first arrived at the Troutman animal clinic, the teenage girl attending the place had been grumpy and unresponsive. She'd been stuck with the Thanksgiving shift, a very lonesome duty. Evidently Sheriff Bearfoot had been the only human face the girl had seen all day.

"They'll take this dog back to Charlotte Rescue tomorrow," she said. "It's sad. Sometimes these animals don't get a second chance. Folks figure something's wrong if the first adoption doesn't work out."

"Then what?" Diana had to ask.

"If no one takes her, they'll put her down."

Mama and Diana groaned in unison, then stared at one another.

"Remember what your daddy always said, Diana: You can always tell a gentleman by his horses and his greyhounds."

It was true. Diana hadn't thought about it for years, but her father, a gentle Quaker who hailed originally from England, had loved to quote the old expression. She'd grown up with horses and a motley crew of dogs, but greyhounds had never entered the mix.

"Be sensible, Diana, you live in a condominium," Matthew said. "They don't even allow dogs at your place."

"Yes, they do."

Matthew's forehead was creased with worry, but she could tell he was weakening. He lowered to his haunches and poked his finger through the mesh. The beautiful, shy creature was watching them intently through dewy brown eyes, but so far she'd neither sampled Mama's yogurt nor approached Matthew's finger. Her coat was a smooth, buttery tan, shattering Diana's preconceived notion that all greyhounds were gray. The dog moved on long legs, like a disoriented fawn who'd strayed from a medieval forest.

"These animals come right off the race track," the girl informed them. "They have a sweet nature and love people, but they've had a very demanding and disciplined life. Sometimes it's hard to make them trust you." The teenager had lost her former truculence as she plopped down on the floor beside Diana and began cooing to the dog.

"Besides, you have that damned parrot," Matthew reasoned. "Perry would cuss himself hoarse if you brought that dog home."

He had a point. Diana had no idea how her African Grey would react to a canine interloper, but damn it, she had inherited Perry against her will. He'd also been a rescue, so Perry had no right to complain. Besides, Matthew had Ursie, the most wonderful Doberman on the planet. He, of all people, should understood about that empty place that only a dog could fill.

"Ooh look!" Mama squealed as the greyhound gingerly tasted the yogurt, then licked Mama's fingers. "She likes me."

"Of course she likes you, you bribed her." Throughout Diana's childhood, Mama had made it abundantly clear that she'd loved their dogs more than she loved Diana.

"What's her name?" Diana wondered.

The kennel girl shrugged. "Beats me. She came without papers."

"She's so graceful." Mama sighed as the greyhound crossed the cage to sniff Matthew's finger.

"She's nothin' but skin and bones," Matthew complained, even as his heart seemed to melt. "But she is amazing..."

"That's it!" Diana cried. Suddenly it was all so clear. "I will call her *Amazing Grace*."

Three sets of eyes gaped at her. Everyone was stunned by the perfection of the title.

"Maybe you could call her *Gracie* for short?" the girl suggested.

Matthew groaned. "This sounds serious. Are you really gonna adopt her?"

Had there ever been any doubt? But Diana allowed the suspense to build.

"Oh, for heaven's sake," Mama huffed. "You'll adopt her. Your name is Diana, isn't it?"

"So what?" Diana huffed right back.

"So, my child, I named you after Diana, Goddess of the Hunt. I suppose you've forgotten which breed the Goddess chose as her hunting hounds..."

The breath caught in Diana's throat. "Greyhounds!" She exhaled. Perfect.

## TWENTY-EIGHT

# Jo Jo Jones

Joanne Early Jones peeled the brown skin off another onion and held it down on the chopping block. She grasped the polished handle of her scalpel-sharp Ginsu knife, inserted the point, and then bisected the onion's white belly. Tears rolled from her eyes as she viciously bisected the vegetable and then tossed it in with the cubed bread, diced celery, sliced oysters, and her own secret seasoning. No doubt about it, Jo Jo made a mean turkey dressing, a recipe so special she refused to submit it to *Southern Living,* in spite of the urging from all of her friends,

She angrily swiped at her tears with the back of her plump hand and glanced out the window at the gathering twilight. Across the manicured lawn, cozy lights glowed in many of the cottages, signaling that families were visiting for Thanksgiving. Dark cottages implied that some of the lucky old folks living here had been taken out to dinner, a result jealously desired by all the retirees at the Evergreen Adult Community.

Jo Jo attacked another onion as the frenetic music of kiddy cartoons blared from the television in the living room. By rights, her two beautiful tow-headed grandchildren—one boy, one girl—should be snuggled on the couch on either side of their grandpa watching Looney Tunes, but instead, her husband watched alone. She visualized Gerald sitting there, his mouth hanging open, unless he was sucking on his apple juice cocktail, his blank eyes glued to the screen. She'd taken great pains to dress Gerald in his suit and tie, in anticipation of their company, but it had proven to be a wasted effort.

She tossed the knife into the sink and washed her hands. She pushed the angel-white hair off her hot forehead and set a stick of butter in a saucepan to melt on the stove.

Gerald was always cold, so the thermostat was set too high. Gerald was the reason they couldn't live in one of the independent cottages, like normal people. All they could afford was a second floor efficiency, where they paid extra for assisted living services. And likely Gerald was the reason their son, Jarrett, had canceled the family visit at the last minute, leaving Jo Jo with the fixings for a Thanksgiving dinner big enough to feed a Boy Scout troupe.

And who could blame Jarrett? Gerald's odd behavior frightened the youngsters and depressed his son. After all, Jarrett had followed in his father's footsteps and was now a successful lawyer in Raleigh. How could he look at his father, who once possessed the sharpest legal mind in the Carolinas, a mind now ravaged by Alzheimer's disease, and not worry about his own fate down the road?

And why should Jarrett's darling little wife, who adored her husband and children, put up with her in-laws' problems? Clearly a visit to the grandparents was not the sweet-as-apple-pie experience they'd hoped for, so Jarrett had made his excuses. Damn him.

Jo Jo poured hot butter into the dressing mix and mashed it with her bare hands. She flattened it into a glass casserole dish, covered it with foil, and slid it onto the lower shelf in the oven, below the twenty- pound turkey cooking in a bag.

She washed her hands again, rolled back the glass door that opened to their deck, and stepped outside. Here she could escape from the insane cartoon music. Here the air was fresh and cool, the breeze actually chilly now that the sun had set. She took a deep breath and sank into a wire patio chair. Laughter echoed from the cottage across the green, while her neighbor's geriatric cat pawed at the trash can on the sidewalk below. Likely the creature could smell a recently discarded turkey carcass it couldn't get at, so Jo Jo made a mental note to save some leftovers for the sorry thing.

She sighed, closed her eyes, and buried her face in her hands. Jarrett had promised that his family would come for Christmas, and he dared not break that pledge. Things could be worse. Her son could have married that slut, Cindi White. Jo Jo remembered it all as clearly as yesterday, how Cindi got pregnant and tried to blackmail their boy into wedlock. Luckily, she and Gerald had put a stop to that nonsense. Otherwise that bitch, Parker White, would be the mother-in-law serving Thanksgiving dinner. Heaven forbid.

Goose bumps lifted on Jo Jo's arms, but as she thought about Parker and the bad luck that had befallen the woman, her lips parted in a smirk. She pictured Parker in disgrace, living in that shabby apartment above the bookstore, and decided it served her right. Parker had always been a self-serving snob. Jo Jo had almost gagged when the other commissioners had welcomed Parker to their ranks. Naturally, Jo Jo had voted against Parker, but she'd been a minority of one. The others had actually wanted Parker, and look at them now—all were dead.

The sobering thought popped Jo Jo's eyes wide open, and she stared fearfully into the moonless dark. First Harold, then Lester B., then Homer, and now her good buddy, Duck. But why? And why had she been spared, or Parker, for that matter? Because they were women?

Jo Jo hugged herself and scurried back into the warmth of the kitchen. On this day of Thanksgiving, she should be counting her blessings. She was, after all, a duly elected commissioner and President of the Flower Club. Plus, she was still alive. She shuddered, poured herself a jigger of scotch, and added a splash of water. The liquor burned her throat and flashed like a fireball in her queasy stomach.

Those deaths scared her more than she cared to admit. Lately she'd been looking over her shoulder and peering into every shadow. She'd heard sounds in the night, but Gerald couldn't protect her. She'd longed to take a vacation to someplace far away, where she'd be safe. But where could she go, especially with a helpless husband in tow?

As she poured another jigger, a little light bulb went on above her head, just like in Gerald's stupid cartoons. If Jarrett was not willing to visit them, then they would visit Jarrett. Her son's big fancy house in Raleigh had two guest bedrooms, and once he understood the danger his mother faced, how could he refuse?

The idea made her spirits soar. They flew out of her body and flapped around the kitchen. When the doorbell chimed, barely audible above the din from the television, her airborne spirits careened towards heaven. *Jarrett has changed his mind,* she reasoned. *They've come for Thanksgiving, after all.*

She sailed through the living room, oblivious to her husband snoring on the couch. Her prayers had been answered, and the muscles at the corner of her mouth, long frozen in a frown, lifted into a smile. She was actually grinning…

Until she opened the door.

## TWENTY-NINE

*Did someone die...?*

Amazing Grace was skittish and disoriented when they brought her home. Diana suspected she'd never been in a house before, so that everything in the new environment scared the poor dog. She startled when she saw her own reflection in the glass doors to the patio, and her initial contact with Perry was a disaster.

Matthew scooped Gracie up in his arms and carried her into Diana's dark condominium. When he put her down, she was wide-eyed and curious, tip-toeing through the rooms like she was walking on glass, clinging to Diana's side and sniffing the furniture as Diana turned on light after light. When they reached the bedroom, and she turned on the overhead fixture, Perry caught sight of the intruder and exploded with a litany of rasping obscenities that would make a sailor blush.

"Good Lord, can't you cover the cage?" Matthew gasped.

"Too late now." Diana tried to block Perry's view of the dog. At the same time, Amazing Grace was frozen in fear, her dark eyes riveted to the bird, her tail hooked under her body.

"Can't you shut him up?" Matthew got down on his knees to comfort the greyhound.

*Shut Perry up?* Yeah, right. In all her long experience with the African Grey, she'd never had one ounce of control over the creature. He was definitely Alpha Bird. But then a strange thing happened. Amazing Grace began to tremble and make an odd hiccupping noise. Then she barked. The sound was a weird series of high-pitched yips that seemed to surprise the dog as much as it surprised Matthew and Diana. She'd begun to think her new pet didn't know how to bark, but had no time to dwell on the theory because the room erupted in a cacophony of squealing and squawking that deafened them.

Something had to give.

Wonder of wonders, Diana's obstreperous parrot gave way first. All of a sudden, he closed his beak, folded his wings tight against his body, and stared at Amazing Grace. His beady eyes were wide from shock. Seconds later, the greyhound stopped, too. She quivered and focused on the bird.

"What just happened?" Matthew breathed a sigh of relief.

The silence was more deafening than the chaos. "Damned if I know. Maybe Amazing Grace is the Alpha, after all?"

They watched them for another long moment, then sat side by side on Diana's bed.

"Where's the dog gonna sleep?" Matthew asked.

Good question.

Diana took Matthew's hand and placed it in her lap. It was warm and comforting, the calluses rough under her fingers. She felt very needy. It seemed like Matthew had been away in Florida forever, and each day of his absence, she'd ached for his touch. They'd never slept together in her bedroom, but she was very willing to give it a try. She was tempted to guide his hand to a more dangerous place, but instead, she raised it to her lips, unfolded his fingers, and kissed his palm.

"I guess Gracie will sleep here with me," she said.

"In your bed?"

Diana's body clenched with need as she patted the bed beside them, and Gracie lifted effortlessly up onto the cover. She laid her long nose on Diana's thigh and looked up at her. "Well, maybe just this first night..."

"Just this once, right?" Matthew's eyes pleaded.

Another good question.

Normally her nights were a lonely ordeal, so that a warm body beside her, even a canine body, would be a welcome diversion. On the other hand, she'd much rather sleep with Matthew.

"What do *you* think I should do?" She glanced at him from the corner of her eye.

"I think these racing greyhounds are usually kept in crates. I bet Gracie would feel more at home in a big old box. You got anything like that, Diana?"

She sensed Matthew was right. They went out to her storage unit and located an enormous cardboard carton, the one her dresser had come in. They wedged it between her bed and the wall, furnished it with fluffy towels, and Gracie took to it immediately. She crept inside, curled into a tiny ball, and went right to sleep. And that, as they say, was that...

Two days later, Diana took one hand off the steering wheel and rubbed Gracie's soft ears. "You doing all right, girl?"

It was Saturday morning, and Diana had been drafted to build sets for *The King and I*. The idea did not appeal, especially since Gracie and she were having so much fun together, and Diana absolutely refused to leave her alone in the condo. But most of the stagehands were gone for the long Thanksgiving weekend, and time was getting short. If the performance was to open as scheduled during the Christmas holidays, someone had to work, and Diana was elected. She was officially in *costumes*, but so far she'd managed to shirk her duties and couldn't gracefully avoid this call for help.

"What do you think, girl?" She scratched under Gracie's chin and conceded she was in love. In three short days, Amazing Grace had lived up to her name. She had brought a sense of peace, or *grace* into Diana's life, so that Diana hardly thought about the murders anymore.

Gracie had taken to riding in Queen Vic just like she'd taken to her box, so they'd spent Friday buying fun doggie stuff together. They'd visited the local pet super store for organic food, a sturdy collar, long leash, and a fashionable winter coat. The girl at checkout had taught Diana volumes about rescued greyhounds, including the fact that they should always wear a coat in winter, since they had so little fat to keep them warm. And while she thought Gracie looked painfully thin, she'd learned that Gracie's ribs were supposed to show, and that she was only slightly underweight.

Racing greyhounds were more comfortable with dogs than with people, since they'd always been kenneled with their littermates. Diana had realized this was true when they walked through the store and Gracie had interacted with the canines, but shied away from humans.

"Don't worry, that'll change," the sales girl had reassured her. "Be gentle and give her lots of love, and she'll come around."

Diana had even told the clerk about Perry's uncharacteristic silence since Gracie's arrival.

The girl laughed. "Count your blessings, ma'am. From what you said, Perry's silence is a big improvement. He's just jealous. Give him a couple of days and he'll be his nasty old self again."

"Something to look forward to, eh, Gracie?" She stopped patting Gracie and concentrated on parking behind the theater building. Her usual space at the backstage door was occupied by a familiar white panel van, and as she pulled up beside it, she saw Danny Capelli unloading lumber.

"Hey, Diana!" He grinned, pushing a paint-spattered ball cap back on his curly brown hair. "I figured I might see you here today."

"Hi, Danny." She clipped the new red leash on Gracie's fancy red-and-white checked collar and eased her out of the car.

"Who's this?" Danny lowered to his haunches beside a pile of two-by-fours and extended his fingers towards Gracie.

Diana made the introductions.

"Yeah, I know. Liz already told me you had this new critter. Awesome. Check out those ribs. I bet you could strum 'em like a banjo."

Diana laughed as a tall African American rounded the other side of the van. He looked like a football player escaped from Panther Stadium, but she recognized him as Danny's friend, Rodney Woods, the Davidson police officer. Rodney was out of uniform, looking very much at home in old jeans and a sweatshirt.

"Hey, Miz Rittenhouse," he drawled and eyed Gracie. "One good thing about that animal—come Christmas you can put some fake antlers on her and folks'll think she's a reindeer."

"Very funny." She stroked her baby, who was pressed against her knee, terrified by the two big men. "Either one of you guys wanna race my girl?"

"No way!" They both groaned.

"So what are you two doing here?" she asked.

"We're good Samaritans," Danny said. "The Community Players were running short of funds to finish the sets, so I convinced Lowes to donate this lumber."

"More like blackmail," Rodney added. "Capelli's a big shot at Lowes. He buys so much paint he kinda twisted some arms. I'd arrest him, only it was for a good cause."

"What about you, Officer Woods?" Diana said. "Are you on the Players' crew?"

"Nope, but I love carpentry. This gives me a chance to practice sawing on some free wood."

By then Gracie had warmed to the strangers. She licked Danny's fingers, then inched closer to Rodney and sniffed his jeans.

"She smells Dawg," Rodney explained. "Dawg's the newest member of the Davidson Police, and he lives with me. Dawg's a drug and cadaver cop, so just like your girl, he works for a living."

Diana made a face. Sniffing for illegal substances and dead bodies did not sound like much fun. She reined Gracie in and held the metal door open as the two men carried in armloads of lumber. She and Gracie followed close behind, passing into the hallway that still smelled like old gym shoes. At the end of the hall, big double doors opened to the stage, where a handful of volunteers crawled around the scaffolding like flies on a bony carcass. They were hammering to the tempo of hip-hop blaring from a portable radio.

Diana was no artist, but someone had decided she could paint sets. Her specific assignment was to create faux palace walls to look like the Siamese royal court. But as she drew closer to the bright light and noise, as Gracie started trembling against her leg, she began having serious misgivings about the project.

The odd sense of dread intensified, so Diana hung back as Danny and Rodney entered the stage. Gracie cowered between her legs and stared into the deep shadows to the left of the door. Diana followed her gaze and saw the framework of a tall ladder rising from the gloom. It was one of those gridiron structures with stairs and wheels that clerks push around to get merchandise off high shelves. As she listened, she heard something strange coming from half way up the ladder. It was a mournful, whimpering sound, like a cat stranded up a tree. As she drifted closer, the crying got louder, and she realized the sound was human.

"Who's there?" she whispered as she nervously stroked Gracie's neck.

All at once the mewing became full-fledged sobbing. As her eyes adjusted, she saw a pair of expensive sneakers, skin-tight black workout pants, and an electric blue running jacket. Above the clothes a woman's stricken face emerged from the gloom. Her bloodshot eyes swam in the pale moon of her skin, and she seemed to be in extreme distress.

"Parker? Is that you?"

Diana's words induced an inconsolable flood of tears.

"My God, what's wrong? Did someone *die*?"

Parker eased herself one step lower on the ladder as Gracie cowered behind Diana's knees.

"Haven't you heard?" Parker moaned. "Jo Jo Jones is in the hospital, good as dead. She's in a coma. The doctors don't expect her to recover."

"My God, what happened?" The news hit like a blow to Diana's stomach.

"She fell off her deck, Diana. It was horrible! Jo Jo landed on the concrete driveway and cracked her skull. They found her crumpled up beside a garbage can, with a ratty old cat licking her fingers."

Diana's stomach lurched. It was worse than horrible. "But how could such a thing happen?"

Parker pawed at her swollen eyes. "Who knows? Jo Jo's always been a klutz. Maybe she was drunk. They found her Thanksgiving turkey burned to a crisp in the oven and her husband, Gerald, sitting in the living room like a dummy while smoke poured from the kitchen."

Parker's account sounded callous and unsympathetic. Diana frowned at the plastic tumbler of tomato juice in her hand and suspected, from the way Parker was slurring her words, that the drink was spiked with vodka.

Is that a Bloody Mary?" she demanded.

"Of course not." Parker bristled. "We were talking about Jo Jo, remember? Or maybe you don't give a shit?" She wobbled to her feet and grasped the metal rail of the ladder for support.

It was unlike Diana's old friend to use vulgar language, and Parker never used to be a daytime drinker, except for the occasional cocktail luncheon. But these were trying times, and Diana tried not to take the rude words personally.

"I'm just as upset as you are," Diana answered carefully. "How can I help?"

Parker's harsh laugh caused Gracie to pin back her ears. The dog got down on her belly and inched around from behind Diana to stare at the woman.

"Maybe we should take up a collection?" Parker said. "Or maybe the old biddies at the Garden Club could do a special arrangement? Either way, what does it matter? Jo Jo's a vegetable, so what does she care?"

Diana was offended by Parker's tone. Her distress was real enough, as were her tears, but Diana knew the truth about Parker's opinion of Jo Jo—she hated the woman. What had her daughter, Cindi, said? *Has Mother killed Jo Jo yet*? The chilling memory caught Diana off guard. Just when she'd begun to believe in

Parker's innocence, and just when she'd begun to forgive herself for doubting Parker in the first place, another commissioner was dying. At best, Parker was a hypocrite and her tears were crocodile tears.

"Was it an accident?" Diana asked.

Parker swallowed the last of her drink and tossed the plastic cup at an industrial waste can. She missed. "Of course it was an accident. Unless you think Jo Jo had the guts to kill herself. Who could blame her, with a husband who acts like a child and a son who doesn't give a damn? If I were in her shoes, I'd consider offing myself."

Quite a speech. Was Parker was projecting her own life onto Jo Jo's? After all, Parker was the one who'd lost her husband and estranged herself from her daughter.

"Why are you here today?" Diana demanded. "I thought you quit the *King and I*?"

Parker pulled a folded piece of paper from her waistband. "They asked me to design this Playbill—cast, crew, and all that crap. Everyone knows I don't have a damned thing to do now that Town Hall's all but closed down. They asked, and since I couldn't think of an excuse fast enough, here I am."

Parker started fanning herself with the Playbill, and Diana noticed beads of perspiration oozing through her heavy makeup, which could never conceal the dark circles under her eyes. Drunk and depressed, Parker was in no shape to help anyone.

"Why don't you go home, Parker?" At least driving under the influence was not a problem. She had only to walk across the street to her apartment above the bookstore.

Parker offered a pathetic smile. "Perhaps you're right, Diana. Jo Jo and I were close friends, you know, so this awful business has taken its toll." As she began to move away, Parker almost tripped over Gracie and made an ugly face. "Jesus, does that scrawny creature belong to you? I'm a cat person myself."

Parker tapped Gracie on the nose with the Playbill. Gracie yelped in fear and crawled between Diana's legs, as Parker giggled in delight. Instead of slamming her fist into Parker's jaw, as Diana was sorely tempted to do, she quickly channeled her anger and mumbled her goodbyes. Diana dropped to her knees to comfort Gracie, then turned her back until Parker was gone.

THIRTY

*The wrong suspect...*

"What's happenin', Diana?" Rodney Woods caught her crawling around on the floor.

She looked up into his smiling dark eyes. "Nothing, really, only Parker nearly scared my dog to death."

He reached down to scratch Gracie's neck. "Aw, she'll be okay, won't you, girl?"

His deep voice soothed Gracie, who climbed to her feet and crept slowly to his side. Soon she was wagging her skinny tail and licking his hand. It didn't hurt that Rodney pulled a dog cookie from his pocket and offered it to her.

"You're her new best friend," Diana said as Gracie crunched the cookie. "But she shouldn't take candy from a stranger."

"I'm no stranger, and it's not like I'm so great with animals. She just smells Dawg, remember?" Rodney extended his big brown hand and helped Diana to her feet.

"And don't let Parker White get to you. She's been hittin' the sauce all morning. Heck, she was three sheets to the wind when Danny and me brought the first load of lumber, and that was just after breakfast. What's her problem, Diana? Seems like she's all torn up about Miz Jones fallin' off her deck. I figure those two are good friends, seein' they're both commissioners, and all."

"You'd think so, wouldn't you?" Diana mumbled.

"Take a break with me…" He took her elbow and guided them out the exit door to a little winter garden between buildings. Although it was late November, the sun was warm on Diana's face. They sat side by side on a concrete bench, and Gracie, the traitor, curled up between Rodney's sneakers. Across the way, a group of students were unloading suitcases from a minivan. They did not look happy.

"Those kids went home for Thanksgiving," Rodney explained. "Now they're back for final exams before Christmas vacation. Doesn't seem fair, does it?"

Today nothing seemed particularly fair. "What really happened to Jo Jo Jones?" she demanded.

Rodney rubbed his jaw. "Tell you the truth, Miss Diana, it's none of your business, but Danny told me you've been following these murders…"

"*Murders?*"

"Fact is, Miz Jones didn't just fall from her deck. We think she was pushed."

His eyes narrowed as he watched her reaction. Diana heard blood pumping in her ears as she waited to hear more.

"Miz Jones is a tiny woman, about as round as she is tall. She's way too short to lean back and fall over the guard railing, and she's too plump to hoist herself over without standing on a chair. And there were no chairs anywhere near the edge. Do you get my meaning?"

Loud and clear. He believed Jo Jo had considerable help falling to her intended death.

"It would take a strong man—or woman—to wrestle Miz Jones over the edge," he continued. "Either the intruder had a gun and forced her out to the deck…"

"Or Jo Jo knew the person and invited her out to the deck," Diana interrupted.

"Her? You think the intruder was a woman?"

"Who knows?" She'd been dead wrong about who killed Duck Wadell, so hopefully she'd learned her lesson. "What about Jo Jo's husband? Surely he saw something?"

Rodney shook his head. "Poor old guy has advanced Alzheimer's. He hardly knows his own name. He remembers the doorbell ringin', but that's about all. I'm sure he saw the person, but he can't recall whether it was a man or woman, young or old. The ambulance crew sedated him and sent him to the Maples Nursing Home. Poor devil. Like as not he'll be stuck in that home if Miz Jones dies, or unless his son in Raleigh takes pity and brings his dad home to live with his family. But from what I hear, the son's a fancy lawyer who isn't likely to put himself out that way. Too bad."

Too bad, indeed. Her heart went out to Jo Jo's befuddled husband. For a few short days, Amazing Grace had lifted her spirits and she'd almost forgotten about the tragic deaths, but now she'd catapulted backwards into the whole messy affair. "Do you think Jo Jo's fall was connected to the other commissioner's murders?"

"My boss, Peter Sokolsky, sure enough thinks so. Before Miz Jones got pushed, he was trying to pin everything on poor Job Little, the man who confessed to killing Duck Wadell. You ask me, he's got the wrong suspect."

Job was the reason Diana had her Gracie, so she felt a weird connection to the man. She reached down to pat her dog's head. Gracie whined and smiled, but didn't leave the sanctuary between Rodney's sneakers. "Look, Rodney, I understand Job killed Duck, but I can't believe he had anything to do with the other deaths."

Rodney hesitated. It seemed he was trying to decide how much he should reveal. Some of Diana's real estate clients played coy about how much they were willing to spend on a property. She had learned to keep her mouth shut and wait until those clients vented all their objections, and in the end, they'd convince themselves, and she would make the sale. Worked every time.

Finally, Rodney cleared his throat. "Sokolsky got a search warrant for the Little's farm. Turns out they found an old bag of Fractol in the barn. It's used to kill rodents, but the government banned the stuff years ago."

"So what? Wouldn't you expect to find rat killer in a barn?"

"Yeah, but the chemical used in Fractol is sodium fluoroacetate, the poison that killed Homer Locksley at the town meeting."

Diana suffered a sudden, vivid memory of old Homer, the art professor, gagging and turning red, foaming at the mouth. "That's awful, but surely Job Little didn't do that? If he's mentally challenged, how could he plan and execute such a thing?"

"I agree, Diana. I'd say Job had about as much chance as my six-year-old son of pulling off that murder. Problem is, Job's old daddy is diabetic, and over the years Job's learned how to inject insulin, so Sokolsky's making the case that Job did indeed have the ability to use a hypodermic and inject the poison into Locksley's bottled water."

"But why?"

"If hating Locksley for the ETJ Project weren't enough, then Job's homophobia might have put him over the edge." Rodney mopped his forehead. "Unfortunately, Job hated homosexuals and everyone else he couldn't figure out, which included anyone different from Job. He went around town blabbing how he hated gays, and old Homer Locksley, much as he tried to conceal it, was a flaming target."

"That is truly sick, Rodney, but if someone with a child's mind is so full of hatred, then someone must have fed him those ideas." She paused to compose herself, because such bigotry disgusted her beyond all reason. "But I still say Job did not kill Locksley. It doesn't ring true."

"Yeah, but Sokolsky wants to burn the guy."

"That's ridiculous! Remember how you people arrested poor Rhonda Smith, Lester B.'s daughter? You claimed Rhonda killed Locksley because she blamed him for putting her father and grandmother out of their home. You insisted she blamed him for her grandmother's heart attack and wanted revenge, remember? The woman lost her job over it, and now you admit she is innocent?"

Rodney held both hands in the air. "Whoa, slow down. I never suspected Rhonda. She and her family are good people, best friends with my folks. That was Sokolsky's theory, and I'd like to wring his neck for putting Rhonda through all that. Now that Rhonda's cleared, she's left town. Maybe it's a blessing in disguise, so she and her kids can start over somewhere they're appreciated."

Rhonda's self-imposed banishment did not sound like a blessing to Diana. "I hope someone offered her a big fat apology. And if you ask me, tagging Job for Locksley's murder is another huge mistake."

"I agree…" Rodney stretched and stood to his full height. Gracie jumped up, too, and they both began walking across the green towards the college students.

Naturally, Diana followed. "What else aren't you telling me?" She recaptured Gracie's leash, determined to keep her own dog.

"It gets worse." Rodney sighed. "Sokolsky's also looking to nail Job for Harold Haver's murder—maybe Lester B.'s, too."

"That is truly insane."

"Don't I know it? But recently Job got his driver's license, and to celebrate, his daddy bought him a little white Honda. Remember how someone spotted a little white car around Haver's place the evening of his murder? Then a bunch of kids high on pot, kids living at your condominium, swore they saw a little white car run Lester B.'s vehicle off the road into Lake Norman."

"*I* never saw any white car at Harold Havers," Diana said.

"No? Then maybe Danny Capelli told Sokolsky about it." Rodney looked puzzled.

"Yeah, right. The whole thing sounds like a fishing expedition to me. Sokolsky's got it all wrong. What's he after, anyhow?"

Rodney stopped walking while three coeds arrived to pat Gracie. Surprisingly, Diana's shy greyhound took to the girls. Maybe she was actually getting socialized. Once the girls were out of earshot, Rodney continued.

"Sokolsky's an ambitious man, and I know he's bored out of his gourd here in Davidson. He wants more action, like he had up in Philadelphia, so he's set his sights on the Charlotte Force. I reckon catching a serial killer would land him a big job in the city."

"That's no excuse, Rodney. I'd rather see him promoted for catching the real serial killer."

"Amen to that." Rodney changed course, and they headed back towards the theater. "Believe it or not, Sokolsky would love to hold Job for the attempted murder of Miz Jones. Someone saw a little white car leaving the Evergreen Adult Community about the time Miz Jones fell."

"You're kidding!"

"Nope. The old folks saw it speeding away. The guy was doing thirty-five in a fifteen-mile-per-hour zone."

"Guy?"

"Yeah, the witnesses say they saw a young man, a stranger, walking real fast to the car."

"But Job was in jail at the time, right?"

"Right. Besides, that night was Thanksgiving, and Evergreen was full of strangers. With children and grandchildren visiting, the young man likely belonged there. Besides, we have hundreds of little white cars in the area."

They had reached the stage door, where Rodney retrieved a big circular saw. With his free hand, he held the door open for her.

"It's been great talking with you, Diana. You sure do have a knack for greasin' a man's jaw. I never intended to talk so much, and I sure do need to be getting back to work. How 'bout you?"

They entered the building and walked onto the set, where the same volunteers were still crawling around on the scaffolding like a swarm of flies. All at once, Diana was uncommonly tired, with no desire to paint faux palace walls. She waited until Rodney disappeared behind a scenery flat, then turned to Gracie. The greyhound's eager eyes said she was ready to run. Clearly she would prefer an all-out race through the park to being leashed on a stuffy old stage.

"What do you think, girl?" Diana whispered. "Can we sneak out of here?"

Gracie whined and wagged her approval.

But as they slipped out past Danny's van and quietly climbed into Queen Vic, Diana knew she had mislead her dog—no park today. She was thoroughly exhausted by her encounter with Parker and the conversation with Rodney Woods. What she principally needed was a good restorative nap. But instead of counting white sheep jumping the fence, which Gracie would no doubt prefer as sleep inducers, Diana would be counting little white Hondas speeding away from crime scenes.

THIRTY-ONE

# Matthew

Matthew unlocked the door of his Jayco RV trailer, while Diana held a big white doggie bag of leftover barbeque. As he eased the door open, Amazing Grace escaped into the lot where only a few other campers had hooked up off- season.

Diana screamed and dropped the bag. "Catch her, Matthew! She'll run out in the road and get hit by a car!"

"No, she won't." The magnificent greyhound was racing in circles around the parked vehicles. Her long legs flashed, bending and extending in perfect rhythm as she smiled at them from the corners of her eyes.

"Please stop her, Matthew!"

He had good instincts about when dogs were fixing to bolt and run, and from that twinkle in Gracie's eye, he knew she was only teasing. "Here, let me show you an old trick…" He opened the white bag and took out a cold hushpuppy. "This dates back to the bad old days of slavery. When the women were cooking out back in the summer kitchen and the hounds were howling for a handout, the cooks would fish hunks of cornbread scrap out of the hot grease and toss 'em in the yard. *Hush, puppy!* They'd shout, and sure enough the dogs would come running, gobble the scraps, and shut their yaps."

Diana crossed her arms and gave him one of her *very funny, but get on with it* looks, so he squatted and extended the hushpuppy into the cold night air.

"Come get it, girl!"

Gracie stopped on a dime and followed her long nose to the morsel in his fingers. Seconds later, all three of them were safely locked in the trailer. Diana sighed in relief as Gracie trotted to her box, the same old box Matthew had salvaged the night Diana adopted the dog.

"Maybe you were right, Matthew. Maybe we should have left Gracie at home and rented a motel room here in Wilmington."

His sentiments exactly. He had argued that Gracie would be fine staying at his place with Ursie. It was high time their pets got acquainted, and Hoke Bodine had offered to look in and feed the dogs while they were gone. But Matthew knew it would never happen. Diana and Amazing Grace were still in their honeymoon phase, so they had allowed Gracie to tag along on their romantic vacation.

Matthew eyed the rear of the trailer, where a tiny double bed was tucked away in a stepped-up closet. "Does Gracie still sleep with you, Diana?"

She laughed and maneuvered her hips onto the cramped bench between the dining table and the wall, so that she was seated directly across from him. She took his hand.

"Even Gracie knows three's a crowd. She'll choose her box—I hope."

Diana's fingers were cool in his hand. He gave them a squeeze and watched a warm blush creep up her neck. She smelled like fresh ocean air, a tangy blend of salt and her own distinctive lilac, and her soft white hair was ruffled from the coastal breeze.

"Should I make coffee?" he asked.

"I'll do it…" She eased out from the bench, crossed to the tiny kitchenette and found a small coffee maker in the cupboard. "All the comforts of home."

He watched in silence, appreciating the smooth movement of her breasts under her white cable-knit sweater. It was an intimate domestic scene, and the close quarters made him more acutely aware than ever of her physical presence. Suddenly he could hardly wait for nightfall. He'd just as soon skip the coffee and take Diana to bed.

Reading his mind, she turned and gave him a long, searching look. Her sensuous mouth curved in a smile and her blue eyes sparked with mischief. "What's wrong? Can't you wait?"

Her tone caused a familiar tightening in his chest and a sudden ache in his groin. Matthew had not experienced such passion in years, not since he was a horny teenager, and he realized how very much they both needed this holiday.

"I'm glad we came," he said.

The coffee had finished perking, so Diana carried two cups to the table. She slid back onto the bench, pushed off her shoes, and then plopped her feet in his lap. "Maybe you *can't* wait?" she teased, noting his excitement.

Her wriggling toes drove him crazy, but he decided to play along. "I'm in no hurry. What's for dessert?"

She gave him a final nudge, then slipped her feet to the floor. "Drink your coffee, Matthew."

He closed his eyes, savoring the hot jolt of caffeine, then worked off his loafers and tossed them out into the room. He was mighty grateful for this vacation, especially since Diana had almost managed to delay their escape again. Ever since her friend Jo Jo fell off her deck, Diana had been morbidly obsessed with the murders. It wasn't healthy. He'd had to drag her away from Jo Jo's hospital bed. "The woman doesn't even know you're here, Diana" he had argued. "She's in a coma." So between Jo Jo and Diana's indecision about what to do with the dog, the trip had almost been derailed—until Matthew put his foot down.

"Now what are you doing?" When he opened his eyes, Diana was thumbing through a phone book, the Wilmington directory. She frowned in concentration.

"I picked it up at the Tourist Bureau," she answered.

Matthew nodded. They had stopped at the Tourist Bureau on the way into town because Diana loved brochures. That's how they found out about the relatively deserted beach where Gracie had enjoyed her run, as well as the best local barbeque joint for supper. Both were within walking distance of their campsite, so he hadn't even needed to unhitch his truck from the trailer.

"What's so interesting about a phone book?" he asked. "Do you get a kick out of reading lists of strangers' names?"

"Here it is!" She crowed and pointed her finger. "I knew he lived here."

"Who?" He didn't like the sound of that.

"Randall White, Jr., Parker White's son. I told you about him, remember?"

Matthew's passion wilted. This was another murder-related issue, and he didn't want to go there. "So what?" he groaned.

"So, Randy lives just down the beach from here, on Mayfield Street. I saw the sign about a mile before we turned into the campground."

The coffee turned sour on his tongue. "What do you want to do, Diana?" he demanded. "Go calling on this kid in the middle of the night?"

Diana's eyes were wide and focused. "You sound like an old man, Matthew. It's only eight o'clock, and it's Friday night. No one goes to bed this early."

"I'd *like* to go to bed this early," he muttered as all hope died. "What do you want with this guy, anyway?"

"Think about it, Matthew. Parker's my best friend—at least she used to be. My guess is Randy has no idea what his poor mother's been going through. I bet he doesn't even know about the commissioners' murders or Parker's drug use."

He tried not to roll his eyes in frustration, yet he realized Diana was already on her way to Mayfield Street, already putting on her shoes. "Listen, maybe you should call him first. His number's right there in the book."

She seemed to consider the courtesy as she bit at the edge of her lip, but then said, "No, I don't want to warn him, or give him a chance to make an excuse."

"That's sporting of you." He looked around for his shoes and spotted his left loafer in Gracie's box.

"Please drive me there. Pretty please?" She batted her eyelashes at him.

And Matthew knew he was licked. He collected the right loafer from under Gracie's blanket, stomped outside to unhook the truck from the trailer, and then fired up his rig.

## THIRTY-TWO

## *From mother to son…*

By the time they turned into Mayfield Street, Diana was having second thoughts and feeling deeply uncertain. Why was she doing this, when all she really wanted was to climb between the sheets with Matthew? He had been ominously silent during the drive over, yet he'd continued to hold her hand and massage her fingers with his thumb. He was a good sport. It was one of the many things she loved about him. He never seriously bucked her independence or tightened the reins on her misadventures, although sometimes, like tonight, she wished he would.

The old neighborhood they entered had seen better days. The sky was a black cauldron, the moon a charred sliver of weak light. Yet she could see the ramshackle silhouettes of old wooden houses, all built in the mid Twentieth Century. Because they were several blocks from the ocean, these cottages and larger Victorian-style boarding houses, once fashionable resort destinations, had long since been eclipsed by the trendy towering condominiums farther down on the beach. One could almost read the sad history in the cracked sidewalks and peeling paint, and yet there were signs of rehabilitation.

"What's happening here?" she wondered aloud.

"I read a feature story about this part of Wilmington in the Observer last year," Matthew said. "A bunch of yuppies and artists are moving in. They're restoring the old homes to get the place up and running again. If they pull it off, the properties will be worth a fortune."

It never ceased to amaze her that Matthew's mind was a treasure trove of useful trivia. By the way he said *yuppies* and *artists*, though, Diana couldn't tell if he admired or resented these entrepreneurs. She knew he hated rampant development that raped forests and turned farmers' fields to parking lots, but she would guess that he'd approve of restoration, of saving of the old ways. Maybe it was the profit motive he disdained?

"Here we are…" Matthew pulled to the curb in front of a small bungalow with a wide, covered front porch.

As they picked their way through a yard overgrown with weeds, she wondered if they should have brought Gracie along for protection instead of leaving her in the box. But what a silly idea. Gracie was as fearful as a mouse in the cat's jaw, hardly a guard dog.

"We might as well go back to the camper," Matthew grumbled as they mounted the tilted stairs to the porch. "He's not home."

She clung to his arm and listened. From the depths of the house, she heard the faint sound of music and a single light glowed from somewhere within.

"You're not getting off that easily." She jabbed his ribs. "Ring the doorbell."

"What doorbell?" He gave her a dark look, but then pounded on the door. His knocking echoed through the still house, and soon a shadowy figure appeared at the end of the entrance hall. The figure advanced, and the porch exploded in light.

"Yes? Who's there?" A young man cautiously opened the door.

The overhead fixture illuminated the bare torso and surprised face of one of the most handsome males Diana had ever seen. The man's delicate feet were also bare below his jeans, and his smooth skin was the color of caramel candy. His eyes were as black as his silken hair, and he moved with the grace of a jungle cat. Whoever he was, he was definitely not Randall White.

"I'm so sorry," she stammered. "I'm afraid we've come to the wrong address."

"Who are you looking for?" The young man's voice was a clear, melodic tenor, and he spoke with the trace of a British accent.

"Randall White. Do you know where he lives?"

"Yes, he lives here." The man extended his small hand. "I am Nanjay. Most people call me Jay. How can I help you?"

"Is Mr. White home?" Matthew shook Jay's hand.

"I regret that Randy is away on business."

Diana took an immediate liking to this cultivated young India transplant. His formal way of speaking betrayed a traditional education. Whether he received it in India, Britain, or here in the States was anyone's guess, but she was curious to know his story.

"I'm a friend of Randy's mother, Parker White," she quickly explained.

"Really?" Jay's eyes widened. "Is there a problem? Has Mrs. White taken ill?"

"Oh, no, nothing like that, but we are worried about her," Diana hastened to add.

Jay hesitated as they introduced themselves. He was obviously puzzled by their sudden appearance on his threshold, but he opened the door wide and bowed slightly. "Please do come in. You will have tea with me, yes?"

Diana tugged at Matthew's sleeve, urging him along as their host led them through a foyer strewn with drop cloths. When they arrived in a brightly lit kitchen, sure enough, a blue enamel teapot was whistling on an old-fashioned stove.

Jay waved them to two chairs placed round an antique soda fountain table. "Please sit down. I will be right back." He lifted the boiling teapot to the counter and disappeared into a room off the kitchen.

"What are you up to, Diana?" Matthew demanded.

"His chest was speckled with paint, did you notice?" She ducked the question.

"I wasn't looking at his chest," Matthew grumbled. "But these two guys obviously have a big project under way."

She agreed. The room reeked of turpentine, and just below that odor, she detected the scent of sandalwood incense, a heady combination.

"Sorry to keep you waiting." When Jay reappeared, he wore a carefully pressed oatmeal cotton shirt and fresh comb marks dented his damp hair. He served their tea in silence, adding a bowl of sugar cubes, small pitcher of milk, and a plate of dainty lemon wafers.

They both muttered their thanks for the unexpected hospitality, and then Jay got right to the point. "Tell me about Randy's mother."

Diana searched for a plausible response. She had no plan of attack, nor did she know how much to reveal to this relative stranger.

Jay arched his eyebrows. "Don't worry, Mrs. Rittenhouse, you can confide in me. Randy and I are partners...*life partners*... do you understand? I am part of the family, you see?"

Diana understood quite clearly, but it took her a few seconds to catch her breath. No one had ever stepped out of the closet so comfortably in her presence. She smiled and touched his hand. "I understand, Jay. May I be frank?"

"By all means." A worry line creased his smooth brow.

Diana glanced at Matthew, who was extremely busy stirring milk into his tea. They had never discussed this issue, or the fact that Diana had close friends, gay and lesbian couples back in Pennsylvania. She could only assume that Matthew also believed it was a basic human right to choose a same-sex partner, so that this current situation should be a non-issue.

"Does Randy see his mother often?" She stalled, hoping to find the right words.

"God, I hope not." Jay sighed. "I've never met the woman, but I understand she has severe emotional problems. For one thing, she refuses to acknowledge my role in Randy's life."

This was no surprise. A few moments ago, Jay had described himself as part of the family, but that was wishful thinking on his part. Diana recalled the day in Parker's apartment when Parker said her son was a heartbreaker. For a woman with Parker's obvious prejudices, denial was a powerful painkiller. "So Randy doesn't get up to Davidson much?"

"On the contrary," Jay said. "He goes up almost every week. Davidson is considering hiring Randy as their new Town Planner. I am so proud. He will make a very good salary, and lord knows, we need the money."

Diana almost choked on her tea as Jay explained their severe financial reversals. Jay had lost a highly paid job as a graphic designer nearly six months ago, while Randy had been unable to find work in his field. They barely had funds to finish restoring the beach bungalow, which was intended to be their dream home. If they didn't find employment soon, they'd be forced to sell their investment, rather than live in it.

"I'm sorry to hear that," Matthew said. "I'm sure something will turn up soon."

The men continued to chat comfortably with one another, but their words seemed jumbled as Diana's mind raced. The overwhelming fact was that for some reason Randy had mislead Jay, because Randy must have known for weeks that the commissioners had rejected him for the job of Town Planner. Instead, they had hired the dazed, bespectacled girl Diana had seen the night Homer Locksley was murdered. Why had Randy lied to his lover? Why was Randy still traveling to Davidson, pretending to be interviewing for a job already awarded to someone else? Was Randy in denial, just like his mother?

She did not know the answers to these questions. All she knew for sure was that she wasn't going to be the one to shatter Jay's illusions. When she tuned back in to the conversation, Matthew and Jay were getting on like old friends. In fact, Matthew was filling Jay in on the details about the commissioners' murder investigations.

"Yes, I knew about the death of Homer Locksley." Jay frowned. "He was one of Randy's professors at Davidson College. In fact, Randy attended Locksley's funeral several weeks ago."

Diana's ears pricked as she tried to grab hold of an elusive memory. Once again she saw the photo of the handsome Randall White, Jr. enshrined on Parker's mantel. Even then she had sensed something familiar about the young man. "Do you have a recent photo of Randy?" she asked.

Jay seemed startled, but he took a wallet from his pocket and passed her a snapshot. "Handsome devil, isn't he?"

Not only handsome, but Randy was definitely the distraught mourner who had sat directly behind Diana at Locksley's funeral. She wondered if he had visited his mother that day.

"Randy's mom always upsets him," Jay continued. "Whenever he sees her, he is depressed for days. He drinks heavily, and once he got so low he went back into therapy."

"Has he been depressed lately?" Diana asked gently.

Jay's shoulders slumped as he watched her through fathomless black eyes. "It has been terrible, and it is always worse when he returns from Davidson. He has nightmares. He wakes up in a sweat, screaming in terror."

"Maybe he should get some more professional help?" Matthew offered.

"Certainly he should, but we cannot afford it," Jay said. "Randy was especially down when he returned from Thanksgiving. He was so out of control, that he put his fist through a sheet of drywall." Jay paused to stare at her. "He claimed he had not been to see his mother. Do you think that is true, Mrs. Rittenhouse?"

What could she say? If Parker had spent Thanksgiving with her adored son, then surely she would have told Diana all about it that day at the theater. Whatever Randy was doing in Davidson, he seemed to be following his own agenda, and the profile emerging was one of a deeply disturbed and possibly violent young man.

"Does Randy have a good relationship with his sister?" she asked. "I met Cindi once, and she seemed like a nice person."

"Far as I am concerned, she is more bad news," Jay said. "But when it comes to his sister, Randy is as protective as a lioness with her cubs. He has always taken his role as brother very seriously, and has never approved of Cindi's boyfriends, including her born-again, NASCAR-driving husband. There was an incident a long time ago, when they were both still living at home, when Cindi got in trouble with some guy at Wake Forest. I don't know the details, but Randy still wants to kill that guy."

Diana wondered if Randy's hatred of the guy at Wake Forest extended to a hatred of the guy's mother. After all, Jo Jo had fallen from her deck Thanksgiving Day, and Randy had been in town.

"Randy is the same way about his mother—just as protective," Jay continued. "Ever since his father died, he has worried obsessively. He is sure his mother will hook up with some man in a bad relationship."

Diana pushed her saucer aside as the crumbs of lemon wafer turned bitter in her mouth. How much had Randy known about his mother's affair with Harold Havers, if indeed there had been an affair? Harold had been a married man. He had possibly demanded sexual favors in exchange for the money he'd loaned Parker. The situation was enough to drive an unstable, overly protective son right over the edge.

Matthew cleared his throat. "We'd best be on our way, Diana. Jay's been kind enough to entertain us, but I know he wants to get back to work."

Jay blinked and seemed puzzled. "But what was it you wanted me to tell Randy? Something about his mother?"

Suddenly Diana felt guilty. Clearly this young couple had enough trouble without her laying her concerns about Parker at their doorstep. At the same time, she was gripped by a sense of dread as her suspicions shifted from mother to son.

Matthew came to the rescue. "Oh, we didn't have anything special to say. We just wanted to pass the time of day and bring

Mrs. White's best wishes. She'll be sorry we missed Randy, but you'll say hello for us, won't you?"

Jay was still perplexed, but like most people, he was reassured by Matthew's folksy delivery. "Well, that's fine…" he blustered. "I will tell him."

Matthew stood up and ambled towards the door. "Ready, Diana?"

"Go on ahead, I'll be right there…" Once Matthew stepped outside, she turned to Jay and impulsively took his hand. "I am so sorry for your troubles. I have a son your age, and you remind me of him." This was entirely true. Although they were from different cultures, Jay's gentle, earnest nature was much like her Robbie's. "You know, I believe I saw Randy at Professor Locksley's funeral, and he was terribly upset."

Jay frowned and tightened his fingers around her hand. "You don't know the half of it. Locksley, the bastard, was the one who put Randy off-track. Randy was an undergrad art student when Locksley seduced him. Poor kid didn't know he was gay then, or at least he was unable to admit it, so that after a hot affair that lasted one semester, when Locksley dropped him for a new boy, Randy went haywire."

Her young host released her hand and massaged the bridge of his nose. Diana empathized. This tragic story, along with the turpentine fumes, had given her a headache, too.

"Randy had a nervous breakdown. He dropped out of Davidson College and spent the next year of his life in and out of mental institutions."

"I am so sorry," she said again. "How did Randy feel about attending Locksley's funeral?"

"That's a good question, and I don't know how to answer. He would not talk about it, and I believe his emotions were mixed.

Frankly, I think he wanted to assure himself the bastard was really dead… maybe close that chapter."

Somehow, she didn't think that chapter was closed. From everything she'd just heard, Randy was likely caught in a downward spiral of violent revenge, a desperate rampage even his lover could not imagine.

"Is something wrong?" Jay stared at her.

She forced herself to smile. "You say Randy's up in Davidson right now?"

"Yes, he said something about unfinished business."

Diana realized she'd alarmed Jay, and that was the last thing she'd wanted. "Thanks for everything," she said as she scuttled towards the door. But as she glanced to her left, through a dusty kitchen window, something caught her eye. She saw a security light burning in the side yard, and beneath that, nestled in the weeds, was a white Honda Civic with a WDAV Classical Radio decal on its window. "That's Parker White's car, isn't it?"

"Not anymore," Jay said. "She gave it to Randy a couple of months ago."

Diana's headache escalated. "Is this the car he drives to Davidson?" By then, Jay surely thought she was crazy, or nosey, or both.

"Yes, Mrs. Rittenhouse. Usually he drives the Honda, but the battery is dead, the carburetor needs an overhaul, and the tires are shot."

And, of course, they could not afford to fix it. "So, is he driving a rental car?"

"No, he's driving my car, an antique Volkswagen Beetle. Any more questions?" He frowned and pointedly held the front door open.

She had definitely worn out her welcome, so she murmured her thanks and made a quick exit. Outside the night had turned viciously cold, and a strong wind from the ocean rattled the branches of the ancient oaks in the neighborhood. Matthew opened the truck door, and she was grateful the heater was on, the cab already warm.

"What do you think?" she gasped as she fastened her seatbelt.

Matthew raised his eyebrows. "About what?"

She heard the weary resignation in his voice, and knew full well that he'd followed the maze of her reasoning through each convoluted turn as they'd listened to Jay's story.

"Come on, Matthew, I'm worried. Aren't you? On top of everything else, Randy White drives Parker's old white Honda. What if he was the one who pushed Jo Jo? What if he tries to finish the job?"

He lifted his eyes to the starless sky to stare at absolutely nothing, and then he reached for her hand. "You can always call Wayne and give him a heads up if you suspect Parker's son is up to something."

"Please, Matthew, you know Wayne already thinks I'm overdue for a sanity hearing."

He leaned across the distance and kissed her lips. "I understand. But I hope all this can wait until morning."

## THIRTY-THREE

## *Randy White*

Randall White, Jr. was sweating profusely by the time he hung up the phone. If Jay's news hadn't been enough to boil his brain, then his ratty motel's heating system would finish the job. The noisy under-window unit blew too hot or too cold, nothing in between, so he couldn't get comfortable. He peeled off his undershirt and shorts, stuffed them into a plastic bag reserved for dirty clothes, and then headed into the shower. The old shag carpet was gritty under his bare toes, and the room stank of cigarette smoke under the even more noxious odor of pine aerosol.

No doubt about it, staying in motels was getting old. He thought about his lover, home drinking tea and eating cookies with strangers. Hell, even painting walls was better than this, but it would all be over soon.

Randy stepped into the cramped bathroom, leaving the door ajar so the steam from the shower could escape, and then he glanced at the mirror. His deep blue eyes were underhung with dark circles, while a two-day's growth of whiskers sprouted like fungus on his jaw. He had always prided himself on his appearance, but lately the worry and fear had taken their toll. The images of violent death stalked him through the night, so he could not sleep. Those images sat across the dinner table, so he could not eat. Just now they were camped out on his chest, so he could not breathe. But it would all be over soon.

He stepped under the jerky pulse of the shower. Like the heating system, it couldn't find a happy medium between frigid and scalding, so Randy opted for lukewarm. He replayed Jay's conversation and cursed the woman who had arrived uninvited on their doorstep. Who did she think she was, and what did she want?

Jay had described her as gentle, cultivated, and nosey as hell, but Randy wasn't fooled. All his mother's cronies fit that description, only this one, Diana Rittenhouse, was clearly dangerous as well.

He lathered his body with the cheap soap, but could not get clean. He thought about the victims—Harold Havers, Homer Locksley, and that bitch, Jo Jo Jones. That woman had nearly ruined his sister's life, and now she lay in the hospital, struggling to regain consciousness so she could tell the cop posted by her bed precisely who had pushed her. Was there an officer by her bed? How good was the security?

Randy shuddered as he climbed from the shower and grabbed a towel. No matter what, it would be risky to hang around the hospital, but what were his options? She had to be stopped, and the nightmare had to end.

Next he was too cold. He punished his skin with the towel, hoping to stimulate his circulation, but still he shivered. Blasted motel. He had stayed in a different dump each time, so that no inquisitive desk clerk would be likely to remember him. He had used a different name each time, and the fleabag joints he'd chosen had accepted cash and never asked for identification.

He had even sabotaged his white Honda, because he was certain he'd been spotted on Thanksgiving. Problem was, Jay's yellow VW bug attracted attention everywhere Randy drove, so that this time he'd parked a block away from the motel to avoid being connected to the classic car.

His hand trembled on the razor as he began to shave. He drew blood and stuck a piece of toilet paper on his chin to stop the flow. The razor was sharp, but not nearly as lethal as the little .38 special tucked in his duffel bag. It belonged to Jay, who had no idea Randy had taken it. Long ago, when Jay was called Nanjay, he had traded the slums of New Delhi for the slums of London, where he studied graphic design. Nanjay had purchased the compact revolver for protection when he walked home late at night from the university. It had never been fired, but Randy knew how to use it. Maybe he should put the damned gun to his own head and end it all sooner?

He drank some fake courage from his bottle of scotch, and then drank a little more. He splashed on some of the cologne Jay had given him for his birthday, and then began to dress very carefully. After all, this was a somber occasion. Maybe the guards at the hospital would think Randy was Jo Jo's son? Indeed, Randy looked something like that prick, Jarrett Jones, who'd gotten Cindi pregnant. Hopefully, Randy would just blend right in, so that no one would even notice him.

He thought about what Jay had told him on the phone. It seemed this Rittenhouse woman was getting entirely too close to the truth. From what he'd been reading in the papers, she was certainly more on target than the dumb cops. He thought about Jo Jo, too stubborn to die, and about his own deranged mother…

He had only one choice—she had to be stopped.

## THIRTY-FOUR

## *Really want to know...?*

General Tso's chicken and vegetable lo mein were Diana's absolute favorites. She reached across the wide desk to spoon some Chinese food from the white carton to her paper plate, and a stray noodle slithered from the glob and landed on a termite inspection certification. It left a snake-like gravy trail on the official form.

"Klutz," Liz mumbled without conviction. She was distracted by her own pile of paperwork and the mastication of moo shoo pork. "I'm never gonna catch up," she moaned. "Danny and I should've stayed in the mountains."

And Diana should have stayed at the beach. Both Liz and she were suffering from the Monday night, work-late-at-the-office blahs, and they'd both made major mistakes by cutting their vacations short.

"At least we have some work to catch up on," Diana said. While Liz and Danny were in Asheville, and Matthew and she were in Wilmington, their answering machine had clogged with urgent messages as a half dozen pending deals finally ripened to fruition. It was always like that in real estate—skinny or fat—and they were starving for calories.

"I should have left my cell phone at home, instead of taking it on vacation." Liz complained. "All this work could have waited a day or two."

Diana had not been as virtuous as Liz. She never took her cell phone on pleasure trips, nor did she rank her business responsibilities above her relationship with Matthew. In Diana's case, it was her stupid obsession with the murders that caused her to act against her own best interests and return home early, and now she was paying the emotional price.

"At least you spent one night with Matthew," Liz said. "I swear, Diana, that man has the patience of a hound with a treed possum, but one of these days he's gonna walk off in disgust."

Liz was absolutely right. As always, Matthew had been loving and understanding when asked to cut their vacation short. And their one night in the camper, the sweet lovemaking in his tiny bed, had been even more intense because they'd known they have to leave in the morning. Even now her body ached with the memory, and she realized she was the worst kind of fool.

Liz finished eating and shoved her paper plate into the wastebasket. She tucked a strand of stray red hair behind her ear and beamed her laser green eyes at Diana. "Was it worth giving up your vacation? I know you have some crazy theories about Randy White. You think he's the fox in the hen house, but did Bearfoot buy it?"

Diana stared right back at Liz. What was with her tonight? All this *hounds and possums* and *foxes and hens* talk was strictly out of character for her hip young partner. She seemed in an exceptionally good mood, which was odd, considering the circumstances.

"Why are you so cheerful?" Diana demanded as Liz cleared her desk. "Do you have a date with Danny?" Even in the dim glow of the desk lamp, Diana saw a crimson blush creep up Liz's neck.

"Nope. I know this sounds weird, Diana, but I have a date with Janelle Havers. I'm meeting her at The Sports Bar for drinks."

Diana was stunned. Surely her ears were playing tricks. Janelle was Liz's archenemy, her longtime rival, the object of her undying scorn. Diana knew her mouth was hanging open.

"Yeah, I know it's bizarre, but Danny convinced me it's time to call a truce," Liz said sheepishly. "Janelle's been telling Danny she wants to patch up our differences and make amends."

This was an astonishing about-face. "I thought Janelle had gone back to Charlotte to live with her mother? The poor woman was devastated by Duck Wadell's death."

"True, but now that they've arrested that man for Duck's murder, Janelle's not so scared any more. Did you know they think the same guy killed Janelle's husband, too?"

"Yes, I know, but they are wrong."

"C'mon, Diana, what's your problem? Why can't you be like me and get on with your life? You don't want the intrigue to be over, do you? Besides, you never answered my question. What did Sheriff Bearfoot say about your cock n' bull theory about Randy White?"

Obviously Liz had already decided her suspicions were ridiculous. Diana wanted to reach across the desk and wring her lovely neck. At the same time, she was devastated to lose her best partner in crime. It seemed that Liz had mentally retreated from the mystery, leaving Diana alone with her doubts.

"Well, what did Bearfoot say?" Liz repeated.

Diana put down her fork, abandoning her General Tso's chicken. Matthew had been gallant. He'd driven directly to Wayne's home when they got back to town last night. They'd parked the RV in Wayne's driveway, left Amazing Grace locked in the camper, and interrupted the sheriff and his pregnant wife on their way to bed.

Wayne had been patient and attentive, even took a few notes as Diana built a case suggesting that Randy White was a serial killer. She had laid out all the motives: how Randy had shot Havers to protect his mother's honor—how he'd poisoned Locksley as a final revenge for the sexual seduction that had caused Randy's nervous breakdown—how Randy knew Duck Wadell had cheated his mother, bringing her to the brink of financial ruin—and how Jo Jo Jones and her son had left Randy's beloved sister pregnant and disgraced.

She hadn't been sure why Randy killed Lester B. Smith, except that collectively the commissioners had rejected Randy as their Town Planner, a job he desperately needed, when Randy's credentials had qualified him as the obvious choice.

She met Liz's eyes. "To be honest, I don't know what Wayne thought about my theories. He was worried enough to call Peter Sokolsky, just to be sure the detective had a guard at Jo Jo's bedside. Turned out there was already a guard at the hospital. Other than that, I think Wayne agrees with you, that my worries are a pack of nonsense."

"Sorry, Diana." Liz touched Diana's hand and smiled.

Her tenderness sent a jolt of jealousy to Diana's brain. Not long ago, Liz had felt left out because Diana had shown a motherly concern for Janelle Havers. But now, as Liz prepared to rekindle a relationship with Janelle, Diana childishly resented the fact that she hadn't been invited along for drinks.

She watched in petulant silence as Liz lifted a blank Listing Agreement from the drawer and tucked it into her briefcase. "What's that for?" she asked.

Liz winked slyly. "Oh, didn't I tell you? One condition of my reconciliation with Janelle is that I sell Harold Havers' mansion on Lake Norman. I know *you* were supposed to get that listing, Diana, but you didn't, did you? No hard feelings, right? After all, it's all for one, and one for all, right?"

Diana hadn't gotten the listing because she'd been too busy coping with Havers' dead body. No wonder Liz was so anxious to let bygones be bygones—nothing like a bribe to turn one's other cheek.

"*What*?" Liz grinned as she headed for the door. "Better close your mouth, Diana, or you'll catch some flies."

With that remark, Liz left, leaving Diana alone in the office as a steady drizzle of wintry mix shuffled across the roof. All Diana had to show for the evening was a stack of paperwork and some carry-on baggage full of regrets. Liz was right. She should get on with her life. She was sure Matthew felt the same, although he was too kind to say it outright.

She turned off the lamp and propped her feet on the chair Liz had vacated. The security light from the parking lot glistened on the window, where delicate webs of ice made a lacey curtain. It was December first, too early for a freeze in North Carolina.

She pictured Matthew alone in his store, maybe deciding to close early. He had hired Hoke for a full week in anticipation of their vacation, then canceled the deal when they came home early. She imagined Matthew's long fingers closing out the cash register, toting up the profits, if there were any, and the thought of his hands sent a tremor through her body.

To hell with the paperwork, and to hell with the ice. Diana would coax Gracie into Queen Vic and head over to Matthew's. It was high time his Ursie met Gracie, and although they were both female, Diana guessed the Doberman and the greyhound would get on famously, just like their master and mistress.

That decided, she was putting her work away when the phone rang. She figured it was Matthew, and they'd be on the same wavelength. She lifted the receiver, expecting to hear his deep voice, but instead, she heard silence.

"Hello?" she repeated as the silence deepened and cold shivers raked the back of her neck.

"Diana?" The voice was definitely female, but hoarse with emotion.

"Who is this?"

"Why are you doing this to me?" The emotion was anger, and the speaker was Parker White. "Some damned sheriff called from Iredell County asking all kinds of awful questions about my son, Randall. What have you done, Diana?"

Diana was in trouble. The cold at the base of her neck clawed at her conscience, and suddenly she felt guilty about putting Parker in this position. On the other hand, how on earth had Parker found out she was the one? Had Wayne told her?

"That friend of Randall's called me from Wilmington. That Indian boy—what's his name. Can you imagine the nerve? He told me about your visit, Diana, and about the strange questions you asked. My God, how could you? You don't even know my son."

She'd been caught red-handed. "You're right, Parker. I don't know Randy, but from what Jay said…"

"How could you listen to that terrible man? What does he know? The least you can do is meet Randall and hear his side of the story. You should have done that before you went crying to the police."

Diana felt terrible, suddenly stricken by doubt and guilt. "I'd like to meet Randy someday. But…"

"Well, if you really mean it, you can meet him right now. He's here in my apartment," Parker said. "Can you come?"

A million excuses skittered through her head, but not one reached her tongue. Parker's apartment was only two blocks from

Diana's office condo, and since Parker had called her work number, she knew damned well Diana was only minutes away.

A million questions tortured her reason, like why was Randy still in Davidson? Diana had thought his travels were confined to the weekends. Why was he with his mother, and why did he want to see Diana? Did she really want to know the answer to that one?

"Well, Diana?" Parker was angry and focused.

"Sure, I'll be right over," she said, sealing her fate.

She hung up, then immediately dialed Matthew at the store. But he was gone, closed up early, as she had suspected. She rang his home, but he wasn't home yet. She left a message on his answering machine. For once she was very direct about where and why she was going to visit Parker. And then she put on her coat and went out into the dark and drizzle.

THIRTY-FIVE

*Trust or retreat…?*

Diana drove the short distance to Parker's apartment and found a parking space right across the street. The town was exceptionally silent, with ice beading on the golden glass of the old-fashioned lampposts. As she gingerly crossed the pavement, taking care not to slip, it seemed she was alone in the world. Not surprising. Most Davidson folks were sensible people who tucked into their homes at nightfall and seldom ventured out in treacherous weather.

She twisted the knob on the street-level door beside Hometown Books, and like before, found it unlocked. Taking a deep breath, she prepared to mount the stairs. Diana was dreading this confrontation with Randy White, who was at best emotionally unstable—at worst, a murderer, as Diana now believed. She regretted not talking to Matthew before she came, but he would have tried to talk her out of this mission, perhaps rightfully so. Her only comfort was Parker's presence, for in spite of all Diana's doubts, she was certain her old friend would never let her son hurt her.

Diana's hand was not so certain. It trembled as she reached for the railing to guide her up the dim staircase. Then suddenly, she lost her balance and toppled forward, skinning the ball of her hand on a splintered riser several steps up. What the hell happened?

She crawled upright, trying to make sense of this latest episode of clumsiness, and then she noticed the handrail was missing. Odd. It had been there before. She looked again and saw that the handrail was not missing, merely detached. The long wooden rail had been unscrewed from its mounts and now lay along the edge of the stairs, waiting to be repaired. How very dangerous! Hopefully Parker's landlord had warned her to watch her step, for the hazard was a lawsuit waiting to happen. Bracing her hand against the wall, she made her way up to the single door at the top and knocked hard.

Parker must have been lurking on the other side, for the door opened immediately and a pair of penetrating blue eyes confronted her.

"Don't just stand there," Parker snapped. "You're letting all the heat out."

As Diana eased through the door, she prepared herself for the chaotic mess that had greeted her on her first visit, but instead, her attention was drawn to the gray sling supporting Parker's arm.

"I knew it! You fell down the stairs, didn't you?"

Parker made a face as she dragged Diana into the living room. "Sometimes you are a brilliant detective, Diana, because that's exactly what happened."

"I knew there'd be an accident."

"Aren't you the clever one? But as usual, your deductions are pure nonsense. It wasn't an accident, Diana. Someone loosened all the screws, but left the railing lying in its brackets. It looked okay when I grabbed it to go down, but then I went flying."

"It's lucky you weren't killed!"

"Whoever did this is very unlucky, because the bastard wanted me dead."

They stared at one another as Diana's pet theories evaporated. The implication was obvious. The commissioners, all of them, were the targets. And the motives, far from being the psychotic personal vendettas she had concocted, were political, after all. Even Parker, new to the Board, was not immune.

"I am so sorry..." Diana said.

"Are you really?" Parker's face was cold as ice sculpture.

"Is your arm broken? Did you see a doctor?"

Parker's laugh was bitter. "It's not broken, but my shoulder is sprained. And no, I didn't see a doctor. My husband was a physician, remember? Living with him all those years, I have an honorary medical degree, so I can care for myself."

Diana opened her mouth to protest, but then decided she had interfered quite enough.

"What did the police say about the loosened handrail?" she asked.

Parker moved deeper into the room and Diana followed.

"Well, of course they think it was the same person who attacked the others," she said, her back turned.

A litany of questions gathered in the back of Diana's throat. Was Peter Sokolsky investigating? Did he dust for prints? Did anyone see a stranger at Parker's place? And why wasn't the street door kept locked after the mishap? But when Parker faced her, with her arms crossed and her eyes firing warning shots, Diana swallowed all those questions.

"You seem awfully calm about this," Diana muttered.

"Do I? Everything's relative, isn't it? The truth is, I'm scared witless. But the attempt on my life is not nearly as upsetting as what you've done to my son."

Parker moved in close. Her eyes were clear and sober, her cheeks flushed with a healthful glow Diana hadn't seen in weeks.

Her breath was sweet, with no trace of alcohol, and finally, Diana recognized the scent of White Shoulders. The fragrance rekindled all her original suspicions about Parker, but she pulled herself back to reality.

"Are you listening, Diana? Randall is mortified. The police want to question him. First they came here, and then the cops in Wilmington coordinated a search of his home at the beach, and it's all because of you."

Parker lifted her uninjured arm and touched Diana's shoulder with her finger. Although the poke was gentle, it felt like a dagger tipping into her flesh. Diana felt terribly guilty about what she had done. She'd had no idea that Wayne Bearfoot would take her suspicions so seriously. In light of the apparent attempt on Parker's life, and since it seemed obvious that Randy wouldn't harm his own mother, it was now clear that the murderer really was targeting the commissioners to prevent some public agenda. "I really am sorry," she apologized again.

Parker shrugged and abruptly abandoned the subject. She gestured widely, sweeping the room. "Well, the place looks good, doesn't it?"

Diana's mind stumbled over Parker's manic mood swing, but she dutifully surveyed the apartment. The packing crates were gone, the clutter eliminated, and every surface gleamed. Even the cat box odor had been replaced by the scent of lemon oil.

"Yes, it looks great!" Diana agreed, somewhat surprised. Was the improvement Randy's influence. If he'd been staying with his mother and brought about this change, then he couldn't be all bad. "So, where is Randy?" She glanced towards Parker's closed bedroom door and wondered why her son had not yet shown himself.

This time Parker's laugh bordered on hysterical. "Are you crazy, Diana? Didn't you hear one word I said? The police are after Randall. Would he be stupid enough to wait here, where they would surely find him?"

"But you said…"

"Yes, I lied. I told you he was here, but would you have come otherwise? And I honestly believe you're the only one who can clear up this mess. If Randall persuades you he's innocent, then you can convince the sheriff to leave my poor boy alone. Isn't that what you want?" Parker paused and pleaded with her eyes. "If you want to make this right, you can still have your little chat with Randall at the motel where he's staying."

"Motel?" She wanted to make amends, but the situation was becoming more bizarre by the minute.

"Is there a problem, Diana?"

"Where is this motel?"

Parker's eyes misted with tears. "I wish I could trust you, but I don't feel comfortable telling you Randall's whereabouts in advance. Considering what you've done so far, you might get on your cell phone and alert the sheriff…"

"I wouldn't do that."

Parker held out her hand. "Maybe you wouldn't, but forgive me, Diana, I'm so confused and paranoid these days. As a gesture of good will, why don't you give me your phone for safe keeping?"

Had their friendship really come to this? Parker and she had once shared some good times—luncheons, theatre dates, and first-run movies. Those memories spun like an almost-forgotten carousel in Diana's mind. Now they were more like enemy combatants than best friends, and it was surely Diana's fault. Perhaps she was the paranoid one. Should she trust, or retreat? She decided upon the former, reached into her purse, and handed Parker her phone.

"Thank you, Diana." Parker smiled, then patted her injured arm. "You'll have to drive, okay?"

"Sure, my car's right out front."

Diana helped Parker into a cape she found in the closet. The garment was large enough to close over the sling, and the running shoes Parker was wearing were as good as any footwear for crossing the icy street. As they moved towards the door, a smug smile curved Parker's lips. Had she had known all along that Diana would agree to the adventure?

"Aren't you going to turn off your lights?" Diana asked as they moved into the hall.

"Why? So I can trip over something when I come home? Don't be silly, Diana. Besides, my cats hate to be left in the dark."

Good enough. She followed Parker down the treacherous staircase. Parker was curiously sure-footed for a woman prone to tumbles. Or maybe she'd been drinking when she took the fall? Either way, they reached the ground without incident and crossed the street. Diana helped Parker into the passenger seat and buckled her safety belt.

"Which way to Randy's motel?" Diana asked as they pulled out.

"Stay on Main Street and drive towards Mooresville."

## THIRTY-SIX

## *A caffeine fix...*

By the time they reached the intersection of Highway 150, Diana's shoulders were tense from defensive driving on black ice and her eyes ached with the strain of interpreting the reflections in the headlights. Some idiot had been following too close all the way from Davidson, obviously someone unaccustomed to driving on slippery roads, someone unfamiliar with the concept that it takes a lot longer to slow down under these conditions.

"I wish that fool would back off my tail," she grumbled.

Parker had offered less than three sentences since their departure. She seemed uptight, too. "I could use a cup of coffee, Diana. How about you?"

"Is it much farther?"

"Far enough." Parker lifted her purse onto the seat between them and fumbled with her good hand until she fished out her wallet. "There's a new Gourmet Brews just west of here. C'mon, I'm buying..."

Diana was in no mood to delay this excursion one moment longer than necessary, but she badly needed a caffeine fix. Making a quick left onto 150, heading towards the lake, she hoped to lose the joker in her rearview mirror. No such luck. The unwelcome stalker skidded into the turn, fishtailed, and then continued to follow not ten yards from her bumper.

"Have you been to the new Gourmet Brews?" Parker was oblivious to the car behind them.

"Yes, Matthew took me to the Grand Opening." The thought of Matthew made her eyes sting. His house was only five miles down the road, and she longed to drive directly to the safety of his arms.

"*Matthew* at *Gourmet Brews?*" Parker chuckled. "From what you've told me about the man, the two don't seem simpatico."

Parker was right about that. Matthew considered Gourmet Brews the epitome of yuppiedom, and their attendance at the Grand Opening had been a bittersweet joke marking the ultimate infringement of canned culture onto Matthew's sacred, natural turf. She glanced at her companion, and somehow they seemed back in sync with one another, like they used to be.

Diana began signaling well in advance of her left turn onto Williamson Road, and the stranger behind her eased up, allowing her to make the immediate swing into the coffee shop's parking lot. Much to her relief, the stranger kept going, and she noticed a flash of bright yellow as his car continued slowly away into the night.

"Whew..." She parked and switched off the ignition. "You're right about the coffee, Parker. Do you want cream and sugar?"

"Yes, please." Parker pressed a ten-dollar bill into her hand.

As Diana stepped carefully onto the sidewalk, she realized her knees were shaking. They continued to tremble as she walked inside and placed her order.

"You're nuts, lady..." the kid said cheerfully as he filled their cups. "You know how many accidents have happened in the last half hour alone?" The boy's radio was tuned to the police band,

and a 10-45 code was being called through the static. "That means they need an ambulance." The kid seemed downright gleeful.

He packaged their drinks in a paper bag, and Diana paid without comment. Some people delighted in other folk's disasters, but she was not one of them.

"Be careful, lady," he called as she pushed the door out against the wind, and in the distance a siren wailed—the most lonesome sound on earth.

"Are you okay, Parker?" Diana balanced the coffees in the holders between the seats and lined up the sugar packets and creamers on the dash. Parker was slumped over in her seat, her head bent into her hand.

"I have a rotten headache, Diana, like my brain's about to implode."

Parker's face was pasty white, and when Diana touched her forehead, it was clammy. "I have some aspirin in my purse," Diana said. "Can you take it with coffee, or shall I go back for some water?"

"I can't take aspirin," Parker moaned. "I need acetaminophen."

"Why, for heaven's sake?"

"I'm on Coumadin."

Diana knew this was a blood-thinning drug, which should not be used along with aspirin, and in spite of the worry she felt over Parker's headache, she wondered what illness necessitated her friend's use of Coumadin. Didn't the poor woman have enough trouble already?

"There's a drugstore across the street, Diana. Please, could you run in and get me some acetaminophen?"

She carefully steered Queen Vic over to the drugstore and assured Parker she had enough change left over from Parker's ten to purchase a small packet. She parked and went inside, where the young woman behind the counter, with studs pierced into her nose and around the rim of her ear, was sullen to the point of rudeness. As Diana paid, the clerk kept whining about the weather and cursing the inconsiderate boss who had forced her to stay until the end of her shift.

"Well, drive home safely," Diana told the girl, but received only a snarl in return.

Parker was more cheerful when Diana returned to the car. "Thanks, you're a lifesaver." She tore open the packet, swallowed a fistful of pills. "I'm sure these will help."

Diana certainly hoped so. At this rate, she'd never meet Randy. Hopefully he was staying in one of the many new motels at Exit 36, and their journey would soon be over.

"I took the liberty of putting cream and sugar in your coffee, Diana. I still remember how you like it."

She smiled at Parker, encouraged by the color already returning to her face. Diana took special comfort in the fact that their friendship seemed to be back on an even keel, and took a long, welcome sip of the steaming liquid. With a little luck, the caffeine jolt would get her back on the road alert and refreshed. She sat a moment to finish, because she certainly couldn't drink and drive safely in this weather. "Umm...tastes good," she said as they communed in companionable silence.

Diana closed her eyes and took another swallow, noting how these expensive, trendy coffees tasted a little too exotic somehow. She leaned back into the headrest and listened to the sleet pelting on the car roof. After several more sips, she realized she was getting uncommonly sleepy. With great effort, she opened one eye and stared at Parker, who was watching intently.

"Just relax, dear," she said soothingly. "Finish your coffee."

Diana took her advice, tilting the cup to swallow the last drop, but as she waited for the much-needed caffeine rush, she became more and more drowsy. "That's funny, I feel dizzy," she confided. She squeezed her eyes shut, but when she opened them, Parker's face had begun to dematerialize, or fracture like a Cubist painting. "Something's wrong…" A tiny alarm sounded at the base of her skull. "I feel really sick, Parker." Diana knew her eyes were wide open, but she could no longer focus—the parking lot was a blur.

"Perhaps I should drive now?" Parker's voice wobbled through Diana's consciousness. "Give me the car keys…"

A cold blast of wind chilled Diana's burning face as Parker opened the passenger side door. She looked on in disbelief as Parker reached under her cape, pulled off her sling, and then flexed her bad arm. Another cold blast assaulted the left side of Diana's face as Parker's hands reached behind Diana's back and under her knees, scooting her across the seat like a limp beanbag.

"What's happening?" Her lips were paralyzed, so that no coherent sound came through.

"Don't worry, Diana, I'm an excellent driver."

The engine sparked to life and they began to move. Through a film of haze, Diana saw the sullen girl from the drugstore leaning against the wall under an overhang, smoking a cigarette. Her eyes were empty sockets as the smoke drifted up and into the storm.

## THIRTY-SEVEN

## *Randy White*

What the hell was his mother up to? Randy kept on driving when the two women pulled into Gourmet Brews, but then he turned around two blocks up the road and doubled back. He parked at the end of the shopping center, in front of the bread store, and doused his lights.

The woman driving his mother through the storm was a stranger, but he'd bet the last jigger of scotch waiting back in his motel room, that she was Diana Rittenhouse, the bitch who'd made his life a misery since her visit to their home in Wilmington. He was sure she'd spotted him following, but what else could he do? His mother was as slippery as a greased copperhead and twice as dangerous. He'd been shadowing her these past two days and had actually confronted her at the hospital.

Parker had been hovering outside Jo Jo's room, pretending to be waiting for someone to step off the elevator. In fact, she'd been waiting for the uniformed guard stationed at Jo Jo's door to answer the call of nature and leave his post, so that she could sneak inside and complete the job she'd botched at Thanksgiving. What had you planned, Mother? An accidental disconnect of the respirator, or the old smother-her-with-a-pillow routine?

Randy shivered as he squinted through the sleet undulating across the parking lot. He could just make out the silhouette of the Rittenhouse woman in the glow of the lighted coffee shop. She made her purchase and returned to the Ford Crown Victoria. He tensed and prepared to twist the ignition, to take up the chase once more.

Yesterday at Lake Norman Regional Medical Center, Mother had been shocked when he stepped out of the elevator she'd been pretending to watch. After listening to her usual round of lies: *I'm here to visit my good friend* bullshit, their conversation had gone downhill fast. They'd had those ugly conversations before, after each of the murders, when Randy's efforts to sort out the truth had ended in stone cold denial.

All those weekly visits had left Randy's mind bloodied and his body spent with apprehension. Parker's eyes had been either dead from drugs, or stretched and staring in manic desperation. She'd been in a similar state during her nervous breakdown after Daddy died. She'd gone on a violent rampage when his sister left home. Her breakdowns had been enhanced by Randy's own depression, his horrible sinking into nothingness when his affair with Professor Locksley ended.

Jesus Christ! What if madness was in the genes? What if her insanity had poisoned his blood as surely as she, the avenging angel who'd given him life, had poisoned Professor Locksley?

Randy watched, frozen with dread, until the Crown Victoria's headlights pierced the gloom and moved onto the road. He started the Volkswagen's engine to follow, but the Ford hesitated, and then crossed over to the drugstore. What the hell? He inched forward on the icy pavement, but stayed far enough away to avoid being seen. Again he turned off his engine and watched the Rittenhouse woman go into the drugstore.

He had visited his mother's new apartment several times, but seeing all the family furniture crammed into the too-small space, like junk in a storage unit, made his chest ache. Her medicine cabinet was a pharmacy of forbidden delights, so he had helped himself to some Thorazine, and that brought him down.

If Mother had been telling the truth during one of her recent drunken rants, she'd had a torrid love affair with Harold Havers, the first victim. The concept of his mother in bed with a man, not his father, her sagging, middle-aged body copulating with a wrinkled stranger, made him want to vomit. She was an emotional train wreck. She had no business having an affair.

Neither did he. Randy broke into a cold sweat as he remembered the handsome stranger in the motel bar, how last night he had coupled with less commitment than a rutting dog on a bitch in heat. He thought about Jay, alone with his paintbrush and a storm crying in from the ocean, and he tasted salt on his lips.

Shit! Through his tears, Randy saw his mother step from the car and take the driver's seat. Gone was the fake sling she'd worn when she left the apartment. He'd known damned well his mother hadn't broken her arm, but why she'd feigned the injury was anyone's guess. And what the hell was she up to now?

He had missed seeing the Rittenhouse woman leave the drugstore, but he was sure she was in the car. He reached down and lifted Jay's .38 special from the duffel bag on the floor and placed it on the seat beside him. The clip was loaded, ready to go, but he didn't plan to use the gun. Surely he could talk sense to his mother. If she was responsible for these murders, she needed a mental hospital, not a prison. He had to convince her…

But where were they going? Randy wiped his eyes with the back of his hand and followed at a distance. Diana Rittenhouse wouldn't recognize his car, but his mother had seen Jay's yellow VW on several occasions, so he didn't want to spook her.

He was traveling in unfamiliar territory. The roads around Mooresville had changed utterly since Randy was an undergrad at

Davidson, so that now, as he trailed his mother through the night, he was at a disadvantage. As they moved west on Highway 150, the strip malls and gas stations gave way to rural fields, and the Ford's taillights became two bloodshot eyes weeping in the distance.

He turned up the heater and defroster fan. Ice crisscrossed his windshield like a vicious spider's web and sweat pooled under his collar. This wasn't happening. It was only a bad dream. What did he know, anyway? Mother had denied everything. If he hadn't seen her at the Evergreen Adult Community on Thanksgiving, he'd have been inclined to believe her. But he had seen her flashy new Jaguar streaking in through the back entrance in a blur of silver. He had followed in the white Honda, but had stayed in his car and watched as Mother calmly entered Jo Jo's apartment. His belly had done flip-flops, and he'd choked on the bile of his cowardice, but in the end, he had done nothing. Maybe denial was passed through the genes, too?

A blast of wind swept the highway, and his tires skidded sideways. At the same moment, the red taillights of the Ford disappeared. Randy fought the skid and fought his panic, just in time to see that his mother had made a left turn.

Fuck! He leaned on the steering wheel and miraculously came through the turn without a major mishap. The distance had widened between them, but the Ford was still in sight. His palms were sweating. He touched the gun—it was cold as death.

What was this place? As his mind cleared, he recalled seeing a billboard as he'd entered the turn. Apparently 'Morrison Plantation' was some sort of a new development. The unpaved road was freshly graded. It looked like blood-red clay in his headlights, and it crunched like solid ice. If he didn't slow down, he'd skid off the edge, and God only knew what lay beyond. As he recalled, this was hill country, so a potentially lethal drop-off awaited his one false move.

Randy's heavy breathing fogged the glass. He cranked the window open and gulped the frigid air. Glancing outside, he saw the ghostly outline of an ancient barn. Its roof was white with snow. And beyond that, on the next crest, a yellow backhoe was poised with its claw lifted and open. He imagined the claw reaching out, eating the barn. How very sad.

Get a grip! He swiped at the foggy windshield with his sleeve, then hit the brakes, because a shiny new red STOP sign was dead ahead. The sudden braking killed the engine, and his car slid into the signpost. His heart was beating outside his chest. When he lifted his eyes to look again, he saw the new STOP sign was riddled with bullet holes. How very funny. His maniacal laughter was all but drowned out by the raging wind.

God, he needed a drink. Randy stared at the fork in the road—should he go left, or right? By then the taillights were gone, but Mother must have stopped somewhere. Amazingly, the Volkswagen's engine started up again on the first try, and he had to make a choice…

His chances were fifty/fifty.

## THIRTY-EIGHT

*Alone...*

"What have you done?" Diana's words were slurred and her tongue was completely numb, like someone had administered an overdose of Novocaine.

Parker laughed, Diana screamed, but only a small cry escaped. She had no idea where Parker was taking her, but first they made a left turn, and then she felt rough road under the wheels.

"No one understands I really loved him. Harold loved me, too. I brought him flowers, but then he laughed. I found his gun— not my fault." Parker's words wove in and out through the cotton in Diana's ears. Diana's brain floated inside her head, and Parker was a watery echo.

"Poison—old shed where the house used to be. Homer— served him right." Parker's lips were twisted red worms churning in the pit of Diana's stomach. Sharp turn. Dina reached for the armrest and braced against the floor, but her hands and feet were missing.

"I'm so sorry, Diana. This was never about you..." Parker touched Diana's face, but her fingers were only gloves and smelled like the latex baby doll Mama once gave Diana. "I never wanted to hurt you, but you wouldn't leave it alone..."

Diana tried to answer, but she was like a tiny whimpering animal, trapped in the dark.

"Don't cry…" Parker stroked her hair, then turned on the radio—classical music.

Too loud! Diana's ears throbbed. Parker's face was a swollen balloon.

They stopped. The car door opened. It was so cold. Gentle hands lifted Diana across the seat and strapped her behind the wheel.

"Don't be afraid…" Parker kissed her full on the lips, and the car door slammed.

And then Diana was alone. The sky was black and white with dust. Suddenly the car was rolling. She saw Amazing Grace and Matthew's face…rolling faster…the sky fell away.

THIRTY-NINE

## *Small comfort...*

"My throat hurts." Diana tried to swallow, but the pain burned all the way down her esophagus.

"I'm not surprised." Matthew's voice was warm as a hot toddy. "They had to pump your stomach. Don't you remember?"

She nodded, pulled his hand up to her pillow, so she could cradle her cheek in it—like a baseball mitt. In fact, she remembered very little about her short time in the hospital, let alone the nightmare that put her there.

A cold, wet nose snuffled against her bare arm. "Is that you, Gracie?"

"She's been 'bout as worried as I was," Matthew said. "Underfoot every step of the way. Should I put her in the living room?"

"No!" Diana rubbed the greyhound's ears and was rewarded by a deep canine groan of satisfaction, warm as honey. "Let her stay, she can sleep in her box."

Diana kissed Matthew's fingers. He talked tough, but where dogs were concerned, he was putty in their paws. One thing she remembered quite clearly—the image of Gracie, and then Matthew, two beacons of hope before the darkness closed in.

"What did she put in my coffee?"

Matthew rolled his eyes. "Your pal Parker was a regular Catherine de Medici, with considerable knowledge of poisons.

Doc said she slipped you a Mickey Finn, like the gangsters used to use in the old-time movies."

"But what was it?"

Matthew cleared his throat, averted his eyes. "Something called chloral hydrate, enough to put you under, but a non-lethal dose."

"I don't understand?" Diana knew he was holding something back. "I'm sure she meant to kill me, Matthew."

"I reckon she did, but not with the poison. The cops figure the plan was to make it look like an accident. Folks would easily believe you lost control of the car and skidded on that ice."

"Tell me the rest."

"Chloral hydrate was the perfect choice. By the time someone found you, the drug would've worked its way out of your system, and..." He paused. "It would be untraceable in an autopsy."

The word made her shudder as she pictured herself dismembered on a marble slab, the pathologist wielding his scalpel. She gripped Matthew's hand.

"I'm sorry..." he said softly.

"Did she poison Homer Locksley, then?"

"Absolutely. They also know she pushed Jo Jo Jones off her deck."

"What about Lester B. Smith?"

"Nope. The cops will never have hard evidence linking the car that forced Lester off the bridge to Parker's white Honda, so lacking proof to the contrary, that one's been ruled an accident." He smiled ruefully. "But everything else you suspected was right, Diana."

Small comfort. Tears burned behind her eyes as they scanned the familiar room. This was her bedroom—two cozy reading lamps, Grandma Whitaker's crazy quilt, and of course, Matthew's kind brown eyes gazing down at her, filled with love and concern.

Nurturing as these things were, they didn't alter the horror of Parker's premeditated plan to kill her and the others. She'd never wanted to be right about her friend's guilt, but she now believed that Parker had tried to confess to her in those final moments, before Diana slipped into oblivion. All the rest was a blank, but she closed her eyes and tried to piece it together.

"Just before I blacked out, I heard a loud noise, Matthew. Was it a gunshot?"

He squeezed her hand. "Yes, I'm afraid so."

"But, who...?" As her head cleared, she realized she had absolutely no idea how she'd come to be saved.

"You had a knight in shining armor, my love, a real-life hero waiting in the wings." Matthew's voice was gruff with emotion.

She opened her eyes and stared at him in disbelief

"Yeah, it's true," he continued. "Parker's son, Randy White, saved your life. He followed the two of you all the way from Davidson. He almost lost the trail once or twice, but in the end, he was there when it counted."

She struggled upright in the pillows, ignoring the aches in her neck and shoulders, and propped her back against the headboard. "Exactly what happened, Matthew?"

"He'd brought a gun along, just in case."

"Dear, God! Don't tell me Randy shot his own mother!"

"No, he fired warning shots, and that was enough to stop Parker. She'd begun to push your car off the edge of the cliff, but when she saw Randy, she wilted on the spot. That gave him the chance to rush up and prevent a tragedy. The boy did some quick thinking. He grabbed onto the door to stop the downward motion, yanked it open and pulled on the emergency brake. He found some rocks to wedge under the tires, and only then did he pull you out."

Diana remembered nothing. A thousand questions short-circuited her brain: *what had been beyond the edge, a deep valley or the lake? Why had Randy been following them, and where was he now?* But of all her questions, only one seemed of consequence:

"What will they do to Parker?"

Matthew was very quiet. He pushed off his loafers and nudged her over, so he could lie on top of the covers, beside her on the bed. She scooted down between the sheets so they could touch foreheads on the pillow. He wrapped his arm around her and pulled her close, and she felt the steady beating of his heart through his corduroy jacket.

Parts of the nightmare still flickered at the edge of her memory, like grainy movie film run in reverse. She recalled Parker's fingers stroking her face, and her final kiss.

"Tell me, Matthew," she whispered.

"Randy left his gun behind on the ground when he ran to save you, and then he heard one shot fired. Parker is dead, Diana. She took her own life."

FORTY

*EPILOGUE*

The little princes and princesses of Siam joined hands and began whistling a happy tune. Many wore costumes fashioned from the red silk Matthew had donated, and in the glow of the footlights, the production seemed almost professional—at least to those who had worked on it.

Diana reached across the armrest, found Matthew's hand, and they smiled at one another in the dark. Those muscles at the corner of her mouth were slowly learning to curve up again, but it had been a long process.

Parker's funeral had been excruciating on many levels, but the sight of Parker's family rallying together for the first time in years was a hopeful sign. Randy and Jay came as a couple to be with Cindi, Ray, and little Maya, uplifting everyone in an atmosphere of grief. The funeral had been Diana's chance to thank Randy for saving her life, and together they had wondered which event had tipped Parker's fragile sanity over the edge. Diana had learned about her friend's history of mental illness and substance abuse, and wondered why she'd been so slow to notice those problems.

Randy believed Parker's affair with Harold Havers was the peak of a slippery slope, but no one would ever know exactly what happened that day Diana found his body. Had Parker gone to his home intending to kill him? Then why the flowers—or the condoms in Harold's pocket? Had Parker asked for a loan, only to be rebuffed? Or had Harold ended the affair, perhaps suggesting reconciliation with Janelle?

Diana had peered into the row behind them, where Liz, Danny, and Janelle were enjoying the musical. The trio made her chuckle. Liz and Janelle had been inseparable ever since they'd established a friendship, yet Liz had positioned herself firmly between Danny and her old rival. No sense tempting fate.

So everyone agreed that Parker killed Havers, but the *why* remained a mystery. But her poisoning of Homer Locksley had been quite deliberate, an act of revenge for Homer's seduction of her son many years ago. That fact was very difficult for Randy, who was back in therapy. He hoped to unravel the damage done by a mother unwilling to accept his lifestyle. He needed to ease the guilt he bore, by extension, for the death of his former lover, Homer Locksley.

Detective Peter Sokolsky, acting upon a suggestion by Diana, had explored the old garden shed left behind on Main Street after Parker's house had been moved. There he discovered an opened container of Fractol rat poison, which contained the sodium fluoroacetate injected into Locksley's Aquafina bottle.

Both Randy and Diana agreed that Parker's irrational turn to violence had been the result of not only an ended love affair and a longstanding hatred of Locksley, but also the loss of her home, her financial security, and the rejection by all the commissioners of Randy's bid to become Town Planner. That devastating tangle of disappointments could unravel a stable personality—for Parker, they had proved fatal.

Some in town thought Parker was better off dead, but Diana disagreed. Where there was life, there was hope. For instance, she heard Gerald Jones singing in the row just in front of them. He was remembering lyrics to "Hello, Young Lovers," a song that had been etched into his mind long before the Alzheimer's erased the rest. Gerald was holding hands with his wife, Jo Jo, who was enthroned in a wheelchair in the aisle. She still looked like Mrs. Santa Claus, in spite of the bandage on her head, and her quick recovery seemed like a Christmas miracle.

When Jo Jo regained consciousness, she had added a few missing pieces to the Parker puzzle. To her credit, she even took responsibility for provoking Parker that fateful Thanksgiving night. Parker had come begging Jo Jo to reconsider Randy's application for the Town Planner job. Their screaming match moved outside to the deck, where Jo Jo called Parker's daughter, Cindi, a born-again whore. The argument had escalated to a struggle ending in Jo Jo's fall—which Jo Jo insisted was an accident

Diana leaned across Matthew to catch her mother's attention. Their little corner of the theater looked like a hospital ward, with Lou Turbyfil's wheelchair parked directly behind Jo Jo's, so that Lou and Viv could critique the performances together.

"Pay attention," Matthew growled into her ear. "You'll miss the Grand Finale."

Diana was surprised that Matthew actually seemed hooked on the play. "What's got into you? I never dreamed you'd like musicals."

"The music's okay, but it's the mystery that intrigues me."

"What mystery?" Diana asked as Anna approached the King of Siam.

"You know…will the bald guy get the school marm?"

Diana laughed, but her mind had strayed to the sad story of Job Little, who had indeed killed Duck Wadell. Luckily, the courts had decided that Job's diminished capacity should lead him to a mental health facility, rather than a prison cell, and Diana was pleased with that verdict. After all, Job was the original owner of Amazing Grace. She thought about that concept of *grace*, and decided that one good thing had come from all the tragedy...

She'd got herself a good dog.

Kate Merrill is an art gallery owner and real estate broker with a lifelong passion for writing. She lives with her family on a lake in North Carolina. When she is not writing, working with the art community, or selling real estate, she enjoys swimming, boating, and allowing her two strong-headed Golden Retrievers to take her for a walk.

## Diana Rittenhouse Mystery Series
*A Lethal Listing*
*Blood Brothers*
*Crimes of Commission*
*Dooley is Dead*
*Buyer Beware*

## Amanda Rittenhouse Mystery Series

*Murder at Metrolina*
*Homicide in Hatteras*
*Assault in Asheville*
*The Mayberry Murders*

## Mainstream Romance
*Northern Lights* (as Christie Cole)
*Flames of Summer*

www.katemerrillbooks.com

www.ingramcontent.com/pod-product-compliance
Lightning Source LLC
Chambersburg PA
CBHW070336260626
47160CB00003B/1056